To Jane with a ~~~~~ to and
Nancy S~

PRAISE FOR T[

"Usually I like a few stories in an anthology, but not others. I liked every story in this book. There is something for everyone, and while many tug at the heartstrings, others give you zombies or horses or magical flea market finds. There is even poetry for those who love that. This would make a perfect Christmas gift for the readers on your list, especially those who don't have time to sit down and read a novel."~~Arkansas Reader

"Anthologies can be tricky things. In most, one writer usually stands out more than the others. In this anthology, they must have chosen only the cream of the crop! Each and every short story was well-written, finely tuned, and imaginatively crafted. The poetry was superb. I can only hope that these talented writers will do another anthology together, perhaps on one theme. "~~Emily J. Henderson

"If variety really is the spice of life, then this collection of short stories encompasses a delightful olio. The talented writers supplied me with suspense, inspiration, thrills, reconciliation, retribution, spite, forgiveness - the best and worst which the human soul can display. There truly is something for everyone encapsulated within this collection. The more stories I read, the more I wanted to read. I reveled in the individual voices which each author gave to their characters, closed my eyes and saw the settings which were artfully painted, heard the conversations and background sounds, and was transported, becoming a voyeur. "~~L. Hunter, Texas

"What happens when you open up a writing competition and provide the entrants with a broad topic? You unleash lots of creativity and end up with a collection of work that reflects the attitudes and abilities of a wide variety of people. Elements of Time is a compilation of short stories, peppered with a few poems, all penned by winners of one of the many short story contests sponsored by Accentuate Writers. Newbies to seasoned writers are represented in this collection, each with a story to tell."~~Elizabeth Grace

ELEMENTS OF DIMENSION
Science Fiction, Fantasy, Reality

AN ACCENTUATE WRITERS ANTHOLOGY

AUTHORS:
Lucinda Gunnin
Gillian Taber
Farah Evers
M. Lori Motley
Nancy Smith Gibson
Shannon Lausch
Robert L. Arend
Daniel Thrasher
Shonda Folsom
Chris Williamson
Lindsay Maddox
Terrie Schultz
Thomas Forthe

POETS:
Andi Caldwell
Robert L. Arend
Angee Stonehouse
Laurie Darroch-Meekis
Charlene Key
Lucinda Gunnin
Lisa Lee Smith
Nancy Smith Gibson
M. Lori Motley
Derek Odom
John Morrison
Bobbi Leder

Elements of Dimension: Science Fiction, Fantasy, Reality
An Accentuate Writers Anthology

Library of Congress Control Number: 2010942108

ISBN-10: 0984209549
ISBN-13: 978-0-9842095-4-5

First Edition
10 9 8 7 6 5 4 3 2 1

Authors: Lucinda Gunnin, Gillian Taber, Farah Evers, M. Lori Motley, Nancy Smith Gibson, Shannon Lausch, Robert L. Arend, Daniel Thrasher, Shonda Folsom, Chris Williamson, Lindsay Maddox, Terrie Schultz, Thomas Forthe

Poets: Andi Caldwell, Robert L. Arend, Angee Stonehouse, Laurie Darroch-Meekis, Charlene Key, Lucinda Gunnin, Lisa Lee Smith, Nancy Smith Gibson, M. Lori Motley, Derek Odom, John Morrison, Bobbi Leder

Editor: Michelle L Devon
Illustrations / Cover: Accentuate Author Services
Book/Cover Design: Twin Trinity Media

Wholesale ordering available:
SAN 858-737X

www.TwinTrinity.com
www.AccentuateServices.com
www.AccentuateWriters.com

Michy@twintrinitymedia.com

Published in the United States.

Twin Trinity Media
PO Box 1135
League City, TX 77574

TABLE OF CONTENTS

Spies & Starship Captains
By Andi Caldwell

Brain Restoration 1

By Daniel Thrasher

Miracles 17

By Farah Evers

David & the Outside 26

By Robert L. Arend

The River of Time 45

By Andi Caldwell

Dancing with Sleestaks 46

By Lisa Lee Smith

The Naked Truth 49

By Terrie Schultz

Mirror World 57

By Charlene Key

Imagination 58

By Nancy Smith Gibson

Mavis & the Leprechaun 59

By Nancy Smith Gibson

Creation 83

By Robert L. Arend

Re-composition 98

By John Morrison

To Harriet 99

By Angee Stonehouse

Elven Dreams 101

By Lucinda Gunnin

Death Obeyed 113

By M. Lori Motley

Failure to Communicate 121

By Thomas Forthe

The Call 143

By Bobbi Leder

Into Fairieland 145

By Laurie Darroch-Meekis

Dead Brother 147

By Shonda Folsom

The Roommates 167

By Lindsay Maddox

The Tale of the Suburban Dungeon 174

By M. Lori Motley

I Miss You 177

By Derek Odom

Nightlife 181

By Chris Williamson

Imp 195

By Lucinda Gunnin

A Life in a Mind 197

By Gillian Taber

The Replicator 225

By Nancy Smith Gibson

Past Realities 249

By Laurie Darroch-Meekis,

The Intervention That Wasn't 251

By Shannon Lausch

Unstable Ground 279

By Gillian Taber

Astral Voyeur 301

By Robert L. Arend

ELEMENTS OF DIMENSION

Science Fiction, Fantasy, Reality

ANDI CALDWELL

Andi Caldwell is a freelance writer, fiction author and history teacher. She is a long-time member of the Center for Independent Study, a group that supports independent scholarship.

She and her husband share a home with two cats in New England. Andi began writing soon after she began reading. She has written many short stories and articles for online content.

She has two daughters of whom she is very proud. She has been featured with her story Saligia, in the Elements of Time anthology. The idea for that story came to her after reading about the seven deadly sins. She then looked for a setting that would allow her to explore and personify those sins.

SPIES &
STARSHIP CAPTAINS

By Andi Caldwell

The heroes of my youth were spies and starship captains,
saving the world, one mission at a time.
Encapsulated into sixty-minute segments, we traveled
together fighting all foes of mankind.
Ruthless and kind, smart and sneaky, loyal and larcenous,
these enterprising uncles provided role models for
success, glamour and excitement.
However, biology and destiny bonded me to a more
mundane fate.
My life was filled with scraped knees, swim meets and
convention.
The fantasies of girlhood crumbled before the activities of
a well ordered life.

I have no regrets.

Now the nest has emptied, leaving me to contemplate the
abyss.
My yearnings have not slackened, my dreams remain
intact.
I see not the end of all things, rather my stalwart heroes,
full of justice and truth, saving the world,
beckoning… beckoning…

DANIEL THRASHER

Daniel Thrasher's passion can be summed up in one word: creativity. He's been writing since age five. The day inspiration first struck, he ran to the art closet, grabbed a stack of blank paper, and scrawled out crooked sentences about a fat dog that got stuck in the doggy door of his owner's house.

Since then, Daniel's forays in writing have spanned satire, short stories, poetry, songs, and parodies. He started a literary club in college and released a campus literary magazine, as well as writing and serving as guest editor for the student newspaper. His love for creativity includes art and music as well. He enjoys drawing, and he has taught himself acoustic guitar, piano, and harmonica.

Daniel recently graduated cum laude from The College of Idaho with a B.A. in Creative Writing and History. He will continue to pursue writing wherever his career takes him.

BRAIN RESTORATION

By Daniel Thrasher

"What is a personality but a collection of thoughts, emotions and memories?"

The scientist mused while he swirled cream into his steaming cup of coffee. He took a sip and yelped. "It's still hot!"

Sheila laughed.

"Careful." She took a seat across from him. "So, what are you saying, Stephen? Are you saying that people are no more than just thoughts, emotions and memories?"

She stretched her arms over her head and yawned.

"Not necessarily."

"Well," she said, "you would know."

Stephen replied, "I'm just a man with dreams that are too big for my head."

She leaned forward, a solemn expression on her face.

"Stephen, it hurts me when you downplay your accomplishments like that. You have made some incredible advancements in neurology."

She smiled and put a hand on his. "Look at me, Stephen. I know it's hard to believe that what you do in that lab every day helps people, but it does! Trust me. Remember Thomas Edison and his endless experiments to discover a working light bulb?"

Stephen winced at the comparison. "Sheila, you know that's not the same thing. When people find out what I've been doing, the people I've—"

"Nothing great comes without sacrifice. Those people knew the risks when they agreed. You've done nothing wrong. Do you understand that? Nothing."

Stephen sighed and stood. "That's nice of you to say, but I feel it in my bones. You didn't see what I've seen in these experiments. I can't say I'm a religious man, but sometimes it really feels like I'm messing with things I shouldn't be messing with."

He turned and saw Sheila's expression turn sour.

"Damn it, Stephen! I'm trying to be patient with you. Come on! You've been working on this for years, and a few days before the payoff, you get cold feet? You're a genius. This world needs you, end of story.

"Now, I'm going home to get some sleep before this hellish week begins."

Sheila pulled her sweater tightly around her shoulders and gave him a sympathetic peck on the cheek.

"I'm sorry, sweetheart," she said, her voice softening. "I'm not trying to be impatient. Just… try to pull yourself together before the big speech, that's all. No one else is going to understand how great your discoveries are if you don't show the world that you're behind your work one hundred and ten percent."

Stephen gave her a quick hug, stroked her striped-blonde hair and whispered, "Thank you."

She picked up her purse off the table and winked at him. "Knock 'em dead, Dr. Winters."

～≪⊗≪～

Stephen leaned back in his reclining sofa and put the book *Fantastic Voyage* down on the nightstand next to him. His eyes burned from exhaustion, but whenever he tried to go to sleep, his heart raced with thoughts of what Monday would bring. Bleary-eyed, he looked at the time on his cell phone: 4:14AM.

"Ugh." He groaned, swinging his legs off the sofa. He stumbled to his feet.

Stephen realized he wouldn't be able to get any sleep with his mind swirling. He sighed and dropped into a chair at the dining room table.

"Might as well get some work done on my speech," he mumbled.

He picked up his notebook and flipped through the pages. After a series of equations and drawings, he found a page full of white space.

He took his pen out of the spiral binding and wrote out the sentence:

Brain Wave Charting and Personality Transfer

"How can I possibly explain this?"
He put his face in his hands, to take time to think.

～≪⊗≪～

With a deep breath to calm himself, he wrote:

My studies in neural science began in college at the U of M. I was a Psychology major; nothing in this world fascinated me more than understanding human be-

• • •

havior. If you haven't taken Psychology, you might believe in free will and freedom of thought in general, but when you get right down to it, you are merely a complex system of thoughts, emotions and memories, with a splash of DNA to set you apart from everyone else.

I have studied brain function extensively, and at long last, I believe I have isolated the parts of the brain that contain you. That is, the part of you that makes you who you are. It has taken years of experimentation, but I have invented a way to convert brain waves and patterns into a type of code that a computer can read and store, which means we can store you on a supercomputer and then transmit a modified version back into your brain... or someone else's.

The implications of this discovery are monumental. For one thing, if a loved one has suffered amnesia, they can refresh their memory by re-inputting their neural patterns, or help someone who has suffered trauma by giving them new memories to replace the detrimental ones.

Personally, I'm most excited to see the greatest minds of our time stored and transferred to new people. Imagine if we could have kept the great minds of Isaac Newton or Albert Einstein alive—what would they have to contributed to the world?

Because I expect skepticism, I have elected to be the first public example of this marvelous new frontier in science. I will store my brain waves and neural patterns periodically. In the event something happens to me, my knowledge and memories will be available for a worthy replacement.

I stand shoulder to shoulder with the rest of the scientific community in this bright time in human history.

Stephen read through the short speech. He had glossed over his experiments, hoping no one would think to ask him about his methods and would focus on *Brain Restoration* and the benefits it would provide.

Stephen sighed. He realized society, as a whole, rarely was that optimistic.

⸎

"On behalf of the Neural Research Foundation, please extend a warm welcome to Dr. Stephen Winters."

The auditorium resonated with applause. Backstage, Stephen gave Sheila a quick kiss, and she gave him an affectionate squeeze on the shoulder before she nudged him forward. He concentrated carefully on each step until he reached the podium and shook his benefactor's hand.

"Thank you very much, Dr. Abbot," he squeaked out.

The wiry old man gave Stephen a pat on the back and flashed him a warm smile.

"You'll do great," Dr. Abbot said. "I'm very pleased with your results."

Stephen watched the older man hobble off the stage, leaning heavily on his cane. He then turned to face thousands of eager faces and television cameras pointed at him. He tapped the microphone and nervously cleared his throat.

"Well, hello, there. I'm Dr. Stephen Winters. Dr. Abbot and I have been working on a technique we've named *Brain Restoration*. It started with research to help with Alzheimer's, but today, it is so much more than that. This is a revolutionary way of looking at and analyzing the human brain."

He paused and shuffled through his notes. "You'll have to excuse me. I'm not known for my oratory skills."

A small wave of laughter echoed off the high ceiling.

"Okay, so... the technique. Think of your brain as a computer hard drive, if you will. On it, you have an operating system that dictates how you behave and through what lens you view the world. On top of that operating system is a bunch of data you've collected over the years: a lot of it junk, but some of it is critically important. This is a collection of your memories, your knowledge, your feelings and your aptitudes.

"You might have memories that are buried so deep within that you can't get at them, for example, without therapy. But using my invention, any memory or bit of knowledge you have can be recovered."

A loud murmur rippled through the crowd. Stephen waved for the audience to quiet down. "Uh, wait. That's not all. That's actually only a minor part of what Brain Restoration is all about.

"Back to the hard drive comparison. If a patient gets amnesia or has a traumatizing experience, Brain Restoration will allow patients to replace memories or even erase unwanted ones, much like reformatting a hard drive."

He rushed to add, "It's all very safe, of course."

He paused to take a breath and let the crowd quiet again before he continued.

"Best of all, think of this: The greatest minds who ever lived, like Aristotle, Plato, Socrates, Jesus Christ, Muhammad, Galileo, all the way up to present-day figures like Stephen Hawking—the extensive knowledge of these men could have been preserved and transmitted to intelligent people to continue their work! This could revolutionize education as we know it!"

Stephen was flushed with excitement, one hand

raised with triumph and the other pounding the podium emphatically. The audience was a large blur of moving mouths and gesticulations.

He finished his speech by appealing to everyone to think of the good that could be done, the prejudices that could be done away with, through memory replacement.

The questions and answers segment was a whirlwind of admiration, fearful pleas and furious outcries. Stephen tried to respond as best he could, but the crowd was frenzied.

⊰⊱⊰⊱

"In a stunning ceremony today, the renowned neurologist Dr. Stephen Winters has finally revealed his long-awaited research project, which he has dubbed *Brain Restoration*. I'm John Atkins, and we'll be right back with tonight's episode of *Detailed Edition*."

When the television show returned, the announcer began with, "Thank you for joining us tonight on *Detailed Edition*. I'm John Atkins, reporting from our studios in New York.

"As you can see in the footage behind me, this morning's crowd had mixed reaction when Dr. Winters revealed his long-awaited and controversial new medical technique he is calling *Brain Restoration*."

John turned to face the other camera on the right before he continued and the footage behind him disappeared.

"Tonight, we have three experts in various fields joining us: Doctor of Theology, Leslee Meadows, who represents Hands Together, a national faith-based charitable organization for Christians; medical professional and bestselling author of *Brains Matter*, Dr. Dorothy Meyers;

● ● ●

and Dr. Thomas Abbot, founder of the Neural Research Foundation and a staunch proponent of Dr. Winters's work."

The scene on the television showed the satellite up-link for one of the guests, while the other two guests and the reporter sat in the studio of the newsroom.

"First, Dr. Meadows, your organization is predominately Christian based. What do you think churches or other religious or Christian organizations' reactions have been for the controversial technology now being called *Brain Restoration*?"

"I can't speak for all Christians, but the predominate response from the members of Hands Together has been shock and perhaps even outrage at this so-called advancement. None of us is God, and no one should be trying to do something as unnatural as downloading someone's brain. Computers don't have souls, feelings, emotions. When we put human intelligence into a machine without a human conscience or a soul, how can we even know what the results might be?

"And then, to put that back into a person—and not the person God intended to have those talents, intelligences and memories… it's just unconscionable to consider."

John nodded thoughtfully before turning to Dr. Abbot. "Do you have a response, Dr. Abbot?"

"We're not trying to play God here," Dr. Abbot said, his voice clear and smooth. "We're looking at ways to preserve some of the greatest minds of our time, to help elderly people remember loved ones throughout their lives instead of suffering from dementia and memory loss or God-forbid things like Alzheimer's Disease. It's cruel to put someone through that needless—"

Dr. Meadows interrupts to say, "You talk about cruel. Tell me how the experiments that helped develop *Brain Restoration* were performed? In order to perfect the technology—if it's even truly perfected—surely human subjects had to be used."

John turned to face Dr. Abbot who nodded. "Sure, we had to use human subjects to perfect the techniques, but all subjects signed consent forms, or their families did. They knew what they were helping to create."

"Well," Dr. Meadows retorted, "what type of physical tests and tortures did the subjects of these trials have to endure? What were the risks and dangers they had to face to create this technology and perfect it—assuming it even is perfected and isn't going to..."

She raised her hands in frustration before she finished with, "Who knows? Scramble someone's brain? Destroy everything that gives them a sense of who they are? This isn't our place to delve into. It's God's domain, not ours."

"All of the trials are documented and Dr. Winters's research will be compiled and published in the trade journals. Really," Dr. Abbot interjected, "these accusations are ridiculous. Dr. Winters is a Nobel Peace Prize winner, for God's sake. He's a respected physician and scientist. This is a technology and medicine combination that can advance humanity.

"We can teach children of underdeveloped nations valuable knowledge at the click of a button, erase the prejudices of age-old conflicts, and bring about a new Age of Enlightenment!"

John turned to Dr. Abbott and asked, "What about the misuse of this technology? It seems like a lot of power to whoever controls the technology. For example, what if it is used in interrogations by terrorist factions against United States military members or our agents? Surely the use of this technology to further military conquest and acts of war must be considered."

Dr. Abbot rapidly shook his head. "This is not a weapon; it's a tool for education."

"But surely, Dr. Abbott," John said, "you have to admit the potential for misuse is there."

"Sure, I guess it is," Dr. Abbott conceded, "but the potential for misusing polio vaccines was there too, or any other vaccination. They could have been used as biological weapons just as easily as they were used as life-saving medicine. This is really no different."

There was a pause as the conversation lulled. As a good show host should, John Atkins turned the conversation to the next guest for the evening.

"All right, let's go to Dr. Meyers here via satellite from Chicago. Good evening, Dr. Meyers. Glad to have you with us."

"Thank you. Good to be here," she replied and then smiled for the camera to the satellite feed.

John continued. "Coming from the perspective of someone in the field of medicine and psychology, what are your thoughts on Dr. Winters's research and *Brain Restoration*?"

Dr. Meyers chuckled. "Well, despite my background, I've really never seen anything like it before. It's too soon to tell, but I do believe that, like with all new technology, humanity will adjust."

"Dr. Meyers, let me ask you this: Would you personally use this sort of device? Let's say you wanted to know more about neuroscience, would you be willing to simply click a button and make that happen?"

"John, while it sounds intriguing, I definitely wouldn't risk it at this point. It's too soon to know all the repercussions of taking someone else's memories and knowledge and putting them into your own head. I do think there's a lot of potential, though."

The conversation stayed calm through the remainder of the program. When the half hour was up, John turned to the panel and the satellite monitor and said, "Thank you all for being with us here tonight. Before we go, Dr. Abbott, are there any final thoughts you'd like to share?"

Dr. Abbot nodded and turned to face the camera with an earnest expression.

"I just wanted to say I understand that the unknown can be scary, but generations from now, people will look back on this as the precursor to mankind's greatest achievements. How can we not progress as a species when our greatest minds will be with us forever?"

"Food for thought," John replied. "And for all of us here at *Detailed Edition*, goodnight."

The credits rolled and John and Dr. Abbot both leaned back in their chairs and exhaled.

⚬⚬⚬⚬

Stephen turned off the television, his face was white with worry. Sheila stroked his hair behind his ear with a gentle touch.

"You did great this morning," she cooed. "I'm so proud of you."

He was silent for a moment, hardly noticing her. When she kissed his neck, he jumped.

"Oh, I'm sorry," he mumbled when she drew back.

"I'm just a little distracted."

Sheila sighed and sat up. "Do you want to talk about it?"

"No. I just... I wish people would be more open-minded, that's all. I can't remember the last time there's been such a big leap in human history, and everyone's squabbling over minor details." He stole a glance at Sheila, admired her shining silver-blue eyes, the contours of her flushed cheeks, her pouting lips, her silky neck, the vee of her cleavage. He placed a hand on the small of her back and pulled her close to him.

"Stephen," she said. "I know you're worried, but—"

"Shh," he whispered, and then he kissed her tenderly.

Stephen had never been one to consider the act of intercourse making love, because to his mind, love was nothing more than a fabricated construct of the human condition, just a bunch of excited neurons and a random compatibility of personality traits.

When he shuddered in the throes of pleasure that evening, he whispered in Sheila's ear, "I love you."

∽≪∞≫∾

The fan on the supercomputer whirred, whipping Stephen's hair up.

"How do you think this is going to go?" Stephen asked. He could feel his body trembling in the chair. A brain receptor was strapped to the back of his skull.

Dr. Abbot smiled and gave Stephen a pat on the back. "It's going to be just fine, you'll see."

Stephen tried to relax, but the hair stood up on the back of his neck nonetheless.

While he worked, Dr. Abbot said, "You know, Stephen, you've impressed me. I don't mean any offense by it, but I wasn't sure you had it in you to deal with this kind of media scrutiny. The research and the testing turned out to be the easy part, huh?"

They both chuckled.

"Yeah, the media has been hard on me," Stephen agreed. "Thank God Sheila's been such a big support. I don't know where I'd be without her."

A beeping noise caused Stephen to jump.

"Relax, son. It's just your machine," Dr. Abbot said. He chuckled at Stephen. "I thought you would have recognized that noise by now."

"Well, I do," said Stephen. "It's just—"

He left the sentence unspoken, but his mind was remembering the subjects in the earlier test trials whose brains nearly literally exploded inside their heads right after the sound of that very beep.

"All right, it looks like it's ready," Dr. Abbot said. He came over and knelt in front of Stephen. "Now, listen to me, nothing is going to go wrong. Clear your mind, close your eyes, and concentrate. Good luck, Steve."

"Thanks."

Stephen shut his eyes and tried to think about nothing, but images of exploding brains kept coming back. He shut his eyes even tighter.

"All right, ready?" Dr. Abbot asked. "I'm going to throw the switch."

"Go ahead," Stephen called.

He was clenching the armrests as tightly as he could. His entire body quivered.

❧❀❧

The ceiling of a hospital room; Stephen's favorite rattle; his stuffed alligator and a plastic dinosaur he received for his second birthday; a trip to the emergency room when he split his head open falling off the counter; his first loose tooth; a crush on a little blond girl named Allie; an A+ on his big science project in fifth grade; Mom dead from cancer; electric toothbrush; first bicycle; voice cracking; glasses; dissecting frogs; Calculus; credit card debt; college scholarship; lost virginity in the basement of the science hall; little brother killed overseas; became an Atheist; DUI; met Sheila; declared Psychology major... pain... searing pain...

⚬⚬⚬⚬⚬

Stephen woke in a hospital room. His eyes burned, and he felt tears dried on his cheeks.

"Where am I?" he croaked. He tried to sit up, but his head throbbed. He couldn't move.

He heard footsteps and tried to call out, but his voice just came out as a ragged gasp. Turning his head, he saw an old man limp into the room. It was Dr. Abbot.

"Hey, son, how are you feeling?" he said, kneeling beside the bed.

Stephen tried to reply, but it came out as a cough.

"I know you're feeling bad. I wish this had all gone according to plan. I'll be right back."

Dr. Abbot left the room with the door ajar. Stephen could just barely make out Dr. Abbot's side of the conversation.

"Yes, the device captured his mind.

"No, he suffered from a hemorrhage.

"Yeah, I've found a replacement.

"No, the world can't know about this yet. I have full faith in you, doctor."

The sound of footsteps faded away.

"Dr. Abbot?" a female voice asked. "If you'll fill out this form, he can get started right away."

"Thank you," Dr. Abbot replied. Stephen could make him out through the crack in the doorway. "Let's see. He used to be a Mr. Joseph Pierce. Police officer, actually. Had two children, a four-year-old and a two-year-old. Married seven years. All right, all done. Joseph Pierce officially died in a car accident."

Dr. Abbot came back into the room.

"It's sad, really," Dr. Abbot said. "I know you don't remember this yet, but you will. Stephen is a great man. The world can't afford to go on without him. Fortunately, you are now Stephen Winters, son. And after the surgeon is finished, you will look like Stephen Winters too."

Dr. Abbot smiled when the masked doctor walked into the procedure room.

"We'll have to get rid of Sheila though. She would probably notice the difference."

MIRACLES

By Farah Evers

It was said the age of miracles was long gone. During the long-ago years of social depression and utter chaos, God sent prophets to spread virtue, organization, peace and love amongst mankind.

Different religions formed and oriented people toward a more righteous lifestyle. All those religions held a stack of miracles in their course, which was what convinced many people of the existence of an almighty God.

As time passed, God lifted that outstanding phenomenon away from the lives of generations, and truly, miracles were not experienced by mankind again for many ages. Various opinions and debates conquered people's lives. Everyone wondered about God and his miracles. Until it happened again, once, right in the heart of Beirut.

Strangely enough, the Lebanese never mentioned the occurrence of that miracle after it was over, and the media couldn't bring itself to publish or discuss that incident ever again. People handled the issue in silence.

Stranger than the miracle itself was the fact that no one learned a thing from it. It was, indeed, as though it

* * *

never were.

The beautiful and peaceful city of Beirut was standing high with pride and progress. People were preoccupied with new inventions, wondrous discoveries by scientists, the Internet and all the various means of modern technology.

One calm summer night, something beyond eccentric happened. It was a miracle that started revealing itself at one o'clock in the morning and lasted just a few hours before it perished into the morning sky. Most of the citizens scattered around the Lebanon provinces were fast asleep when it happened, while others were awake to witness the madness.

People have attempted to explain everything but weren't able to purposely tell that tale. They said it was like an earthquake that creeps up on one uninvited and shatters one's life within seconds. The next day, everyone went about their daily lives as though nothing had happened.

Nizar opened his eyes at around one in the morning to the sound of a piercing clamor. The noise rose in pitch as the seconds passed.

Nizar peeled his body off his mattress and headed for the window. His eyes widened at the sight of countless individuals running in every direction. Every single person carried an axe or a mallet in hand. He looked across to the other side of the street and saw a demolition truck driving toward the fancier housing areas.

Could they be construction workers at this time? his puzzled mind speculated.

The streets were filled with people. He saw a child clutching his mother's dress while she tried to forcefully pry him away. She looked like she wanted to run off. On another corner, a man ran around in his underwear. It was all so shocking to Nizar. Panicked, he hurried down the stairs of his building and made his way to the street.

"Can someone please tell me what on Earth is going on?" he yelled out.

Nobody replied or even uttered a word, but the commotion worsened. Every time he tried to stop someone, they shrugged and shook between his hands like freshly caught fish, shoved him aside and took off.

He looked to his left; there was a bunch of kids gathered in a dark alley, sobbing. When his eyes shifted toward the right, he saw a lady scurrying away in her nightgown. Everywhere he looked there were people, rubble and large stones strewn around the streets like ashes in an ashtray.

Some trucks were already picking up the mess, but things were wildly out of control. Outrageous chaos took over the nearby parts of the city, and the shrieks were incomprehensible.

Oh my, God! he thought. *This is the end of the world! It's Armageddon!*

While he tried to make sense of the inexplicable craziness, his eyes fell on an old lady barely able to haul herself along with the crowd. He immediately ran in her direction, knowing that she could not go faster than him. He snatched her by the arm and pulled her close to his building entrance.

"What's going on at this hour of the night? By God, tell me. What's happening, lady? Has everyone gone mad? Is it the end of the world? Are we all going to die now?"

Before he had the chance to finish his questions, the old lady interrupted him.

"Haven't you heard, son? It's a miracle! A miracle bestowed upon us by God!"

"A miracle? Lady, you're out of your mind! What miracle?"

His eyebrows met. He felt a rush of blood leave his feet and surge to his head.

"It's a miracle, you ignorant fool. The walls have *spoken*!"

He could see the terror in her eyes, but for the first few seconds, he wasn't sure he'd heard what she said.

"*What?*"

The old lady repeated "The *walls,* son! They can talk!"

Nizar rolled his eyes in disbelief, grabbed the woman by her weak frail shoulders and shook her.

"Wake up, old lady, wake up! This is not the time to be sleepwalking or babbling gibberish!"

"Get your hands off of me, you fool. I'm telling you, the walls are talking back to people now! I swear. When I heard people say the walls have ears, I used to think it was just a figure of speech. Turns out, son, those walls have been listening to every single word we've ever said. Go and talk to your walls; you'll see for yourself. They'll reply…and they never shut up!"

Nizar stood there, stunned.

Lost in thought, he wandered back into his building and made his way into his apartment. He held his hand up parallel to the wall, and his palm slowly touched the cold grainy texture of unpainted cement.

He raised his head gradually, smiling. *She's nuts. Walls can't talk.*

One thought took him on an endless ride of possibilities, and another returned him to logic. He walked back outside and down to the streets. His urge to understand the situation was far too strong to be satisfied with an absurd idea about talking walls.

He took to the streets, browsing through the crowds for someone who looked a bit more sensible, someone who wasn't panicking as much as everyone else. A middle-aged man passed by, and he was walking instead of running like a lunatic.

"Excuse me!" Nizar yelled out. "Sir, please tell me. What's going on?"

The man did not reply immediately, but instead, he blinked and turned to look down the street and then back at Nizar.

Nizar continued, trying to coax a response from the man. "Sir, what drove all those people crazy? What's with the clouds of dust and all this destruction?"

The man replied in a calm and collected tone, "The walls are talking back to people. Those walls have witnessed events and overheard conversations. They know our secrets!"

Nizar blinked but said nothing.

Quietly, the man shook his head and looked down at his feet, and said, "It's a disaster."

The man then turned and walked down the street, away from Nizar.

Nizar followed the man.

Just when he caught up with him again, the man turned back to Nizar and said, "Go home, kid. Demolish your house and get rid of your walls."

He looked back up the street and then turned back to

Nizar and continued with, "I just did that myself. I stopped my walls from blurting out all of my private moments. Everyone is doing that; it's safer that way."

Nizar stared at the man, his eyes wide. "You destroyed your home?"

"Yeah," the man answered. "I mean, we'll all be homeless soon, but it's better than being totally exposed."

"Exposed?" Nizar asked.

"Son," he responded. "Every person has a secret."

Without another word, the man walked away again, and Nizar simply stood and watched him go.

After a few stunned moment, Nizar too walked away, disappointed. What he had heard was depressing, but it also made him curious to find out what his walls had in store for him, if he even believed it was true.

He wondered if it might simply be a case of mass hysteria. While he stood in a corner and contemplated the matter, he watched while his neighbors destroyed their homes, right in front of his eyes.

Should I believe all this? Should I really go tear down my walls? Or should I ask my walls questions first?

While Nizar watched a busy demolition truck driver tear down a house, some people were heading downtown. Nizar figured many would be heading toward mosques and churches. In difficult times like those, people prayed to their God.

Those not heading downtown or who were not tearing down their homes and apartments were instead nosily asking the standing walls about all their occupants' secrets.

Nizar heard people talking, planning to rove around famous peoples' and governors' mansions, to ask all sorts of questions, to hear others' wild, furtive stories.

⋘⋙

Nizar sat crouched in the corner of the street, away from people and walls. He didn't know where to go or what to do while he watched the remains of his own apartment begin to crumble as the walls fell in.

Before long, small rockets and bombs landed on one side of a province and another set of rockets were fired back in that direction in response.

The blast sounds later would be talked about by the elders as reminding the people of the Civil War. More fearful than war, though, it seemed people were looking for the fastest annihilation method to get the gossip, betrayal and secrets contained within the walls over and done with.

⋘⋙

When morning finally broke, the city woke to a destroyed Beirut. People still wandered around the streets, wondering, pondering what had happened. They eyed each other with great caution. Some were preparing for emigration, and others sought help.

Nizar opened his eyes to find he'd fallen asleep on the ground in the same corner he had sat in the night before. He picked himself up and looked around in bewilderment.

A wealthy real estate agency owner announced in the streets that he would buy most of the properties and renovate or rebuild everything at his own personal expense, but it was unclear if it was an impulse of basic altruism or if it was a method of greed yet to be seen. Nizar couldn't be sure what the man's motives might be.

Beirut has been destroyed, was all Nizar could think.

❋ ❋ ❋

He watched an old woman he knew tread sluggishly through the rubble. It was Mrs. Hassoun, the woman who lived in the old house previously occupied by a military base in 1978, during the Beirut Civil War.

Nizar had been in the house before, and he knew of its creepy history. From what he'd learned in history and from his neighbors, the old woman's house had at one point contained torture chambers and questioning rooms in which officers frequently held captured militia militants and persecuted them to death.

He walked up to her, his heart filled with joy at the sight of a familiar face. "Mrs. Hassoun! It's me, Nizar, the son of Omar."

He smiled reassuringly at her.

The old lady looked up at him.

"I hadn't lived in my house for fifteen years! It was occupied by those damned... went back to it recently..."

"Did you see what happened? They destroyed Beirut!"

He pointed around.

She looked down and replied, "I spent the night alone, behind the walls. Alone..."

"They destroyed Beirut, Mrs. Hassoun," he repeated.

"You're going to grow a root soon?" She placed her palm near her earlobe.

"I said: Beirut! It's gone!"

"Don't grow the root in the sun," she mumbled.

He took her hand and walked beside her. When he looked up and scanned the distance to find her house still standing. He couldn't stop gazing at the only house holding its weary stones together.

"I can see you are looking at my house," she said. "It's

pretty worn out; my house is old."

Nizar quickly assumed she was deaf. He figured she must have missed out on everything her walls had to say.

"If only you heard what your walls had to say!" he screamed out, making sure she'd hear him. "There must be endless stories from the war days, but God gave you the best blessing ever: being deaf!"

The old lady waddled away, murmuring to herself as she approached her beloved house. "The idiot thinks I'm deaf. I scared the living daylights out of those walls! The military base is just a phone call away!"

She wagged her finger.

FARAH EVERS

Farah Momtaz Evers was born in Beirut, Lebanon, on April 1, 1978. She graduated from the Lebanese American University in correspondence with the University State of New York, carrying a BS in Liberal Arts (Major: Interior Architecture), in 2000.

She then moved on to studying German and Dutch and received certificates in both languages.

Farah is a member of the International Society of Poets, and has attained an Editor's Choice Award for her poetry. Most of her short stories and articles have been featured online.

In addition to, her passion for writing, Farah is a song writer/singer. Her singles have reached Soundclick's Top Ten charts in Jazz vocals, and are available here:

www.soundclick.com/farahevers

DAVID & THE OUTSIDE

By Robert L. Arend

David turned his eyes from his teacher. Barack Obama had been dead for years, yet there he was, teaching a ninth grade civics class about government and the Constitution, as much a holographic image created by molecular processors as the open fields of grass David could see through the walls of glass.

"Mr. Tripper," the see-through former President of the United States of America calmly called out to David, "I'm here, not where you are looking."

"Sorry, Mr. President," David murmured under the subdued laughter of his classmates.

"Perhaps you could answer my question," the president quipped.

"What question was that, sir?" David, privately, ridiculed the hologram's big ears.

"Where in the Constitution is slavery outlawed?"

"Um, something about involuntary servitude—"

"The Amendment, Mr. Tripper."

"The Amendment was about involuntary servitude —"

"The number, Mr. Tripper. One? Two? Three? Twen-ty-two?"

I'll bet it isn't any of those, David thought. He squirm-ed, unable to think of anything but his birthday the next day.

"I'll be thirteen," he thought out loud.

The President raised his chin and looked down stern-ly at David.

"Correct," the hologram said. "The Thirteenth Amendment it is."

David couldn't believe his luck. He was barely pass-ing the president's class. A wrong answer would have re-duced his points to failing.

"Oh, and happy birthday," the president leaned down to whisper. "Class dismissed."

The school day over, David ran through the corridors, weaving in and out of the paths of other kids to get to his cubicle. He wanted to flop himself on his bed, put on his virtual reality headgear and experience fishing on the banks of the Mississippi River.

⚬⚬⚬⚬⚬

"I don't know, Huck. They aren't biting today," David told the other boy.

Huck's eyes were hidden under his straw hat, the fishing string tied to his big toe. He was snoring.

"David," the woman's voice seemed to come from the sky. "Dinner's ready!"

The fishing bank, Huck and the Mighty Mississippi faded out.

Darn it, David thought when he fumbled for the re-lease button of the head-enclosing helmet. He knew some really bad words, but he didn't dare say them, let alone think them. He placed the helmet on the shelf, and then climbed down the ladder into his parents' living quarters.

"How was school today," his mother asked when she handed him his plate. She was still wearing her climate-control uniform.

"Okay, I guess," David shrugged. He sat at the table, letting the steam and smell of the hydroponic vegetables waft up his nose. He wondered what fish tasted like.

His mother joined him at the table.

"Your physics instructor had me leave my worksite at eleven-hundred hours to meet with him about you. He told me you daydream too much in class. You know what happens to students who develop no essential skill."

David nodded.

"They're put outside, David," his mother reminded him, tears welling in her eyes.

"But I want to go outside, Mom," David said. "I want to see real sky. I want to see a real river. I want—"

"No. You don't, David," his mother pleaded, cupping his face in her hands. "Don't you understand we live far below the outside because—"

"The war," David interrupted impatiently. "How long ago was that, Mother? It was in 2054. It's 2129 now. It must be safe to go there by now."

"Well, it isn't," his father scolded. He was so tall he had to bend his body sharply to enter the cubicle, straining the fabric of his water works uniform.

"How do you know?" David asked.

His father sat at the table.

"None of the boys and girls and the old men and women have ever come back after being banished outside," he said without looking at his son.

David's eyes followed the path of another plate from his mother's hands to his father's.

"Maybe they didn't want to come back."

"I'm sure all of them did," his father said. "But there is no way to get back in once you're out. Nothing can live outside. The radioactivity and lack of food and water would kill within a hundred and sixty-eight hours."

"Maybe fifty-years ago, but who's to say people can't live outside now?"

David toyed with his food. He wasn't hungry. He wanted to eat fish.

An expression of terror came over his father's face before David felt the sting of the man's hand. David pushed away from the table, hand over the left side of his face, and ran to the ladder.

"That know-it-all will get himself killed," David heard his father whisper.

Back in his cubicle, the boy put the helmet back on and rejoined Huck for fishing on the bank of the Mighty Mississippi.

⋙⋘

David's parents did calm down enough to go through with their planned birthday celebration for him. In the phony outside, on the patio, they sang *Happy Birthday*. He blew out the thirteen candles. After cake and chocolate soymilk ice cream, David opened his present, a shiny red single-seat transporter. Red was his favorite color.

"You're old enough to drive now," his father said, proudly. "It's got anti-collision sensors, but I think you should just practice driving up and down our corridor before you start using it to drive to school."

David climbed inside and the seat harness automatically wrapped around him. He wrapped his fingers around the steering wheel, thinking of all the places he could drive to explore in the underground city.

What is down Corridor 5, or Corridor 6, or Corridor 7? he thought. *If I can't go outside, I may as well check out every place there is on the inside.*

"Can I drive around our corridor now?" he asked.

"You can drive until seventeen-hundred hours, then it'll be time to come in," his mother said.

"I'll levitate it out there for you," his father said, aiming the crescent-shaped moving device at the transporter.

A gray bubble immediately surrounded the transporter, and then both rose from the floor and floated out of the cubicle while the Trippers followed. When the vehicle came to rest on the blue floor of the corridor, the bubble silently burst.

In the car, David strained against the safety harness to touch the security button. The car told him to press the fingers of his right hand on the screen of the console. When he did, light strong enough to make his hand near-transparent rolled from fingertips to the wrist.

"Fingerprints logged," the car said. "What is your name?"

"David Tripper," the boy answered.

"Searching... You are qualified. Happy birthday, David Tripper. You may proceed," the car droned.

"Ignition," David ordered.

The low hum of the engine excited David. He gripped the steering wheel and commanded, "Transport!"

The transporter lifted two inches off the surface. David steered it to the center of the corridor, straightened the trajectory and then sped away from his parents at the programmed 11.176 meters per second.

The corridor of family cubicles was 8046.72 meters long. The cubes had a juncture midway for the school and shopping districts, but David obeyed his father by taking no detours off the thruway. Still, he had never before been so far away from his own neighborhood by himself.

The transporter automatically eased to a stop before the gigantic arched wall. David had to tilt his head so far back it touched his spine in order to see the buttressed ceiling. There were many manholes and vents up there and panels that beamed down the light. Letters above and below each manhole spelled: WARNING: CONFINED SPACE.

They identified each to be entranceways to *Electrical, Climate, Water* and *Waste* and the other vital systems of the underground nation.

How do they get up there? David wondered. He looked at the row of security doors in front of him, each identified with a labeled manhole for ground-level entrance to each system.

That must be the door Dad goes through to work every day, David thought when he saw *Water Works* stenciled in red on the shiny white entrance. *Climate Control,* his mother's work area, was to the right of his father's. Each entrance had a screen with a hand identifier like that in David's transporter. David mused that the noise of so much machinery behind those doors leaked not a decibel outward.

"You have a caller," the transporter announced.

"Answer," David ordered.

"It's time to come home, David," his mother said, her holograph standing in front of the transporter.

"I'm on my way," the boy said.

He turned the steering wheel sharply for the U-turn that put him on a path home.

"Transport," he ordered.

The transporter hummed and made the turn and sped forward at the instant David saw a lone door at the far end of the systems corridor identified in red: **OUTSIDE**

∕✦✦✦✦✧✧∖

Stephen Hawking roamed the classroom in his powered wheelchair, undeterred by the narrow space between the rows. He simply passed through the desks and his students like every hologram instructor could.

"The Higgs boson, though isolated, has never been observed directly," his voice buzzed. "The question, therefore, has yet to be answered as to whether human observation would or would not have an effect on the particle's properties, even to where observation may cause it to change into something else entirely."

David daydreamed he was running through the holographic field of tall grass beyond the wall of glass. Suddenly, physics instructor Hawking's transparent face blurred the view.

"Do you think if you do not see nor hear me I do not exist?" Hawking demanded.

"No, s-sir," David answered.

"You were assigned to my classroom because genetic and mental scan data indicated your ability to grasp particle physics and apply them as a skill to benefit the Underground United States," Hawking reminded. "Too often, it is as though you're not here, David. You demonstrate zero interest. There will be serious consequences if your inattentiveness doesn't change. Do you understand?"

"Yes, sir," David murmured.

So they'll put me outside, he thought. *Why should I care when that's where I want to be anyway?*

"The vacant desk behind you, David," Hawking said. "Linda Fochler used to sleep through every class. She won't sleep in here anymore."

Good, David thought. *I really like Linda. If they put me outside, at least I can be with her.*

Hawking returned to the front of the classroom. He stared at the wall-to-wall blackboard until white words appeared:

Assignment: course work/fusion

Compile a report on current usage and suggest improved methods for generation. Due: 1400

❦

"You may leave now," Hawking said.

When David sat in the seat of his transporter and the harness secured him, some of his classmates surrounded him to admire and touch the machine.

"Gosh, Davy," Andrea said, "this must have emptied your parents' access points."

"Don't know," David replied. "Maybe."

"Heck, look at you," Brian scoffed at Andrea. "Dave's parents are rich. Both have Level 2 jobs. Both of mine have Level 12 jobs. We're lucky if they can keep me and my sister in shoes."

"I'll be rich, someday," Eddie said. "If I can get a job with Fusion Systems when I graduate—"

"Hey, Dave, when they kick you outside, can I have your transporter?" a kid named Michael asked.

"You know something I don't?" David shot back.

"Who doesn't? My kid brother's smarter than you.

Everybody knows you're going to be kicked outside."

"Then I'll be better off than you bunch of earth-worms," David replied.

David saw Michael's right hand become a fist.

"Ignition," he ordered. He heard the low hum.

"Forward," David squealed, but, because the other children were in the way, the transporter's anti-collision system activated and the transporter did not move forward.

The punch was powerful. David had never been hit like that before, and held tight by the safety harness, he could only hold his hands and arms to his face in defense.

A robotic sanitizer traveled through the corridor with spidery arms waving. David's classmates ran to it and climbed on for a ride. When their laughter had faded, David ordered his transporter home.

<hr />

"Ain't nothin' to be afeared of," Huck told David. "I live on the outside. I hate bein' too long cooped up."

David picked up a dirty fragment of a whiskey bottle and tossed it in the Mighty Mississippi. The sun was blinding, but he wished he could feel its heat on his bare skin. Virtual reality helmets had limitations that prevented it feeling like the real thing, no matter how much it might have looked it.

"I'm supposed to be doing my physics homework," he told Huck. "If I go into Mr. Hawking's class tomorrow without it, it'll be here-come-the-goons."

"So what's the worst could happen?" Huck asked, wiggling his big toe to test his fishing line. "You and me can fish all day instead've jest when you put that thing over your head."

"What about my parents? If I'm banished to the out-side, it'll kill them."

"Naw," Huck said. "Your folks'll get by. They'll jest make another kid and ferget you soon enough."

David nodded.

Huck reached into his pocket and extracted his corn-cob pipe. From his other pocket he took out his tobacco pouch.

"My Pappy's dead. He ne'er cared what I did. He ne'er cared much fer me more'n spit."

He struck a match on the crust of his foot and lit his pipe. He stared across the river, and David respected Huck enough to know when to leave his friend alone.

David descended only two rungs on the ladder before he froze. He could hear his mother crying, pleading with someone.

"No, no, no, you can't do this! We'll make him buckle down."

"Calm down, Mrs. Tripper," a strange male voice said. "Nothing's been decided, yet. You and your husband will attend this hearing—with your son, of course—and all of you will have a chance to defend against banishment."

"Maybe he just needs some medication to help him pay attention better."

"We don't allow drugs like that here anymore. You know that. Everyone here must be without mental and physical defect so as not to be a drain on the survival of the whole."

"How very fascist," David's mother hissed.

"Call it what you want," the man replied. "The surviv-al of this ship cannot be compromised."

"Even by a little boy?" David's mother spoke through her clenched teeth.

Ship? David thought. *Some ship, sunk in a big hole in the ground.*

David stepped down to the living cubicle.

"When's dinner, Mom?" he asked.

David glared at the strange man.

"You know what is expected of you," the man said to the boy's mother. With a stiff snap to the briefcase, the man stood and departed.

"Sit, David. We need to talk."

David took a seat at the table.

"I heard everything," he said.

"Then you know how much trouble you are in," she said. "I'm about to lose my mind, son. You've got to help us hold on to you."

David was about to shrug, but he stopped when he realized that attitude would only worsen his mother's despair. "What do you want me to do?"

She stood and went to the small desk in the corner, opened the drawer and found her not-so-secret stash of hydroponic cigarettes. She put one in her mouth and lit it with her pocket laser. She inhaled deeply, coughed, and then inhaled again.

"The hearing won't be for another two weeks, right after the school year ends," she said, the side-to-side tilting of her head telling David her mind was analyzing the situation. "There's time to change everything, get your grades up to passing, get you prepared for finals."

"But, Mom, you tried to help me before. Dad too," David said. "You and Dad don't know much about particle physics."

"Not in depth, but we both had some instruction for what was necessary in our fields," his mother said. "I don't think they'll really care about your performance in Obama's class. Besides that and physics, you're passing your other classes. What matters is the physics. Get your study kit. We'll go at it together."

Along with David's father after he arrived from work, and even through dinner, David and his parents studied. David had to admit his parents' basic knowledge was helpful, somewhat. As before, though, there came a point where going beyond the simple equations stretched his mother's and father's limits. They tried to learn, to understand more and help David, way past the point of mental and physical exhaustion.

"I don't understand it," David's mother said, exasperated. "All the pre-school scans strongly concluded our child was some kind of genius. His brain was mapped and tested, and the data fed into the school system's computer. A mind geared to the sciences, especially physics was what that screwed-up thing decided!"

She slammed her fist on the table and bowed her head to cry.

"We'll go at it again tomorrow," David's father said. "At least the homework is done. Hopefully Hawking will find the review and arguments good enough for a passing grade."

"Hawking's brain is inside another damn computer!" David's mother sneered.

"Go to bed, son," David's father said. "Tomorrow's another day. We'll get through this."

David stood and shuffled to his ladder. He paused, looked back at his grim parents and said, "Maybe we can all go outside together."

"Son, when you are in high school, you're going to learn that things are not quite what they appear to be. The government keeps many secrets, and adults who know those secrets are forbidden to discuss them among themselves, let alone their children."

"Do you know those secrets, Dad?"

"Only those that are critical to my job. I don't even know what your mother knows."

"Does that mean you can't go outside with me?" David asked.

"I'm afraid that's what it means, son."

David stared for a moment, watching his parents, before he softly said, "Goodnight, Dad. Goodnight, Mom."

He climbed into his cubicle, dropped onto his bed and soon fell asleep. He dreamed of rolling through the grass in the sun of the beautiful great outside.

On his way to school, David spotted a robotic trash collector sucking in waste at the central collection chute. David studied the gigantic machine, wondering where it went to empty itself. He reasoned that what was collected inside had to be disposed of somewhere else. When the vacuum tube retracted and the hatch of the chute slid shut, David decided to skip his first class and follow the collector.

The collector traveled slower than the programmed speed of David's transporter, so the boy had to order his vehicle to stop whenever it moved too far ahead of the waste machine. Progress was slow due to the number of stops the collector had to make to empty the other chutes. At the wall of entrances to critical systems, the big machine pivoted and moved to and disappeared into the dimly lit side corridor.

David felt his heart beat faster. That was where he had seen a door with **OUTSIDE** stenciled on it the day he had first driven his transporter. The boy made the turn and continued behind the collector.

The waste machine halted in front of the **OUTSIDE** door. David ordered his transporter to stop.

A clang was followed by a humming when the **OUT-SIDE** door slid open. The collector emitted a slight screech and then moved into the brilliantly lit room.

"Ignition," David ordered. "Forward." But the transporter had barely moved before the **OUTSIDE** door slid shut.

Almost as quickly as the collector had entered, the **OUTSIDE** door slid back open to allow the waste machine to exit. The transporter's anti-collision system activated and David jerked when his vehicle went into abrupt reverse and sped backward out of the corridor. David turned the steering wheel sharply.

"Forward," he commanded. The transporter executed the U-turn and took David to school in time to be late for his first class.

❦

The surface of David's desk instantly booted to the forest and animated animals. The creatures were searching for his composition. Whichever located the short story would reveal the boy's grade: the skunk a F, the shrew a D, the squirrel a C, the bear a B or the antlered buck an A. There were no plus or minuses in instructor Shirley Jackson's class, no middle ground.

While the other animals continued to sniff and search,

the shrew began to frantically dig, and David's heart sank. Suddenly, the buck reared and charged the shrew. The shrew burrowed into the ground, but tossed out a folder in the spray of dirt. The buck caught the folder in its mouth, tossed it in the air where it opened and its pages spread like a deck of cards over the screen:

Grade: A

David's sigh of relief merged with other such sighs, all smothered by the groans of the less fortunate. The grade would bolster his overall ninth grade average, but writing, though important enough to be taught, was not considered a vital skill.

Instructor Jackson had posted a note at the bottom of the last page:

David,

Your short story: Turning Inside Out, *was so reminiscent of some of the important fiction writings of my own era. I think I may have written something quite similar had I been confined underground, never to be able to physically experience all the wonders of the outside world. Should I dare to compare your story to* The Lottery, *the one I am most identified with? I think I shall dare to compare and decide the two to be of comparable literary weight.*

The desktop cleared to announce the book report on Mark Twain's *Adventures of Huckleberry Finn* was due tomorrow.

Another cram session with his mother and father began after dinner. David made small progress, but found his parents had better ability to absorb the information in their newfound fascination with particle physics than he himself had.

David had submitted the report on ideas for better fusion generation to Instructor Hawking. The boy knew the writing was good, but the substance not likely as good. String theory analysis was due on Monday. It was obvious Hawking detested the subject himself.

At least I have the weekend to get that report done, David thought.

David did not need his parents' help with the *Huckleberry Finn* assignment. He completed that book report by bedtime. Dreams of Huck and steering a raft in the strong currents of the Mighty Mississippi made for a restless sleep. The raft pitched violently, but Huck had a firm grip on the steering oar. David held on to the other steering oar at the bow of the raft, more to hang onto than to steer. A steamship whistled from the bend in the river before the bow of the raft jumped steeply upward. David lost his grip and was flung backward into the river.

Muddy water invaded David's mouth. An undertow sucked him beneath the river. Quickly exhausted, the boy's body relaxed for the drowning.

Sweaty pajamas clung to his bare skin when David awoke. The boy was happier than he could remember to be alive. The panic brought on by being unable to breath underwater lingered along with the pain of his lungs filling with the Mississippi until his chest was about to explode. He stripped and stepped into his shower.

Powerful jets sprayed a programmed exhaust of hot water, cleanser, disinfectant and skin and hair conditioners from scattered ports. After the shower, David dress and then gathered his dirty clothes and dropped them in the laundry shoot for cleaning and decontamination. He climbed down the ladder to the living quarters, ready for breakfast, but his mother was on the patio, smoking a cigarette and staring at the holographic storm clouds that the weather center projected for the comfort of variety. When his mother saw him, she quickly dropped the cigarette in the hazardous waste portal.

It was a quiet breakfast. His father and mother talked about the phony weather, and it was clear to David that the storm clouds were viewed by his mother as an omen of the worst sort.

"Can I have my allowance?" David asked his father. "There's a new virtual reality program I want to buy."

After the drowning experience, David had decided to take a break from Huck for a while.

"What program is that?" his father asked in that intrusive tone of voice that always gave David the creeps.

"It's a Harry Potter adventure," David blushed, seeing his father's disappointment that the program was not something less childish. "All the kids are talking about it."

He handed his wristband to his father.

The man sighed, but went over to the points scanner and programmed fifty points into the wristband.

"Thanks, Dad," David said. He touched the open band to his left wrist and the band closed and was sealed by the unbreakable bond of a mini-unified field. After another swallow of soymilk, the boy bolted from the cubicle to his parked transporter.

David's was not the only transporter on the thruway that day, but more adults were driving than the few other children who owned one. He was thinking about it being the first time he had driven his transporter to the shopping district when he spied the backend of a waste machine about eighteen meters ahead. He decided to follow it.

The drivers of other transporters gave David angry looks when they needed to pull out around him.

"You in some kind of hurry?" David would yell at each frown.

Progress was slow. *So many disposal units to suck out*, the boy thought. He wondered how so much waste could accumulate every day.

All units emptied, the waste machine made that abrupt turn with David only about two meters behind.

When the waste machine stopped in front of the **OUTSIDE** door, David parked his transporter and stepped out. He ran to the back of the waste machine, grabbed a handrail and stepped onto its rear bumper. He heard the **OUTSIDE** door clang and then hum. He braced himself when the mighty machine started to move forward again.

David trembled a little when he was completely in the brightly lit room and the **OUTSIDE** door slid shut. He jumped down from the waste machine to look around. There was another, much smaller, round door that buzzed.

Warning lights flashed. Alarm sirens blared. David covered his ears and had time to feel the horror at the moment the round door opened and sucked all of the air and him out of the room into the field of stars. The boy's body froze instantly and tumbled away, surrounded by the refuse from the waste machine.

⋘⋙

David's transporter was found easily enough, and the cameras had recorded the boy's fulfilled dream of escape to the outside. The information about what was really outside had been top secret, however, shared only with David's parents—who had known for a long time to where and what the OUTSIDE door led.

Most tragically were the results from a lengthy investigation of David's data files, which were found to have been accidentally switched with data processed on another child when both had been toddlers. The mistake had resulted in the wrongful banishment of one toddler, and thirteen years of life for David that would have otherwise been denied.

"What a horrible mistake," the chairperson of the secret governmental commission that had conducted the investigation said.

His co-chair cried. "That toddler was my son."

THE RIVER OF TIME

By Andi Caldwell

High up in the mountains, the trickle of the spring begins.
It flows downwards,
picking up water, silt, and experience.
As it reaches the middle, diverse streams join it
to form a strong and powerful entity.
By the time the river meets the sea, the water is steeped in
wisdom and detritus.
It is impossible for the human eye to follow a single drop
of water on its journey from the mountains to the sea.
Past, present and future all exist simultaneously as does
the beginning, middle and end of the river.
It has already happened.
It is happening.
It will happen.
The poor, feeble human is able only to access the present.
He mourns his losses and ponders his fate, thinking him-
self the master of his karma.
Listen to the sound of the river; the bubbling, gurgling
noise of water over the rocks.
Eternity is singing.

DANCING WITH SLEESTAKS

By Lisa Lee Smith

There's my fluttering heart and
my nervous laughter
and the uncomfortable reality
that I want whispers of reassurance
every bit as much as the scary green face
says it wants Dorothy's ruby slippers.

I'm still slightly afraid of flying monkeys
but luckily I'm not the pretty little prey
anyone has in mind.

Besides, there will always be plenty of other
assorted things left to worry about when it
comes to lost creatures from unfamiliar lands
and the gathering of nonexistent monsters
for a perfect midnight storm in the
blank space between clarity and confusion.

There's a genuine possibility
I'll be chasing inspiration or
asking for truly divine intervention
just as soon as I am finished
running from giant chicken statues
laughing at futile tornado warnings
riding with headless horsemen
losing my own way
and dancing with hissing Sleestaks in my dreams.

LISA LEE SMITH

Lisa Lee Smith grew up reading novels, poetry and the occasional cereal box, while letting her thoughts run wild around the western United States. A copy of Island of the Blue Dolphins *by Scott O'Dell remains on Lisa's crowded shelves, a reminder of those days when she fully realized a vivid imagination and a good book could take her anywhere in the world.*

After college and graduate school, Lisa began to follow her heart through freelance writing. About nine years later, she discovered Accentuate Writers Forum and joined the online forum.

In addition to the written word, Lisa believes that life with her husband, time spent with animals, the love of old movies and a view of snow-covered mountains are among the best gifts the universe has to offer. Uncontrollable laughter is right up there too.

And yes, she is still just a little afraid of those flying monkeys.

TERRIE SCHULTZ

Terrie Schultz has wanted to be a writer all her life. Inspired by authors she loved as a child such as Madeleine L'Engle, Mary Norton and J.R.R. Tolkien, she started writing a fantasy novel in elementary school. Her writing was laid aside as she pursued a career in the biological sciences, but her desire to write never faded.

She is fascinated by mythology and the way similar motifs and images appear in myths from diverse cultures, pointing to a commonality deeply rooted in the human psyche. She particularly enjoys reading and writing fantasy and fairy tales, and sees these genres as providing the most creative means of expression of our universal hopes and fears.

In addition to reading and writing, she loves traveling and nature, gardening and art. She lives in a rural part of California with her husband and various pets and has two daughters in college.

THE NAKED TRUTH

By Jerrie Schultz

I first met Gloria the day I had moved into the studio on the third floor of the Cedar Lane Apartments. She lived in a one bedroom across the hall and popped out of her door like an overzealous jack-in-the-box while I hauled up the last load.

After she introduced herself, she fired off a barrage of questions: "What's your name?" "Where are you from?" "Where did you live before?"

It was the last thing I needed. I was exhausted from the move, on top of the ordeal I had just gone through with my disastrous relationship and ugly breakup with Rick. The bruises had faded to a sickly green-yellow color, but it would take the emotional wounds much longer to heal.

All I wanted to do was get my stuff into the apartment and collapse, but Gloria was relentless in her friendliness. She insisted I come in for a cup of tea and a piece of homemade cake.

She sat across the table from me in a magenta housecoat with yellow hibiscus flowers. Her bony elbows rested on the blue checkered oilcloth and an unlit cigarette teetered between her fingers. After she placed an enormous serving of chocolate cake in front of me, she proceeded to fill me in on everyone who lived in the building. She spared no details about their love lives, extended families and health problems. I pretended I was interested while I tried to figure out how I could make a graceful exit.

That was when she blindsided me. "Now, surely a lovely young lady like yourself must have a special young man?"

I might have guessed it would come.

"Actually, I just got out of a dysfunctional relationship," I replied. I hoped she would let the subject drop without pressing for details.

"Seems most relationships are dysfunctional these days, judging by the divorce rate. I certainly hope there wasn't any abuse," she said, her expression a peculiar mixture of sympathy and eagerness.

"There may have been something along those lines." I hedged, not wanting to provide her with material to broadcast to everyone else in the building behind my back.

"Oh, honey, I know just what you've been through. My first husband was a drinker. After he had a few highballs, he'd start hammering on me like a prize fighter. He pushed me down the stairs and kicked me in the stomach when I was pregnant. I lost the baby. It would've been my first."

I was rather stunned and wasn't sure how to respond.

"I'm really sorry to hear that," I finally managed.

"Just a bump in the road of life," she replied. Her voice was dispassionate. She drained her teacup and re-filled it.

"Well," I said, trying to get the conversation back on a more positive track, "my relationship with Rick is over now, and I'm putting it all behind me."

"That's the spirit, girlie! Everything always works out for the best." She took a bite of cake and chewed it. "My son, Andrew — he goes to Harvard Medical School — he's just about your age," she said.

"That's nice," I said, but I doubted she had told the truth. It was more likely her son was a garbage collector in some armpit of a suburb than going to one of the most prestigious universities in the country.

I managed to extricate myself from Gloria's hospitality and vowed to myself I'd do my best to avoid her in the future. As it turned out, that would be easier said than done.

The next afternoon, when I came home from work, her door flew open the moment I turned my key in the lock. I suspected she had waited in ambush with her bright beady eye glued to the peephole.

"Janelle!" Her raspy, nicotine-stained voice was filled with delight, as though I were a dear friend she hadn't seen in years. "Come on over for a bite of something and a chat!"

I didn't see any easy way out, short of being rude, but I had a gnawing fear that it would become a familiar scene each time I came home. I dreaded setting a precedent.

"How are things at work?" she asked.

She set a cup of tea and a plate of gingersnaps in front of me.

"Not that great, to tell you the truth. There's an employee in my department out on maternity leave, and my boss expects me to do most of her work as well as my own. He's being totally unreasonable about it. He refuses to extend any deadlines, and I'm really getting stressed."

"Oh, honey, that's not so bad compared to what I had

to deal with back when I was working at the meat packing plant," Gloria responded. "There was a strike, and I had to work twelve-hour shifts, seven days a week for three months straight!"

"You don't say?" I said. My voice was dull.

"It was brutal, let me tell you!"

She proceeded to bore me with a vivid description of how standing for twelve solid hours every day for weeks on end had aggravated her lumbago and corns.

"That sounds pretty unpleasant, all right," I said. "I think what I really need is a vacation. I'd love to take a few days off and go to the coast. Just north of Jackson Point, there's a place with cute little cottages right across the road from the beach. It looks charming and I've always wanted to stay there. There's no way my boss will let me take any time off."

"Funny you should mention Jackson Point," Gloria said. She perked up even more, if that was possible. "I just saw on the news that a young woman was murdered there recently. They found her body stuffed into a dumpster, strangled. The killer is still at large."

"Well, then, I guess it's a good thing I'm not going to Jackson Point anytime soon. Maybe they'll catch the murderer by the time Felicia comes back from maternity leave."

"Or you might just find someplace you'd rather go that's closer to home. Do you know how many traffic accidents there are on that stretch of interstate between here and the coast?"

I said I had no idea. I concentrated on finishing my cake while Gloria recited traffic fatality statistics.

I felt a pang of annoyance. It seemed that I couldn't

say anything to this woman without her bouncing right back with a gruesome anecdote. She probably read the obituaries for pleasure.

A similar scenario played out every afternoon for the rest of the week. Every subject I brought up produced an immediate and horrific response. I heard all about gangrene, botched plastic surgeries and freak accidents involving gas ovens.

By the following Monday, however, my attitude had shifted. The annoyance had disappeared, and I began thinking of it as a bizarre game of one-upmanship in which I tried to come up with a story that Gloria wasn't able to top. I quickly decided that sticking to the truth was unnecessary, and I began to embellish my tales.

My father's angioplasty became a heart transplant. My sprained ankle in third grade became a compound fracture.

While at work, I found myself thinking of tall tales to spring on Gloria when I went home, determined to render her speechless. Even though my lies became more and more outlandish, she instantly and effortlessly managed to surpass every one. My cousin who had his leg ripped off by an alligator in Florida was topped by her nephew who was eaten by a great white shark while surfing off the coast of Australia. My uncle who shot himself in the head with a nail gun and drove himself to the hospital was trumped by her brother-in-law who fell into a crevasse while cross-country skiing and dragged himself five miles through the snow to safety with two broken legs and a fractured skull.

It seemed that Gloria's morbid imagination knew no bounds. I just couldn't seem to conjure up anything that she couldn't beat, no matter how hard I tried.

"You look a little peaked, dear," Gloria said one afternoon a few weeks later, while I sank wearily into her kitchen chair. "Are you feeling all right?"

"Well, Gloria, I didn't want to say anything because I didn't want to upset you, but I've just been to the doctor. I've been diagnosed with breast cancer."

"Oh, honey, don't let that get you down! You can beat this! Why, I had a double mastectomy seventeen years ago, and look at me now. Still going strong!"

Gloria's eyes shone with a fierce intensity.

I wanted to scream. I don't know what I had expected. I should have said I'd been infected with the Ebola virus.

Suddenly, she stood and began to unbutton her housecoat. I stared as she shrugged out of it, and then pulled off a prosthetic bra and cast it down onto the black and white linoleum.

Her scars were extensive and horrible.

Gloria stood there displaying her ravaged chest, not to sock or solicit sympathy, but rather to lift me up. She showed me the evidence of her appalling pain and suffering to inspire me and give me hope and determination to beat a terrible disease, just like she herself had done.

In a blinding flash of understanding, it became clear just how grievously I had misjudged Gloria. While I had written her off as a pathetic old fool, all of those elaborate disasters she'd spun had been for my benefit. It was her peculiar way of telling me I should appreciate life, stop complaining and be grateful for everything I have.

"You're strong, girlie," she said, stooping down to

pick up her bra. "You're a survivor, just like me!"

A survivor?

I wasn't sure I would ever be able to survive the shame I felt at that moment. I mumbled something about not feeling well and left as quickly as I could.

Safely behind my own locked door, I paced the floor and agonized over what I had done. What on earth had possessed me to say I had breast cancer? Did she realize that almost everything I had told her for the past several weeks had been lies?

If so, she never seemed to let on.

I didn't see how I could go on living in the same apartment where I would see her every day. I figured if I started to look for another apartment immediately, I could move out by the end of the month. I'd gladly forfeit the last month's rent if I never had to face her again.

Then it hit me: the only way out of the hideous mess was to go to Gloria and tell her the truth. Make a full confession. The nail gun, the alligator, the breast cancer—all lies. If she hated me afterward, so be it.

At least I would have rid myself of the tormenting guilt.

The next day after work, my hands were shaking when I turned the key in the lock. What if she didn't come out? Would I have the guts to go knock on her door?

I felt a rush of relief mixed with terror when I heard her door open behind me.

"Janelle!"

She sounded like the same old Gloria who always seemed so surprised and delighted that I had come home from work.

I turned and saw her there in a turquoise housecoat

with orange and green parrots and a huge, welcoming smile on her face.

"Got a minute for a bite and a chat?"

"Sure," I replied.

I followed Gloria into her kitchen. There was a freshly baked apple pie in the middle of the table. I decided not to waste time, but to get it over with right away.

"Gloria, there's something I need to tell you," I began.

She looked at me expectantly through her smeared bifocals.

"That biopsy... there was a mistake, and I don't have cancer after all!" I heard myself blurt.

"Oh, honey, that's terrific!" Gloria reached across the table and patted my hand. "Didn't I tell you not to worry? Everything always works out for the best!"

In December, Gloria's son Andrew came home for Christmas. She invited me over to meet him, and we had a nice chat over tea and cookies. He told me about how he had been inspired to enter the medical profession after witnessing his mother's battle with breast cancer.

He'll finish his residency program at Harvard Medical School in the spring, and he wants to come back to his home town, where his mother and I live, to set up a practice.

He's just about my age.

56

MIRROR WORLD
By Charlene Key

I stand between two worlds
in wonder.
I've lived in both.
I've loved in both.
But only one has love that I can see.

A room reflected in
a mirror: Which room is real?
Which world is real?
The concrete facts? Distorted fantasy?

I've lived where love brings joy and peace,
Respected, wanted– free to take or share.
I've lived with pain, destruction of the mind,
Respected, wanted– loved but yet ensnared.

Reflected images of love:
Selfishness guised selfless, false hope appearing fair,
Sacrifice of gentleness in love's name: Pain
becomes the measure– to ache is thus to care.

I choose between two worlds
with terror.
Which world is real?
Which love is real?

Distorted facts then concrete fantasy.

IMAGINATION

By Nancy Smith Gibson

Where have all the faeries gone
That used to dance upon the lawn
When I was a child?

They wove intricate patterns
In their games
Leaving circles in the grass
For me to find the next day.

They have been replaced by fireflies
Darting aimlessly to and fro
On a summer's eve
Leaving no evidence of their being.

I wish the faeries would return
And bring back
My youth and imagination.

MAVIS & THE LEPRECHAUN

By Nancy Smith Gibson

I won a leprechaun in a raffle.

No, not a stuffed doll—a real, live leprechaun. You didn't think they were real?

Well, I didn't either. Then I got my prize, and my life was never the same.

It all started on St. Patrick's Day, which was appropriate, wouldn't you say? I mean, after all, you don't win a leprechaun every day, so it was fitting for it to happen on St. Paddy's Day.

My boyfriend Cole and I often met at O'Brady's Pub after work, sometimes for a beer and sometimes for supper. O'Brady's is located halfway between his apartment and mine, so it was convenient to go home after work, change into jeans and sneakers and meet at the pub. After we ate, or drank and maybe played darts, he would walk me home and then walk home himself. Sometimes he came in and stayed a while. Or overnight.

On that particular night, the waitress, Annie, said, "You guys want to buy some raffle tickets? The money is going to buy playground equipment for St. John's School. They're five dollars a ticket or five for twenty dollars."

So Cole and I bought twenty dollars' worth each. Of course, I never thought I would win. I just thought of it as a donation. It was not until Annie brought our dinner — corned beef and cabbage with potatoes and a special sauce only O'Brady knows how to make — that I thought to ask her what I would win if I won the raffle.

"A leprechaun," she said.

Cole laughed and said, "A real one?"

"A real one," she said. "Sean Fitzpatrick is donating him. He says it is a leprechaun who cleans the house for you, from top to bottom. A real expert house cleaner."

After dinner, we filled out our tickets with our names, addresses and phone numbers and dropped them in the box by the door as we left.

I said, "Boy, it sure would be nice if I won the leprechaun and got my house cleaned."

Cole said he thought Sean owned a maid service or cleaning company or something and this was the way to get good advertising.

Was he ever wrong.

We walked the two blocks to my apartment and Cole came in. He stayed a while. I was just drifting off to sleep when Cole got up and got dressed.

"I'm going on home, babe," he said as he kissed me on the cheek. "I've got to be down in Oak Grove by seven for that 5K race. I'll call you tomorrow."

I mumbled something and went on to sleep. He knows I sleep late on Saturdays, and he was being thoughtful going home that night so he wouldn't wake me early the next morning.

The crashing and banging of pots and pans woke me at dawn.

Hadn't Cole gone home last night? Had he come back for some reason?

I got up and started toward the kitchen, when it occurred to me that someone might have broken in. It was probably best I not go into the kitchen starkers. I put on my robe, picked up my cell phone and dialed 911. I held my finger on the send button so I could hit it in a hurry if I needed to.

I peeked around the corner, and there, standing on the kitchen cabinet, was the leprechaun. It was obvious that was what he was: he was about four feet tall ("Four feet three and three quarters inches, thank you very much," he told me later). He was dressed in an emerald green satin suit covered by a big white apron. Around his neck was a long scarf of green chiffon. His feet were shod with green slippers that turned up on the toes, more like a Santa's elf might wear.

My mind told me, *That is a leprechaun standing on my cabinet pulling out all the pots and pans.*

So of course I said, "Who are you and what are you doing in my kitchen?"

He turned toward me and took his green cap off his head. He bowed low and said, "Faith and Begorrah. I'm your own personal leprechaun, come to straighten out your life and home, I am."

With his cap off, I could see his pointy ears that poked through the abundance of red curly hair on his head. He hopped down to the chair, which was pulled up to the cabinet, and from there to the floor. He bowed again.

"I can see I've caught you unaware," he said with an

Irish brogue. "Ye've won me, y'see, in the raffle, and I find it best to begin me workday early."

He turned toward my cabinets.

"I see that I'll have lots of work to do here. Lots of work," he repeated, putting his hands on his hips.

"I won the raffle?" I asked.

"Isn't that what I said? Would I be here if ye didn't?"

"I guess not." I turned back toward the hall. "I'd better go get dressed."

When I returned to the kitchen, the dishwasher was going. I assume it was filled with the pots and pans, since they were nowhere to be seen. The leprechaun was wiping out the cabinets.

I filled the teakettle and put it on to heat.

"Would you like a cup of tea?"

Quick as a wink, he hopped down and drew the chair up to the kitchen table.

"Sure an' I'll join ye in a cup," he said. He sat while I fixed mugs of Irish Breakfast, my favorite waking up tea.

"My name is Mavis," I introduced myself. "And what should I call you?"

"Me name be Greenberry Muldoon, but ye can call me Berry."

"I'm very pleased to meet you, Berry." I stood and found some yogurt in the fridge. "Would you care for some yogurt?"

"Ack, I can see the need to stock yer pantry as well. The day should begin with some good Irish oats to tide you until midday. Proper nutrition canna be slighted or yer health will suffer."

Well, la-di-da!

Cleaning my kitchen was one thing; telling me what

to eat was another. I stood and started toward my bedroom. "I'll just get started with my Saturday chores."

"That is me job, dinna ya know? To do all your housework. Now, ye don't want to be taking me job away, do ye?"

I thought it over a minute (well, a split second) and decided he was right. I won a housecleaning, the whole shebang. I would leave it all to him.

"I'll just go to the grocery store then, and buy groceries for the week."

I grabbed my purse and started for the door when he grabbed me by the arm.

"Sure an' you wouldna be thinkin' of going out in public looking like that?" I looked down at the jeans and sweatshirt I had put on. There was a rip in the knee of the jeans and a bleach spot on the shirt, but they were clean.

"I'm okay to go to the store," I said.

"Ye just think again, missy," he said, one hand propped on a hip.

He flung the chiffon over his shoulder. "It just won't do, won't do at all. I cannot have my reputation sullied by allowing you to dress like a rag-tag urchin. My name would be besmirched forever."

He leaned his head back and covered his eyes with his hand.

"Everything you do reflects on me. Someone might think that I dressed you like that." He took his hand down and shuddered when he looked at me. "Let me see what else you have in your closet."

I stared at him. *He's going to dress me?*

Then I had another thought. "What happened to your Irish accent?"

He fidgeted and scuffed his shoes against the floor.

"You see, it's like this. I've been in this country so long I've lost it. But a leprechaun is expected to talk like that so I do my best to oblige."

"How long have you been in the United States?"

"Hmm. A hundred and twelve years come November."

"A hundred and twelve years! You don't look that old."

He looked very pleased at that. "Well, wee folk live a lot longer than you larger ones, and besides, a youthful appearance runs in my family."

He pulled off the apron and hung it over a chair.

"Come along now. Let's look at your wardrobe," he said while he pulled me toward the bedroom. I wondered if that was going to be his habit, pulling me around.

He opened the double doors of my closet and set about discarding what he found, muttering to himself as he went.

"A disaster.

"Dowdy.

"Horrors.

When he looked unfavorably at an item of clothing, it went into a pile on the floor.

"*Passe!*

"Never tell me you wore this!

"So wrong for your coloring.

"This looks like an old woman's dress."

I never wanted to be on that TV show where Clint and Stacey throw away all of someone's clothes and then send them out to buy more, but I was getting the same treatment. Well, at least the throw away part.

Finally, he came to a pair of gray flannel slacks that met his approval. "Do you have any sweaters?"

I pointed him toward the chest of drawers. After all my sweaters went in the reject pile, he kept the last one, pink cashmere, and thrust it at me.

"Go put this one on while I look for accessories."

I did as he told me. I wouldn't have dared do otherwise. When I came out he had a paisley scarf in one hand and my black leather jacket in the other. When he was done with me he stood with chin in hand studying me as I turned slowly around.

"Well, it will have to do for now. Something needs to be done with your hair and makeup." He reached up and flipped my hair. "You have a nice color, but we must get you a better haircut." He took one of my hands. "And a manicure too."

I started off to the grocery store with firm instructions not to come back without some McCann's Steel Cut Irish Oatmeal. I decided to drive across town to Albertson's, since I knew our neighborhood market wouldn't have anything like that.

"What's so special about McCann's Oatmeal?" I had asked. "Wouldn't Quaker Oats do?"

He bounced up and down on his tippy-toes.

"It's made in County Kildare," he said with agitation. "Since 1876. When you taste it you'll know why it is special!"

So off I went to do my weekly shopping, which included the items Berry added to my shopping list, including cleaning supplies. Evidently, I was sorely lacking in the cleaning department as well as proper food, having not enough to clean the whole apartment and not enough food to properly sustain me.

When I returned, the kitchen was sparkling clean and Berry was vacuuming the living room. The drapes were gone (in the dryer spinning the dust out, he told me). The books and papers on the table I used as a desk for my computer were in neat piles. While I put away the groceries, Berry cleaned the windows with the spray and paper towels I had bought at the market. By the time I was finished, he was rehanging the drapes.

"You really need a paint job in this room—in the whole apartment, actually." He stood, one hand on his hip, studying the walls. "I'll have to give it some thought. I need to learn your personality better before I decide."

Before I could respond, he was off to the bedroom, his chiffon scarf trailing behind him.

By the time the day was over, there was not a nook or cranny Berry had not vacuumed, dusted, mopped or scrubbed. From the insides of the cabinets and refrigerator to the corners of the closet floors, everything was spotless. I had never had such a clean apartment.

"It is almost dark, so I'll just say ta-ta." Berry stood in the door to the kitchen.

"Thank you so much, Berry. You did a marvelous job. It really was my lucky day when I won the raffle. And it was very nice to meet you."

I bent and gave him a little kiss on the cheek. He turned a bright pink.

"Ah, um, yes, well," he said and then he disappeared.

Really! Just disappeared into thin air. One minute he was there and the next *poof* he was gone.

Cole called later. "I won the leprechaun, Cole. He's a real leprechaun, and his name is Greenberry Muldoon. He

came and cleaned the whole apartment and then just disappeared."

"That's great, babe. Listen, the gang is waiting for me.
I finished 27th in the race, which isn't bad, considering the
competition. We're all going out to celebrate."

"Okay. See you tomorrow?"

"Tomorrow... I've got to work on a case I have coming up for trial. I'll call you."

Cole was an attorney who wanted to make partner at
Quincy, Stearns and Hart in less than five years, so he
spent a lot of time working. Lots of evenings were spent
studying for upcoming cases, so we didn't get to see each
other but once, maybe twice per week, often at O'Brady's.

The next day I washed my hair, gave myself a manicure, and worked on some personal things I had neglect-
ed. It was lovely to have a day with not one bit of
housework, thanks to winning the raffle and Berry.

Monday morning, when I stepped out of the shower, I
thought I heard the teakettle whistling and a delicious
aroma was in the air. I stuck my head around the corner
and there was Berry.

"Good morning, my dear. Which tea do you want this
morning, Irish Breakfast or Cinnamon Spice?"

"Berry? My apartment is clean. What are you doing
here?"

"I thought you knew! I am your permanent leprechaun. I'll be here every day from dawn until dark, except
Sunday. I have the Sabbath off."

"Every day? But what will you find to do?"

"Don't worry, my dear. You still have plenty of work
to be done."

Little did I know then how much Berry was going to

change my life. He began with breakfast. Mornings started with hot tea and either oatmeal or eggs and biscuits. Berry packed a nice salad for me to carry for lunch. When I came home from work, supper was ready. Berry was an excellent cook, presenting me with a variety of delicious meals. As time went on, he taught me how to cook some of his dishes, including O'Brady's special sauce to go on corned beef and cabbage.

Every day, Berry appeared dressed in different costumes. That was how I thought of them, as costumes. There were lime green trousers with a silver shirt and silver shoes and his green chiffon scarf. And forest green pants topped with a green and white striped shirt accompanied by knee-high boots of soft brown suede. His wardrobe was limitless. I never knew what to expect.

Once I said, "In pictures, leprechauns are shown wearing red caps, but yours are always green."

"Those pictures are of leprechauns who are the guards for the pots of gold in the main treasury: the bank, if you will. The red cap is a sign of their office, you see?"

Every day I learned something new about leprechauns.

When I woke the next Saturday morning, I found Berry standing in the kitchen wearing a completely different costume. He had on a black pinstripe suit, an emerald green shirt with a darker green tie, a black bowler hat with a green feather in it, and spats.

Yes, I said spats. Those things that cover part of your shoes. Not your shoes or my shoes, his shoes. And his shoes were black patent leather. The stickpin in his tie appeared to be a diamond. He was wearing a large diamond ring on his pinkie finger and a green carnation in his buttonhole.

"Are you ready to go buy a new wardrobe?" he asked.

Stunned, I stood there in my pajamas. "Uhh, sure. Just let me go get dressed." Then I thought about the shape of my bank account. "Uh, Berry? I can't afford much of a new wardrobe right now. In fact, it will be payday before I can afford anything."

"Pish, posh. Don't you know all leprechauns have a pot of gold?"

I thought about telling him I hadn't even believed leprechauns were real, much less their pots of gold, but I just kept my mouth shut and went to get dressed.

We took my car and he directed me to a shop in a part of town that was new to me.

McGillicuddy's Pawn Shop
We Buy Gold.

The sign was in neon green.

"I'll just wait in the car," I said, but he shook his head.

"No. That won't do. I am your own personal leprechaun you see. I must either be in your home or in your presence from dawn until dark. I cannot go in there unless you go with me."

Obviously there were more leprechaun rules than I was aware of.

A jingling bell over the door announced our arrival. The man behind the counter in the rear of the store could have been the model for Shrek, except he wasn't green. He was tall and big enough to make several normal-sized men and a whole bunch of leprechauns Berry's size.

"Sure and isn't it Mr. Muldoon come to visit today.

And what can I be doin' fer ye today, sir? It has been a fair long time since I have had the honor of yer presence."

"And a good day to ye also, Mr. McGillicuddy. I hope the world has been treatin' ye well." I noticed Berry's Irish accent was back. "May I present Miss Mavis Hannon to ye."

Berry whipped off his bowler hat and held it in front of me.

"It is an honor to make your acquaintance, Miss Hannon. And to be sure, any friend of Mr. Muldoon's is a friend of mine." He smiled a Shrek-like smile. "And how may I help ye today?"

"Mavis, me dear, if you will be so kind as to wait here, I shall transact my business with Mr. McGillicuddy at the back of the establishment."

I spent the next few minutes looking at the varied merchandise displayed for sale: guitars, guns, TVs, amplifiers, drum sets, silver tea sets, nail guns, anything and everything. The jewelry counter kept my attention for some time. Although I was curious, I was trying not to be nosy, but one time I heard the clink of coins and glanced that way to see the glint of gold in a hanging scale. After about twenty minutes, Berry returned to me.

"We can be going along now, me dear."

"Always a pleasure doing business with ye, Mr. Muldoon, a pleasure. Come again any time."

When we were in my car again, Berry gave his next instructions. "Now we shall proceed to the beauty salon. Do you know where *Chez Jon* is located?"

"Yes, Berry, but we could never get in there without an appointment. That is the most exclusive salon in town. There was an article in the society section of the newspaper about it. Women wait months to get their first appointment there, and then they will only keep you as a standing appointment if they approve of you. And it costs a fortune."

"Just do as I say. Drive to *Chez Jon* and don't worry about the money, my dear. I *have* a fortune."

We arrived at the salon and entered through a door that reeked of elegance, sophistication and expensive perfume. I was prepared to be embarrassed when we were turned away, but instead we were greeted with enthusiasm, to put it mildly.

"Mr. Muldoon!" gushed the tall blonde receptionist. "How nice to see you again! Look, Jon, at who's here."

I recognized the famous Jon from his picture in the newspaper. He was tall, thin and impossibly blonde with his hair pulled back in a ponytail tied with a lavender ribbon.

"Berry, darling," he said. He bent to give my companion a hug and air kisses beside each cheek. "Rolando, come, see who's here! It's Berry!"

An equally tall ebony-skinned man with a shiny bald head came from the back to embrace Berry and tell him in some sort of odd accent how they had missed seeing "darling Berry". Rolando was dressed in purple and green clothing with splashes of pink here and there, and he had a large gold hoop in one ear.

"And who is this?" he asked. "Your latest protégé?"

"Indeed. This is Mavis, and she needs a complete re-do. Hair, nails, facial, makeup, everything you have to offer."

Jon and Rolando proceeded to look me over. Jon lifted my hair and ran his fingers through it.

"Good hair," he pronounced. "Terrible look. We can do lots with her. She will be a new woman when we are finished."

He called to the receptionist, "Tatiana, when Mrs. Gates comes in, send her to Misha for her styling. Tell her a member of the British royal family is visiting in the States and I must see to her personally. If Misha needs me for a consultation, I can spare a minute or two, but that is all."

With that, they took me back to a private room, where I indeed became a new woman, in appearance if not in fact. My hair, which was too brown to be red and too red to be plain brown, became a glowing chestnut color. It was cut short and stuck up at angles in all directions.

"Now if you want to go conservative, although with hair like this I don't know why you would want to, just brush it down when you dry it," Jon told me, "and it will be a pixie, which, of course, would look wonderful on you too."

My hands and feet were pampered and painted and after a facial, which was both soothing and invigorating, I was taught how to apply makeup. When I looked in the mirror, I saw a girl I had never seen before. I was someone much more sophisticated, someone who was hot and cool at the same time. It wasn't me.

"Now," said Jon, "you go out and get a man."

"Oh, I already have a boyfriend," I said.

"You do?" said Berry. "Who?"

"His name is Cole Windsor. He's an attorney. He's been very busy this week getting a case ready for trial, that's why you haven't seen him."

"Cole Windsor," said the manicurist named Susie. "Isn't that who—ah."

She stopped as Rolando pulled her out saying, "Come on, Susie, and help me get the shampoo and makeup together for Mavis to take with her."

They put together a big sack of products to take with me: shampoo, mousse, cleanser, moisturizer and lots of makeup. Then Jon told me he wanted to see me once a month for a trim, facial and manicure.

"I just don't think I am going to be able to afford that, Jon. This was Berry's treat, but I can't go on letting him pay."

"What a precious girl! Thinking about Berry instead of using him! Sweetie, Berry has taken care of it already. Rolando and I can never repay all that Berry has given us. You are paid for the rest of your life. Now, when is best for you?"

We settled on the first Thursday of every month, right after work.

When we left, Berry suggested we have lunch at a little tearoom right around the corner.

"We need sustenance before shopping," he said. After chicken salad and peach tea we were ready, he proclaimed, to dress me as I should be dressed.

"So, go to the mall?" I asked.

"Heaven forbid! Never shop where the hoi polloi obtain their clothing. You are one of a kind, Mavis, and it is time you recognize that fact."

He then directed me to first one, then another, and another, small shop. He sat in a chair and had me model everything the saleslady suggested. By the time the afternoon was over I had dozens of bags filled with everything Berry had decided on: dresses, suits, slacks, blouses, jackets, shoes, lingerie, scarves, costume jewelry. I had more than I thought I would ever wear.

"That will do for a while, my dear. Let's return home now before I must go."

Everyone at work exclaimed at my new look, and Cole couldn't take his eyes off me when we met at O'Brady's Tuesday evening. He finally came home with me to meet Berry. We had to hurry home before it was sunset and Berry disappeared. Afterwards, Cole told me he though Berry was creepy and that something was weird about him buying me clothes. Cole never came over again when Berry was there, and since the days were getting longer, that meant Cole didn't come over except on Sunday, sometimes.

I often came home after work to find Berry watching TV. His viewing habits were varied: some days he watched Oprah, Dr. Phil or Judge Judy. Other times I would catch him weeping into a handkerchief while watching an old movie. He especially liked Tom Cruise movies. He said Tom was a darling boy.

As summer neared and the days grew longer, I cajoled him into eating supper with me. He asked many questions about my work and enjoyed hearing the stories I told about people I worked with and the buildings that were being designed.

I finally persuaded him to tell me about the Old Country and how he came to be in virtual servitude to people in America.

"It was this way, you see. I am from a very wealthy and powerful leprechaun family. It was expected that I marry into an equally wealthy and powerful family. To this end, I was betrothed to a pretty little thing. Her name was Kathleen. It was a marriage arranged by both our families. I did not love her, nor she me, but she was very taken with marrying into my family. We are a very prestigious clan, you know.

"But another caught my eye, and I became besotted with a member of her immediate family. I was determined I should bond with the one I loved. Many extravagant arrangements had been made for the nuptials when I was caught in a very compromising position, you might say, with the object of my fancy, and all hell broke out.

"Oh, Berry! A member of her family? How very hurtful. You seduced her sister?"

"No, hmm, ah, it was her brother, actually."

"Her brother? Berry! She must have been very humiliated."

"Ah, yes, both families said they were extremely humiliated and the decision was made to send me away so they would never have to set eyes on me again."

"Oh, Berry. That is so sad."

He looked so despondent.

I patted his arm and asked, "So you were sent to America? How is it determined who you will work for? Surely not by raffle?"

"My sentence, if you call it that, is that I must stay with each person until I have straightened out their life, then I move on to the next person. Since I fu--,er, that is, I messed up the lives of two families I must now straighten up the lives of others, literally. I must go to the person who wins me. It can be by raffle, game of chance, or auction. Anything that counts as winning moves me along to the next place."

"That must be very unsettling. I hope everyone treats

you well."

"No, my dear, not everyone does so. There have been times — well, I don't really want to go into that. It's best to put all that behind me."

"Where do you go when you disappear at dark?"

"That is my secret, my private life, not for you or anyone else to know."

Berry's next project was redecorating my apartment. I came home from work one day to find the living room redone in shades of brown, caramel, terra cotta and gold. He said those were my colors. Indeed, much of the clothing he picked for me was in those shades. There was a new living room suite in soft suede cloth with lots of toss pillows. Lamps offered soft lighting all around the room. But the pièce de résistance was the whole wall of bookshelves with a desk section for my computer and printer.

"But Berry," I protested, "I don't have anything to put in all those shelves!"

"You will, my dear, you will. I have read those stories you are always writing and they are good, very good. It is time you spread your wings and write a novel. Therefore, you will need books: grammar books, dictionaries, several thesauruses, reference books and most of all, books to read. You do like to read, don't you?"

"Oh, yes, Berry. I love to read." I gave him a hug. "Thank you so much, Berry."

From then on we spent many Saturdays in bookstores. Sometimes we browsed through the big chain stores, but more often we went to small bookshops that sold used books, where both Berry and I found the most interesting volumes. Gradually, my shelves filled.

After redoing the living room, Berry decorated my

bedroom in soft shades of turquoise and ivory. It felt like the most luxurious room in the world. Last, he redid the kitchen in cherry wood and granite with the very latest stainless steel appliances.

When fall came, Berry took me shopping for clothing again, this time for warmer clothes for winter, as well as coats and boots. He seemed to have such a good time choosing what I should wear, and he told me why he chose each item, pointing out which features I should look for and which I should avoid.

It was almost time for the Harvest Ball, the biggest charity event of the year. I was hoping Cole would have time off from work to go and that he would ask me to attend. I was looking forward to picking out a ball gown, and this was certainly the only opportunity I would ever have to wear one.

Thursday, I was at my appointment with Jon when a pretty blonde woman walked by, talking to Rolando. "Yes, Cole is taking me to the Harvest Ball. We are going to announce our engagement there. He is buying me an enormous diamond ring and I am planning..."

Her voice trailed off as they proceeded to the back of the shop.

I must have looked stricken, because Jon closed the door to his private styling room and turned to me.

"You are worth a hundred of her, and he is a stupid fool."

"Who is she?"

"Missy Hart. Her father is a senior partner in that fancy law firm."

"Yes, that is where Cole works. He wants to make partner. I guess one way to do it is to marry the boss's daughter."

I wiped the tears that began to trickle down my cheeks.

"Sweetheart, don't you cry over that no-good cheater. A much better man will come along. See if I'm not right."

"Oh, Jon, all these months I've just been a bootie call," and with that thought, I cried for sure. Jon patted and talked and Rolando came in and patted and hugged and talked and finally I calmed down enough to get my makeup repaired and go home.

The next time Cole called to see if he could come over after Berry left I told him I was busy, that I was seeing someone else, please not to call again. I didn't tell him I knew about Missy Hart.

At last, everything was done that Berry could find to do. The apartment was spotlessly clean and redecorated. I was redecorated, too, and taught how to choose flattering clothes. I could cook all the dishes Berry had shown me, and could set a table 'fit for the queen', as he put it. My bookshelves were almost full, and I had a novel almost finished, with an idea for another one simmering in my head.

At last, Berry came to me and said, "My job here is done, my dear. It is time for me to move on."

"Oh, Berry, no! You can't go! What would I do with-out you?"

"It is time, Lass. When a job is done, it's done. I have nothing more to offer you. I came to straighten out your home and life, and I did."

"But you offer me your friendship. That is worth more than housecleaning or clothes shopping."

Nothing would dissuade him. Now, he said, we must

plan a way for someone to win him.

"I've been thinking on it," he said, "And I've heard much about this thing called eBay. It is an auction, am I right?"

"Yes, Berry, you put up things for auction and people bid on the computer and pay on the computer. The high bidder when the time is up wins."

And so it was decided that Berry's services would be listed for auction on eBay. He liked the idea of someone far away winning him, instead of a local person. He wanted to see the world, he said.

Together we wrote up a listing for the "...*complete and thorough organizational skills of a trained professional who will put your home and life in order. This professional, who goes by the name 'Leprechaun' guarantees he can organize anyone's clutter.*"

We settled on a seven-day auction, ending on a Friday night, shortly before sunset, so he could start to work the next morning.

The following Friday evening we sat in front of the computer, refreshing the screen every minute or so. The bid was bouncing around among three bidders: 2gud4u, Kelly_N_Mom and biker4ever.

All the other earlier bidders had dropped out. I was feeling sadder by the minute. I could not imagine being without Berry, and I was worried about the treatment he would receive at his new employer's house. Even though Berry had been assuring me that he would be fine, I knew that I would continue to worry after he'd left.

"Now, don't forget, Lass, there is a large pot of Irish Stew simmering on the range. You have enough to feed a party. If you don't want to eat it all, remember to put it in containers in the freezer so you will have it later."

"I won't forget, Berry."

At last, the final refresh revealed that he had been won by Kelly_N_Mom.

"That sounds good, doesn't it? It sounds like there is a little girl in the house," I said, trying to convince myself. "And as soon as she pays by PayPal you'll be gone, right?"

I wiped a tear.

"Yes, lass, that's right. And before I go I have one final thing to do."

He stood, leaned toward me and kissed me on the forehead.

"That is just about the best thing you could ever hope to have, a kiss on the forehead freely given by a leprechaun. It assures that you will always have the best of luck, a long and happy life that includes both good health and wealth, and that you will always love and be loved. It is luckier than all the four-leaf clovers and rabbits feet in the world. Many men would kill to get a leprechaun's kiss. I give it freely to you for being my friend."

I took a wavering breath to thank him, when *poof*, he disappeared. The PayPal payment had gone through.

I sat there listening to the rain on the window and trying to decide whether to give in to the tears and let myself have a good cry, or to see if I had any wine or liquor in the house and get drunk, when a knock sounded on the front door.

When I opened the door, I looked at a denim shirt containing a wide, muscular chest. Raising my view a little, I saw a ruggedly handsome man with auburn hair and dark brown eyes.

"Hi," he said. "I'm your neighbor from across the hall.

My name is Ryan Malone. I just moved in today and I don't have any food in the house. I wonder if you know the name of any deli or pizza place close by that delivers?"

"Thank you, Berry," I whispered.

NANCY SMITH GIBSON

Nancy Smith Gibson has always loved to read, especially stories with a bit of magic. *Poppy the Fairy* was a favorite. As a child, she imagined finding a fairy in her garden and bringing it in to live in her dollhouse. *The Little White Horse*, a story where lions are dogs and nothing is what it seems, enthralled her. Perhaps this is why she likes to write 'magical reality' stories.

Having to get her four children raised first, she only recently began writing when 'story dreams' insisted upon being written.

Nancy lives in the country near Hot Springs, Arkansas, with three cats, two dogs and possibly fairies in the garden.

ROBERT L. AREND

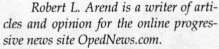

Robert L. Arend is a writer of articles and opinion for the online progressive news site OpedNews.com.

He served as the president of an AFSCME union local for a total of five terms, retiring in 2007. Yet, throughout Robert's adolescence, he was encouraged by teachers to pursue a career as a professional writer.

He came to the realization that he did so too early, still a teenager, without a basis of enough life lived to establish important skills and credentials to avoid rejections to his work.

In marriage, Mr. Arend abandoned artistic pursuits for 35 years of dependable paychecks that permitted his family the modest expectations of the American Dream.

With retirement, the itch to write was reborn upon a fateful visit to the Accentuate Writers Forum, where the friendliness of the online writers colony caused Robert to decide to make it his online home/school. The writers contests geared to themes eventually resulted in a number of his short stories being awarded inclusion in the series of Twin Trinity Media "Elements" anthologies: "Elements of Dimension" with the short stories "Creation" and "David and the Outside".

Robert believes his inclusion with such a group of remarkably talented authors dwarfs all other accomplishments of his life. His advice for others dreaming of being writers is to get to know the authors in "Elements of the Soul", "Elements of Time", "Elements of Dimension", future anthologies and other Twin Trinity Media offerings and by joining the online writer's colony that is Accentuate Writers Forum.

CREATION

By Robert L. Arend

Beyond the Universe is the source of all we see,
Where dwells the true Real, here only a hazy facsimile:

Projected Reality, illusion, a hologram of time and space;
our sham 3-D reality dreams from that distant place.

"I think, therefore I am," is the greatest of delusions;
All around us massive, spinning confusion,
And we dare not dwell on the true source of our being,
Fearing we'll cease to be, along with all we are seeing...

No past, no present, no future. No here and no there. I am where the physical is created and spun to produce time; both are illusion. I am discussing expectations with those who are to be my parents.

Our auras dim with a shared sense of how dreadful this is all going to be.

Why do we have to do this over and over again?

I will try to prepare my manifest, even in the womb, to resist notions of learning how to love as life's purpose. Love has nothing to do with going from here to there. We go to have something to do, to create and to learn how to forgive.

Too bad a good creation requires suppression of what

* * *

is for what *is not*. False memories require so much energy and skill. However, it is necessary of the successful manifestation that the unbelievable be believed: a grand amnesia vital for our manifests to navigate in a dream projected from here, there and everywhere. Hunger and pain, poverty and oppression, great sorrows and infirmity are the best scripts to win praise from the audience.

Shame is the only discord here—not real—felt whenever a poor creation lingers, like a vapor between the virtual and the abrupt return to reality. So I went the lazy route of wealth and privilege after a prior creation of miserable slavery. I wanted to pamper myself after all that suffering.

I was not the first to create the plantation experience, but I added such dazzling forces of degradation and brutality to the concept that most here still study the work.

The psychic damage of my slavery transcended the sixty-two-year-old Negro's last breath. That last gasp of, "I forgive you," directed up and into the hateful eyes of the overseer who kicked me.

I required an extended stay in intensive aura care. Discharged still too early, I dared to disappoint the Watchers, who expected even grander creations from me.

Everybody here is a critic.

My last creation was not well received, scripted as it was for little discomfort. I manifested to rich parents, rich experiences, all leisure and few troubles. I lingered at the end, not wanting to part from my luxuries. My favorite, a French prostitute, drowned me in my bathtub after I married her. She had been twenty-two and I eighty-four.

What a sweet way to die.

Death? How quaint the notion becomes when the

physical burns away slowly, like fog under a rising sun. I never lived, so never died. I imagine everything and create accordingly. None of us ever leaves here entirely. We collaborate on scripts, rehearse our lines and then project. Our projections never know how phony they all are.

After the shame of my last creation, few volunteered to risk their reputations in another project with me. Only interns agreed to participate, none with even a single manifestation to bring to the work. The interns had to enlist in a creation projection or be relegated to background fixtures: trees, sidewalks, lamps, furniture, whatever cannot move by will.

Two interns were sent ahead to be my parents. The father would be a drunkard and jailbird. The mother would be the dumb sort, who trades her teenage years to a handsome but brutal alcoholic. She births five children. I will be baby number three, and because I am the only one amongst the seven to have ever manifested, I will be the smartest child.

⊰❈⊱

My mother does not know I am beside her at the hospital. Her face is wet, not from sweat, but from crying. Her husband can't be found—too many bars where he could be loitering. According to the script, Dad will be arrested this night for breaking into a warehouse to steal whatever he finds to steal. Pretty Mommy, so alone, will birth me into her world of poverty and violence. Dad will not see me for four years. He will not like me. I will not like him either.

"Please, I can't go on," the intern pleads. Partially dislocated from the flesh that is Mom, the intern continues to struggle to leave and can now notice my presence.

● ● ●

"This is too hard," the intern says.

I try to push the intern back into the Mom manifest. I have always been amused that I cannot touch what is of my imagination. At this point, I can only touch the intern who is not of my imagination. I try to sit on the intern.

"If you quit, the entire creation will be wasted," I warn. "You will slow your expansion into other cooperative manifestations with the other Creators, and you will be unable to create on your own."

Something penetrates my aura, causing my vibration to pitch wildly. I abandon the effort to force the intern back into the body of the Mom manifest and rise up through the ceiling to safety.

"Get a substitute, or I shall have this body destroy itself," the intern threatens, bobbing into and out of the Mom manifestation's body in tantrum.

Peeking through the ceiling, I tell the frantic intern, "Seeking a substitute will require a pause of the time element here, until I can convince another to take your place."

"Then do it," the intern demands. "I thought I was ready for this, but I need more practice."

Lest my entire creation be ruined, I reduce the three-dimensional universe to a single dimension, stripped of space and time.

The fate of the entire creation depends on convincing an experienced Creator to take the intern's place as an illiterate, heartbroken and horribly abused young mother of three, eventually five, children.

───※───

I summon all who participated in my previous creations and those Creators for whom I interned. Their auras let me know none are pleased to be within my space, even the one who was Matthew to my Luke in the creation manifested by the most heralded Creator in the Multiverse.

"I truly am sorry about my last creation," I tell them.

"I understand many of you don't want to waste your energies on anything less than what was achieved by the Creator of the Christ Saga."

The gathered pulsate in agreement.

The adulation for the Christ manifest was so great, the Watchers could only helplessly roll above their seats, unable to applaud. We all aspire to create like that, to develop elements of glorious promise crushed by the most unforgivable betrayal, yet transcend on a cloud of absolute forgiveness. Until we do, we yearn to be working with the Great Creator.

"But we can only work to achieve enough recognition of our creations to be elevated into the Great Creator's classroom," I remind them. "The Creator of the Christ Saga teaches, no longer required to create. I have designed a creation that may earn me entry to the teachings of the Great Creator, and all other participants will be rewarded some elevation if I succeed."

The dull buzzing tells me the gathered are doubtful.

"An intern who agreed to manifest as my mother is unable to cope with the challenges and wishes to withdraw at the point I am scripted to manifest into my creation. I require a walk-in, lest the entire creation be scrapped. The one who volunteers to take the intern's place will be offered a full collaborative partnership with me. Should my creation impress the Watchers enough, the walk-in may be elevated into the Great Creator's classroom with me."

One after another expands then vanishes. A well-crafted creation is about to be undone. In my despair, I roll up into a ball.

"I'll do it," the only one remaining, the one who manifested as my vicious overseer on the plantation, volunteered. I fan myself full circle. The abuser of slaves will enter the abused wife and mother manifest out of respect for our prior collaboration.

It is easy extracting the intern from the single dimension. Though a tight fit, the substitute manages to squirm in before I restore space and time. There will have to be changes to the script to accommodate the walk-in's level of vibration. More frequent rehearsals might be necessary. The walk-in has a right to suggest changes.

The intern streaks past, obviously embarrassed, yet relieved.

My essence leaves and forms an undulating tunnel around me. A scream narrows the walls. I am sucked through time and space to be born.

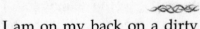

I am on my back on a dirty blanket. I pooped in my diaper some time ago, but Mom doesn't seem to have noticed yet. This is the part of manifestation I hate the most, the helplessness of the baby stage. It would be better if it didn't take so long to completely forget reality. Still, for a short time after manifests enter a creation, we can remember reality. During this time, we are free to come and go from our bodies when we want to, but not so often that doing so retards the development of the human bodies. For me, that means I must remain here long enough for the baby to achieve enough misery from the mess drying all over his ass to cry.

Two interns are in the playpen, although there is nothing in there to play with. The oldest is a toddler. The other intern is out of the other baby's body, glaring at Mom. Mom is reclined on the sofa, smoking a cigarette and reading a paperback novel.

"I didn't sign on for this," the out-of-body intern tells me. "My manifest is full of mucus, and that woman's smoking is making it worse. Why doesn't she take me to a doctor?"

"She will," I tell the intern. "You need to be more persistent in crying. Let the snot pour from your nose and refuse to eat."

"She's such an idiot," the intern says.

Without looking up from the page, my collaborator speaks from within Mom's body. "I'm just following the script. Don't take it out on me. Take it up with poopy-pants."

Poopy-pants being me, I respond to the unattached intern. "You did sign on for this. Mom is an experienced manifestor, staying within the limits of her predetermined personality. She will only mother us when we make her mother us. Let me demonstrate."

I begin to cry. Mom continues to read. I raise the volume of my crying. Mom remains unaffected. I cry and scream. Mom gets off the sofa, clearly annoyed. She checks me out.

"Poo-tink! Poo-tink," she says. Then, with amazing dexterity, she removes my diaper, cleans me and secures me in a fresh diaper.

"What about us," the out-of-body intern says about the two manifests still in the playpen. "Okay, let's cry, then," he tells the oldest brother.

The room fills with cries and screams. Mom abandons me to pick up the wheezing baby, forcing his intern to return to his body. Mom tries to get the manifest to drink formula, but he refuses. My brother smears his snot on Mom's neck and shoulder, then vomits to emphasize his distress.

"You're learning," I tell him.

Mom telephones her mother for help.

⋘⋙

"Why does she remain committed to him?" Mom asks. "While he sits in prison, she barely earns enough to feed the kids. She moves when she gets behind on the rent. She's had utilities billed under more names than she can count.

"I mean, she's still young and attractive enough to interest a better man, but not for much longer."

We are gathered in a circle. Mom and I are inside the ring. Our manifests are asleep, allowing us to leave them so we can go over the next day's script, perhaps make some minor changes. Due to their complete lack of experience, the input of the interns is only tolerated.

"Her hair will be all gray by the time she's thirty," I respond. "Her teeth will be gone before that. She must love him and stand by him in order to create all of the challenges I've scripted for my own manifest. Any positive change in her circumstances will diminish my challenges, and consequentially, be of little value for our audience."

"Hey," my mother derides, "they are Watchers, not an audience."

I respectfully nod, still grateful my collaborator agreed to replace the intern as a walk-in for the Mom manifest. After the cruelty inflicted upon me by the plantation overseer, this volunteer seeks harmonic balance by suffering the brutality I script for my mother.

"Is there any redeeming value in my manifest?" the intern who is Dad asks.

"If you desire to create on your own, you must adhere to the personality I predetermined," I reply sternly. "You must strive to make Mom hate you."

"But turning love into hatred causes my vibrations to drop almost to nothing," Dad whines. "I am risking long-term meld with the physical realm."

"You must manage the risk of harming yourself to utilize the energy needed to be so cruel to Mom," I explain. "First, love must become hatred before there can be forgiveness."

"I must admit, the Dad, Tom, manifest is doing a pretty good job of making me wish I didn't love him," Mom says. "Sometimes I think of killing him."

"That's further along in the script," I reply.

The Watchers pulsate their approval. Many of them passively participate in my creation as background manifests, barely real, such as neighbors, background celebrities, the President and politicians, but mostly, only unfamiliar faces seen in malls, convenience stores, restaurants and bars and numerous other settings that flicker on when needed and vanish when not. The Watchers can observe and be scenery without anchoring into space and time, unlike interns who are stuck until a creation's end for refusing to collaborate when assigned to do so. The sense of being watched, even when alone in a creation, is real.

All interns are summoned for rehearsal. My dialogue is still limited to "Momma", never "Dada", "Bye" and "Big Bird" because my manifest has aged only a year.

Scripted directions require me to observe my two-year-old brother to learn how to walk without falling. The intern who is my oldest brother hates to rehearse and, when in body, stutters because he can never remember his lines—and stuttering for his predetermined personality is not in the script.

⟋᪦⟍

On my manifest's fourth birthday, Dad is released from prison. Of course, his intern spent little time in body those four years. It is not necessary when out of my physical sight in a flicker setting. This creation requires the intern to manipulate Dad only in the most critical scenes in solidly projected places, where the influences on me are immediate and predetermined.

According to script, Mom and Dad spend an entire day and night in their bedroom. Their orgasms breach time and space to signal another intern to prepare to become my first sister. When the lovers finally come downstairs, they find we three boys in the kitchen, jelly and peanut butter smeared all over us and whatever we had touched. Dad's anger is instant and his punishment so severe that Mom can only look away, too frightened to try to stop her husband.

⟋᪦⟍

My memory of my reality is fading. Another year or so will bring total amnesia, except sometimes in dreams. Of course, though centered inside the boy manifest, I still guide everything. I am here and there at once, both the star and director of my own creation. The boy me will believe me to be God. I will let him believe that.

I first pray to myself the night I witness what I had only heard before. Upstairs, through the rails, still only four, I see Dad hammer his fist on Mom's head. She is unconscious, allowing her walk-in to get away from the beating. Dad kicks Mom, and then takes the purse she had fought so desperately to keep from him.

Dad empties the purse on the hall floor, grabs the green papers and then goes away.

My brothers watch with me. Ricky, the oldest, runs down the stairs to Mom.

"Mommy! Mommy!" we younger brothers cry, joining Ricky.

According to the script, Dad will use Mom's green papers to get drunk. He will break into a car to find something to steal. A policeman Watcher will see him. I will not see the Dad manifestation again for two and a half years.

⚬⚬⚬

Mom is always counting her pills. They make her headaches go away. Her hands tremble when she counts. Her thin face is moist skin over bony bones. Her forehead is taut against the veins and drips of sweat. This count is easy, only one pill left. She hungrily swallows it.

She cries.

⚬⚬⚬

A strange man visits Mom one night. In the morning, she makes him breakfast. He gives her green papers. She will never see him again, but she thinks about him often.

⚬⚬⚬

"It is good to be out of her body," the walk-in says. "I need a break from those awful headaches. Can't you understand how close the Mom manifest comes to suicide to end the pain?"

"I broke her jaw," Dad says. "That is why she gets those headaches. I am very sorry."

His aura shrinks and his vibration becomes an irritating buzz.

"That's all right," Mom soothes. "You did what you had to do."

The Dad intern is attending script review because his manifestation is scripted to be released from prison.

"You need to get inside and practice with Dad's body," I advise. "You've barely been in contact with Dad in the lockup."

"He really didn't need me much," Dad says. "He is such a dullard. He obeys the Watchers—um, guards. He likes not having to think for himself. He likes prison."

"We are at a very important part of the script," I tell Dad. "For the remainder of my Troy manifest's life, nothing will impact his future behavior more than what takes place when he is six. You have the opportunity to impress the Watchers to such a degree they may accelerate your vibrations, even grant a higher pitch."

"I'm just glad I'm done birthing," Mom says. "I have to admit though, that Watcher made the last one worth it. Great sex, and cash too!"

"Slut," Dad says, teasing. "Don't flicker your aura at me. I'm just staying true to my manifest's character."

All the interns are summoned to rehearsal. We rehearse and rehearse and rehearse; the lack of maturity among these interns—laughing and playing silly aura tricks on one another—troubles my vibrations.

I am scared. Since Dad came home from prison this morning, he has been quiet, though clearly angry. The family sits at the table—except for oldest sister Tiffany in her highchair and little Britney beside Mom in her bassinet.

I pass the meatloaf to Ricky. Ricky takes a piece and passes the platter to Danny. Danny uses his fingers to slide a piece onto his plate, and then hands the platter to Dad. Two pieces left, Dad takes both, leaving none for Mom.

Ricky cuts his own meatloaf in half, and then he cuts mine and Danny's. He forks a half piece from each of us onto the empty platter and carries the plate to Mom.

Dad grabs the back of his shirt and, with his other huge hand, smashes Mom's meatloaf into Ricky's face.

"Tom!" Mom screams.

Dad kicks Ricky into a corner.

"Your mother, the slut, can starve," he shrieks.

He tilts the table, causing everything to crash to the floor. His fist strikes Mom's mouth with such force, one of her teeth hits me in the eye. When I open my eyes, Mom is on the floor, trapped under her chair. Baby Britney starts to cry.

Dad stiffens. His eyes narrow at the bassinet. "Shut the fuck up, you little bastard," Dad mumbles, standing.

Then louder: "Shut the fuck up!"

Britney's cries change to screams. Dad kicks the table out of his path. His big hands grip the edge of the bassinet. He lowers his face to the baby's and shouts, "If you don't shut the fuck up, I'll shut you the fuck up!"

⚬⚬⚬⚬

I hear a swarm of tinkling. The melodies blend into a

high-pitched whistle. I see the Watchers huddle so close they form a radiant cloud that fills the entire house. The walls and ceilings are transparent. The floor becomes a circle of light, bathing us manifests. Confining us as well.

The physical Dad grunts when the meatloaf knife plunges into his back. He howls, but his intern sings a symphony. Dad pivots to present his chest and abdomen to the blade. Blood splashes Mom and Britney. The red spray changes to a rainbow of colors, some I have not seen since before my birth into this space and time.

Dad drops to his knees and grabs the knife from Mom's hand.

Too late; his intern has escaped the flesh so Dad can die.

Dad's blue eyes roll up to look for the last time into Mom's. He drops the knife and gently clasps her hand. He forgives her while she sheds tears of forgiveness for him.

Free at last, Dad's intern bows to the Watchers. They all project appreciation, so much they form a universe of stars and the sound of a colossal bell rings in the void. The intern's aura expands and fills in the spaces between the stars until all are blinded out and there is only one star, no more an intern, twinkling alone in the multiverse.

~∞~

Life goes on for those left behind.

Dad's death is ruled a justifiable homicide. Mom is receiving treatment in a state mental health facility, mostly staffed with Watchers to watch over her. We child manifests are scattered to foster homes until Mom is judged as recovered. We will never see her again in space and time.

Rehearsals continue without the Mom and Dad manifests. New interns will create the manifests needed when the script requires them. My manifest will forget his mother and father in favor of his new adoptive parents. Fully developed to cope in space and time, he will forget me too, except when he prays.

Re-composition

By John Morrison

Let music be my transitional shroud
Strong, to pierce old pores — loud!
To vibrate this abandoning clay
That clings to bones of yesterday

Transcending care of Mother Earth
Guide me toward a spirit birth
With no pause put between Her beat
And the astral sounds that wait to greet

Grant my heartbeat pace the drumming
Syncopated by guitar strumming
And let a string bass
Walk my soul toward its resting-place

Turn Jacob's ladder into a keyboard
Where music's mystery is freely poured
And to Gabriel's calling trumpet tone
Add comps of soulful saxophone

As rhythm takes me to Summer's Place
Where unheard melody fills the space
Help my song earn angel nods
And maybe win the smile of God's

Then...
If some young lovers at play in spring
Should attune to the thrill I sing
Let me be plucked through ether's door
To play the notes of earth once more

To Harriet

By Angee Stonehouse

~~ Harriet, a Galapagos tortoise, was a former resident of the Australia Zoo. She died at an estimated 175 years of age. She was thought to have been brought on board one of the ships in Darwin's expeditions to the famed Galapagos Islands.

Young claws etching Galapagos sands
Specks of ships approaching
Rising and falling
In undulating waters that encased
Your home.

Shifting waves of open sea
Embrace your rigid shell
Promising legends
Yet imagined.

Industry unfolding
Human creation building
Growing
And crumbling
As you endure.

Sweet hibiscus blossoms
Delight unspoiled senses
Simplicity of living
None but you recall
Unbroken, unremitting, unfazed

As time makes lab rats
Of fleeting invention,
Your eyes close in slumber
When others seal in death.

'Til wizened claws yield
To earth, to time
Your breath faded
Nature's selection fulfilled.

ANGEE STONEHOUSE

A poet and aspiring novelist, Angee Stonehouse has been writing since childhood. Her work focuses on near-reality sci-fi/fantasy for young adult and adult audiences. She finds inspiration in twisting perspectives on history and current events, and in never ceasing to ask, "What if?" She plans to complete and hopefully publish a novel in the next few years.

ELVEN DREAMS

By Lucinda Gunnin

"The ears tipped them off," he said. He laughed too loudly at his own pun.

Cora groaned. She hoped her father would not launch into yet another tale about the world before the age of Elves.

For generations, the Elves had hidden among the human race without any problem at all, but when the threat of nuclear annihilation loomed too close on the horizon, the goddess ordered her people to take over the world once again.

Suddenly, Elven children sprang up like spring seedlings. Even Cora's parents, far beyond the normal fertile years, were gifted with a child.

Lord Lindmere had announced the Elven presence and the human threat had been diminished. Along with fertility, the goddess had granted Elves the ability to stop certain dangerous human technology via magic. Safe from the human armies and nuclear weapons, the Elven Lord simply announced his court and the formation of the Elven Nation.

Negotiations were ongoing to cede land to the Elves, but many had bought up huge tracts in Central America and the southern American states, so the land was already legally theirs. The United Nations simply had to approve the membership of the new nation.

Cora had been born before the Elven presence was well known. Because of that, Cora's ears had been cropped soon after her birth, a minor plastic surgery performed by the hospital without her parents' permission, to, as they had said, "...correct her birth defect."

While she stood in a room full of Elves and those who fawned over them, the self-consciousness over the hospital error led Cora to reach up surreptitiously to run her finger along the jagged cartilage where her eartips should have been.

"Daddy, please, let me see a surgeon to have them fixed," she had begged once.

"Absolutely not! No daughter of mine will have fake eartips. You will not be some *poseur*! Your scars will serve as testament to the cruelty and xenophobia of the humans," he insisted.

Thus it came to pass that Cora Bellingwood, sole daughter of Lord and Lady Bellingwood and the Heir Apparent to the Elven throne through her Uncle Lindmere had mutilated human-looking ears instead of the graceful pointed eartips she had at birth.

Sometimes to Cora, her father's bad puns seemed deliberately cruel, designed to call attention to his daughter's pain.

"It's not like the whole world doesn't know anyway," she mumbled.

She was bitter about the situation, and the fact the National Enquirer had made sure everyone knew about her eartips didn't make her feel any better.

* * *

Cora was sixteen years old when Lord Lindmere came forward. Soon after, his entire family was fodder for the evening news and tabloids. Cora had been at school planning a homecoming dance when the photographers had first found her. Once they had seen her and her human ears, they had claimed she was not the royal heiress. Some had even supposed her parents had adopted a human child, which caused her father to release her medical records to quiet the rumors.

Whether he didn't realize that it would include information regarding her menstruation and her battle with acne or he simply didn't care was the subject of much debate in the Bellingwood household. After the revelation, Cora was whisked off to a private school with bodyguards and absolutely no freedom.

That argument hadn't gone her way either.

"Daddy, I'm an Elven. I can absolutely stop anyone who tries to hurt me. I want to stay here with my friends," she argued.

"You're royalty. You don't need to try to protect yourself," he said. "Besides, royal Elves do not go to public schools."

She knew her father was compensating for the years he'd had to use his glamour to cover up his true form. He'd had to appear as a middle-aged, overweight bank vice president for so long. He stood before her in his true form as six feet five inches tall, with flowing blond hair past his waist.

She feared the reason he was being so strict with her was because of his own inferiority complex.

Get over it, Daddy! She kept the thought to herself, though. To her father, she said, "Daddy, I'm not royalty.

I'm just Uncle Lindy's heir. It's not that big a deal,"

Within a year of Lord Lindmere's revelation, the nuclear disarmament treaties were in full negotiations and the Elves seemed to be coming out of the woodwork.

Everywhere Cora looked, someone was claiming to have always been an Elven. Celebrities and others with the means were having ear enhancements to pretend to be Elves and all Cora wanted was for life to go back to the way it was before.

Cora could have used her glamour to make the eartips appear, but she never bothered. The truth was already out there, after all.

Despite her flawed ears, Cora was a very popular companion at the embassy's coming out party. Since it was no longer necessary to cover her Elven appearance with glamour to make her look more human, her striking beauty was finally allowed to shine. Still not as tall as many Elven women, Cora had added six inches to her height since she had dropped the glamour. Her brown hair, once described as mousy, revealed itself as a deep chestnut. That night, she wore it off her neck, up with ringlet curls on either side to emphasize her graceful anatomy.

The dance lessons that were mandatory at her private school seemed even more useful when, one after another, the eligible bachelors at the party led her to the dance floor. Her feet ached from exhaustion, and she longed to stop smiling for just one moment.

Cora sought out her mother and intended to offer her regrets and retire for the evening when she saw a familiar face. Troy Connelly, quarterback at the public school she had attended and boy of her dreams, stood near the buffet table, sipping a glass of punch.

Cora's face lit up, and her feet suddenly seemed well rested and ready to find their way again to the dance floor. Brazen though it seemed, she went directly to him, offering her apologies to those people along the way who tried to garner her attention. She had almost made it across the floor to where he stood when she realized she had absolute no idea what she would say. Setting aside the nervousness that comes with being a teen, she reminded herself that she was, in fact, Elven royalty.

Her inner shyness came through when she walked up to the man she looked in the eye even without heels.

"Hi, Troy. Enjoying the party?"

His blue eyes sparkled when he smiled. Cora looked toward her toes, wishing her eyes were more interesting than the pale shade of jade she had been cursed with.

"Wow! You look great. Wanna dance?"

Cora had dreamed of hearing those words since they met as freshmen. That night, as seniors, she hoped the dance would be the start of something beautiful.

"I'd love to, Troy," she said. She took his hand and strolled toward the dance floor.

"Did you say something, Cora?" Miss Nestler asked.

The smile on her face disappeared when Cora recognized the voice of her English teacher. She looked around the room and saw her classmates staring and smirking.

Behind her, Ashley Thompson leaned in close and whispered, "Daydreaming again, four eyes?"

Panic crawled up her back, and Cora scrunched down in her seat, trying to hide herself in the oversized sweatshirt she wore.

* * *

"Sorry, Miss Nestler. I was, umm, caught up in my reading," Cora said.

From across the room, she saw Troy's eyes on her as well, a knowing smirk on his face.

I wish I could die!

"Try to read more quietly," her teacher offered, a look of condolence in her eyes.

Cora looked up at the clock and was relieved class would be over in a few minutes. As soon as the bell rang, she gathered her books and practically ran to the restroom, tears of embarrassment streaming down her face.

Cora went to the nurse's office and pleaded to call her mother so she could go home sick. She couldn't explain what was really wrong, so she claimed that she was having really bad cramps. That got the old nurse's sympathy and a call to her mother.

Her mother was not so easily fooled, but came to get her anyway.

"So... your period isn't due for a week yet. What's up?" her mother asked.

"How do you even know that?"

"Every mother with a teenage daughter knows, or at least they should. Between PMS and pregnancy, sometimes I wish you'd get knocked up."

"Not likely," Cora said, staring out the window.

"Ah. So it's about a boy," her mother said.

Lady Bellingwood from Cora's daydream, who was known by everyone else as Helen, saw the look on her daughter's face and explained. "It wasn't that long ago that I was a teenager. I remember the feeling. What happened? Did he ask someone else out? Tell you that you are a great friend? I always hated that one."

"Worse. I was daydreaming in English and might have said something, like his name, where everyone could hear it."

Helen stopped the car at the red light in front of them, looked around cautiously and then turned on her blinker, changing lanes in preparation for a right turn.

"Mom? Where are we going?"

"Trauma like that requires serious therapy. I'm thinking ice cream and new shoes," Helen said, remembering how devastating the social *faux pas* of being a teen could be.

"Could we skip the ice cream, Mom? It's horrible for my skin, and I'm fat!"

Helen looked at her daughter in glasses and braces and a sweatshirt that hid most of her curves. "You're not fat, sweetheart, but we'll skip the ice cream anyway."

"Thanks, Mom," Cora replied, but Helen was lost in thought and almost didn't hear her.

A few minutes later, when they pulled into the mall parking lot, Cora slid her finger across the rough cartilage of her right ear. Where the cartilage was smooth for every other person she knew, hers was rough and uneven, as though it had been torn or badly cut.

"Mom, what happened to my ears?"

Helen's eyes grew wide for just a second, and she was thankful her ever-present sunglasses masked the reaction to her daughter's question. "What do you mean, Cora?"

"They're bumpy and uneven. Ugly. Your ears don't look like this. Dad's don't," she said, holding her mousy brown hair away from her head so her mother could see her ears.

"Why, I never noticed them, sweetheart," Helen lied. "They're beautiful, just like you."

"I just could swear I heard Dad telling Uncle Lindy they got cut off at the hospital."

"We haven't seen Uncle Lindy in years. I'm sure you misremembered. Now, let's go look at those shoes."

※≫◎≪※

"Ted, I'm changing Cora's glamour. She's starting to feel uncomfortable and even ugly in the one she has," Helen said, whispering to her husband while they lay in bed that evening.

"You'll need to be careful, so people don't notice. Take her to the salon to get a makeover, maybe?" he replied. "Why are we whispering?"

"She told me today that she heard you tell Lindy what happened to her ears."

"She can't remember that. It was a decade ago. She was only six," Ted insisted.

"Well, she does. And I'm concerned about her day-dreaming. I can't get her to tell me all the details, but I did manage to get out of her that she was dreaming of being a princess."

"All little girls dream of being a princess at some point," he said, trying to dismiss her worries and snuggling deeper into his pillow.

"Do they all say, in the midst of a classroom day-dream that they are Elven royalty?" she asked.

Ted bolted upright, his attention fully on his wife instead of his sleep.

"Who heard it?"

"The entire class, according to her English teacher. She called me right before Cora called to ask me to let her come home early. She thinks Cora may need counseling."

Ted chuckled. He dropped the glamour he used to interact with mortals. "Do you think I ought to go see her like this?"

His pointed ears peeked out from beneath golden waves of hair.

"Damn it, Ted, be serious for a minute," Helen said, tempering her words with a smile. "How did she figure it out?"

"Hey, the psychics are on your side of the family, not mine," he grumbled, half under his breath. "What do we do now?"

"I have no idea."

"I guess I'll call Lindy tomorrow. I'd like to tell her, but we can't without his permission. It's really his decision, after all. Until then, let's get some rest. Maybe things will make more sense in the morning."

⋙∝⋘

The ringing of the alarm clock woke Cora the next morning.

Wait, the alarm doesn't ring. It beeps, she thought. She wiped the sleep from her eyes.

Five in the morning? Who calls at this hour?

Cora slipped on her slippers and went down the stairs to the kitchen. Her father was on the phone.

"Are you sure it's time, Lindy?" he asked.

Cora was excited he was talking to his brother. Her Uncle Lindy was one of her favorite people in the world, and she rarely was able to see him.

"No, we haven't told her yet. I was intending to call you about it today, at a more reasonable hour," Ted said into the phone. Cora suppressed a smile. Her father was always so cranky when he had to wake up early.

"You're right, of course, Highness. Better that she learn it from us than on the morning news." He paused, listening and then continued. "As soon as we hang up. She's sitting at the table now, hanging on every word I say. Yes, I'll have her call you after school."

Ted hung up the phone and then sat. He eagerly accepted the fresh coffee Helen sat in front of him.

"Cora, we need to talk —" he started.

She interrupted. "I really did hear you and Uncle Lindy talking about my ears, didn't I?"

"Yes," her father said. He explained that her mother suffered hemorrhaging during labor, requiring sedation and an emergency Cesarean section, so she could not extend her glamour to the newborn. The Elven doctor that was supposed to be there to prevent any mishaps had been delayed on his way to the hospital, so they saw Cora's eartips, he said.

"And that tipped them off..." Cora giggled. Her father looked confused. "Daddy, when the papers claim I'm not really Elven, please don't release all of my medical records to prove them wrong. We can prove I'm Uncle Lindy's heir without the whole world knowing when my next period is."

Ted wrinkled his brow. "How do you know about Lindy's heir? He just told me. I mean, we promised mother a hundred years ago, but he just confirmed it."

Cora thought to question his exaggeration of time and then thought better of it. "Do we really live forever? Am I supposed to be taller? Please don't send me to boarding school."

Her questions and requests all came running out of

her mouth as one long stream until Helen interrupted her.

"Cora, hush. Your father and I don't have all the answers. In fact, I think you may know more about this than we do. Why would we send you to boarding school?"

While she recounted her daydream from the previous afternoon, Cora saw her mother nod and her father clench his coffee mug tighter, until his knuckles were white with the strain. When she was finished, Helen spoke again.

"It's true then, Ted. She has the gift. We will be blessed indeed to have a High Lady with the goddess's gift.

"Cora, you won't be going to school today. We have some catching up to do and some shopping. Uncle Lindy will want you to look like an elf, not a human, when the press comes calling. We need to go shopping to get you some clothes that fit."

Helen unwove the glamour she had placed on her daughter. Cora felt nothing at all, save the slight tingle of the magic leaving her.

"You should go look in the mirror. Get used to your true reflection," Helen told her. "I suspect we don't have long before the press wants to know about Lord Lindmere's heir and family. You really should have something respectable to wear. I'll call Elise."

Cora suddenly felt important, knowing her mother rarely went to the expense of having Elise tailor-make clothing.

Standing in the hallway, Cora looked into a mirror and saw her own reflection for the first time, the girl of her dreams in flesh and blood.

Suddenly, she bolted back to the dining room. "Dad, does this mean there was a nuclear war?"

"No, sweetheart. Your Uncle Lindy stopped the missiles from firing last night. Today, he expects the world will want to know why they didn't work."

"Okay, cool. And, Daddy?"

"Yes, Cora?"

"Maybe the whole 'ears tipped them off' is kind of funny. Just don't use it all the time, okay?"

He agreed, but Cora smiled, knowing he still wouldn't understand a word she said.

LUCINDA GUNNIN

Lucinda Gunnin is a short story writer working on several first novels from her home in Carterville, Illinois. Her award-winning short stories were included in Elements of the Soul, published in 2009, and have been accepted for inclusion in Elements of Dimension scheduled for release by Twin Trinity Publishing in 2010. In 2009, she also had a short story and an essay published in the Southern Illinois Writers' Guild anthology, Writer's Voice, Volume 8. Cindy is current the vice president and program chair for the guild.

Cindy came to fiction by way of journalism and has spent more than two decades as a reporter. She has worked for several local newspapers and had her articles reprinted in several national magazines under her maiden name, Lucinda Morgan. She has work published at several online sites as well.

Currently, she spends her days managing a self-storage facility and writing. She lives at the storage facility with her husband and fellow author, Steven Thor Gunnin, and her adorable and adoring cat Rain. Cindy has degrees in journalism and public affairs reporting from Adams State College in Alamosa, Colorado, and the University of Illinois at Springfield.

DEATH OBEYED

By M. Lori Motley

Her hands rested on her chest—her child's chest—and Death hovered in the shadows in the corner. Asla's gaze flicked toward it then away, her mouth hardening to a grim line.

One year ago that very day, Jasic Dorl—cantrip artist and potion seller—had bested Asla Talean.

The memory was as fresh as yesterday. It pulled her grim countenance into a fierce scowl, incongruous on her unlined adolescent face.

Asla swung her feet out of bed and eased forward toward the floor, pulling her emerald velvet robe tight around her shoulders. She swished into the front room where Hobb was setting out breakfast.

"Good morrow, Milady," he muttered, raising a palsied hand to his forehead and bowing as far as the pains of age allowed.

"Is it?" she snapped, and climbed onto the chair by the window. She clenched her ankles together, lest her feet swing playfully above the floor.

Hobb backed out of the room. She had hired him out of necessity a few days after her transformation and had not bothered to lighten the burdens of propriety he inflicted upon himself. It made her feel more like her old self.

She drank scalding tea and broke bits of honey cake into her mouth, her mind casting back to that night. She had been lounging on cushions in the parlor with the book of Harrig the Elder open before her.

Jasic had surprised her. That, in itself, was worth a lifetime of shame. The triumphant grin plastered on his face when he burst into the room still burned in Asla's memory.

Two rooms away from any casting runes or weaponry, Asla had been nearly powerless to deflect the spell he attempted to cast. Nearly powerless.

While he muttered the unfamiliar words of a spell prepared by another, she whispered the summons she had learned years ago when she had won her immortality.

The sunlight that streamed through the high windows dimmed; the warmth of afternoon turned cold as a grave. Death spread his pall over the room. Jasic was wise enough to recognize what walked there and fled.

✦❧✦

A week and a half later, the pride she took in her unprepared defense shattered. Jasic's awkward spell had not killed her. Yet her life and power were still diminished. She woke to find her nightdress pooling on the floor around her feet, the sleeves dangling a foot below her wrists.

In the mirror, she saw her face as it was when she was ten. Her body was androgynous and weak.

In her weakened condition, she had been unable to retaliate against Jasic Dorl. She saw him at the guildhall or on the street, but never let him have the satisfaction of seeing what he had done to her. Her hatred festered, and she filled her spare hours studying particular agonies she could unleash upon him.

One year later, Asla was no closer to regaining her previous form. She had attempted almost more than she dared by herself. She had approached countless magicians and sorcerers.

Once she had convinced them who she was, all had refused to attempt disenchantment. Some made excuses, while others truthfully admitted they feared repercussions: either from the spell itself or from her should they fail. All knew of Asla Talean's dominion over Death.

Asla licked honey from a tiny finger and scowled. She knew what she had to do, however much she dreaded it.

"Hobb! I must find my sister. Pack light."

Sliding off the high chair, she strode back into the bedroom to dress.

The road out of the city was paved with wide flat stones for several leagues west of the river. Farms, orchards and inns lined the road on either side. The road gave way to hard packed dirt, and the farms became meadows covered with strawflowers and grasses.

Hobb carried a pack too heavy for his stooped shoulders. Asla's pouches and purses jounced off her legs in time to her small steps. The hilt of a silver dagger flashed at her hip.

As darkness fell, Hobb's feet stumbled against each other.

"We will camp under the trees," Asla said, indicating

a dark green band ahead.

His hand wavered upward but fell to his side before reaching his forehead.

"As you wish, Milady."

Asla frowned, and she became even more aware that Death followed close behind. She knew it stalked Hobb, and she should not interfere.

She sighed and then led him off the path and to a convenient glade near the edge of the forest. He unshouldered the pack and sank to the ground.

"I wish you would let me help you," Asla said, and the old man's head whipped up, shaking from side to side.

"There is nothing evil in it," she insisted.

Night shadows closed around them and Death waited.

"No, Milady," Hobb said. "I won't be having any magics done over me. You are what you are—and I have no problem with that—but it's just not my way."

His breath came in harsh wheezes, and Death pressed closer.

"I could at least—"

"No," he repeated, and his tired eyes peered up at her in the forest gloom. "Though I thank you for the offer."

She sat on a fallen log and listened to the coming night and watched the twilight mists wind their way through the trees. Hobb slipped into a quiet sleep, wrapped in his traveling cloak near the fire. Death filled the night; the air in the clearing lay thick and still.

Asla cast her mind away, a seer stone clutched in her hand. She saw the fae dance in the deep woods and heard the mind-numbing music of their flutes and lyres.

Hobb's breath caught in his throat, his foot twitched once, and then all was still. Death gathered his prize and withdrew. A soft breeze sighed through the leaves, and a nightjar chirred somewhere deep in the forest.

⚒

The next morning, Asla flagged down a merchant caravan heading toward the city and paid for Hobb's body to be taken to the churchyard. The man hesitated, but Asla glared at him and added another silver piece to the pile. He silently loaded the old man's body onto his wagon and hurried away.

On the quiet morning road, Asla walked west toward the place of her birth. Almost two hundred years had passed since the midwife had laid two squalling bundles in her mother's arms. Her wizard father stood in the corner and mumbled a litany of blessings and enchantments upon them both. Her mother, a simple town woman, died the day after.

Her father had been destroyed thirteen years later in a foolish battle with another wizard. Asla and her sister finished raising themselves, delving deep into the magic that their father left behind. Asla moved to the city and joined the wizard's guild. Sylla took a different path.

The entrance to the cave was overgrown with decades of creeper vines and weeds, but Asla found it without hesitation. She stood at the mouth and peered into the gloom, her mind toying with the possibility that her sister had moved on long ago.

Her left hand clutched a rune of protection, her other the hilt of her dagger. She stepped inside, plunging into the still blackness.

A soft susurration of breath drifted through the

gloom, barely audible, but it told Asla what she needed to know. Her sister lay within. She crept forward.

"Who disturbs me?" The voice rasped out of the dark.

"Sylla, it is Asla, your sister. I come seeking your aid."

Something slid across the floor like the low rasp of a snake on stone. The darkness before Asla solidified when something rose up unseen before her. A dank breath blew across her face.

"Asla? No, my sister is dead."

"Death cannot claim me, Sylla."

The low hiss came again and the sound of something large shifted in the shadows ahead. "You are so young! So young! And come to me for help?"

"Caught by another's spell. I have been reduced to this body and wish to rid myself of its constraints." Asla paused, her fingers playing over the rune in her hand. "I come to offer my youth to you."

A green light flared in the darkness, and Asla squinted. Inches away from her face, her sister loomed. Sylla crouched on the floor, her skin mottled green and gray with mold and moss. Her hair was a matted cloak of black, her eyes wide, black orbs. Her breath was swamp fire.

"Your youth? I could take it easily if I wanted," she said, prideful bravado tingeing her words. "You offer it to me? I could be young again?"

"A trade, sister. I do not want this youth, and you need it. It benefits us both, and leaves neither in debt."

Sylla inclined her head. Her tongue slipped over cracked lips.

Asla shucked her clothes and shoes, tossing them behind her toward the entrance. As soon as she stood upright again, Sylla pounced.

Bone-thin fingers wrapped around Asla's arms and throat. The rotten-toothed mouth opened wide while the child's body stiffened. Asla felt it happen. A hard tug simultaneously from heart and mind and she could feel her body lengthening and fleshing out under her sister's grip.

Her mirror image stared at her from where Sylla stood next to the green fire. Curling deep brown hair, long white limbs and firm breasts, the two women were perfectly matched.

"Death will take you eventually," Asla muttered, but Sylla shook her head and grinned.

"Death cannot touch such beauty. I can go out now and feed. I will keep him at bay, as always."

She turned, and passed a hand over the fire, plunging them into darkness.

Asla paused at the mouth of the cave. Under the gaze of waiting Death, she slipped the old gown she had brought over her head. She tossed the child's dress on a bush by the side of the road, expecting some farmer's daughter would find and make use of it.

She spared a last glance at the black entrance to Sylla's lair, her lips pressed together in a grim line. No enchantment existed to free her sister from her half-life.

Eventually, Sylla's youth would fade once more, and she would be forced to retreat back to monstrous form in the cave. All Asla could offer her then was a swift end to existence. She shook her head and turned her back on her sister. The shadows under the rocks writhed hungrily.

"Not for you," she whispered to the dark. "Not tonight."

She turned and headed toward the city, her feet hurrying down the rocky path. The destination was etched in her mind: the house of Jasic Dorl.

"Follow me," Asla commanded. "Your hunger will be sated."

The shadows coalesced on the path behind her.

Death obeyed.

M. LORI MOTLEY

M. Lori Motley is a divorced Mom to two boys, one autistic, whom she homeschools. By day, she is an internet business owner and freelance writer of mundane web copy and articles. By night, she delves into the realm of mostly fantasy and horror fiction. She began her writing habit when she was six with a scintillating story about a giant cow attacking a city. Since then, her writing experience has grown to include several not-yet-published novels, dozens of short stories, and some rather awkward poetry that no one seems to understand but her.

Whether the desire to write fiction is a fever to be doused through finger-cramping, late-night typing, or a muse-fueled blessing, it is an integral part of Lori's existence. The day-to-day input of suburban New Jersey and family life offers inspiration, but requires tweaking to release it from the ordinary. She seeks to suspend reality whenever possible and produce fiction that can transport readers to other times, places or fantasy worlds.

More information about current projects and her self-published "Roll the Dice Fantasy Fiction," a fantasy genre story generator book, can be found at:

http://www.MloriMotley.com.

FAILURE TO COMMUNICATE

By Thomas Forthe

Eric ran down the halls of East High School. He slammed students and teachers aside and screamed at the world to listen. He accosted Ms. Evans first and yelled at her to leave town before it was too late. Next he caught Maryann, the head cheerleader, and backed her into the lockers. He begged her to get her family out of town. It took four male teachers to wrestle him down amongst the scattered books and debris to restrain him until the sheriff arrived.

John Malcolm had been the elected sheriff of Hanstead County for nearly twenty-five years. In those years, he had dealt with quite a few strange things, including that same kid several times. Hanstead was a decent place to live with little major crime of any kind, mostly minor cases to keep John busy. There had been a burglary or two, a car chase that involved a drunken townsman, and the infamous chicken theft at Bartlett's farm, but little real trouble until Eric Finnely had started high school.

Eric was a good-looking kid and far from dumb, but it was John's third trip to pick up Eric that year. He was tired of it. John wondered if the kid was yanking people's chains or if he might actually be nuts. The sheriff delivered the teenager in handcuffs to his parents, along with a stern warning to get him some help or else.

Eric's long dark bangs could not hide the blaze of his deep blue eyes when he glared at everyone within his vision.

"Next time, I aim to lock him up," John explained. "Unless you care to explain to the judge why he's on the warpath again, I suggest you get him to the clinic or something to get a handle on his behavior."

The sheriff left Eric in his parents' custody and drove off. He hoped they'd see reason.

"I got expelled today." Eric made the statement with no emotion. He had always been a problem child: problems at school, trouble at home, but this latest escapade had his mother in tears. Eric's father said little, as usual. He kept his thoughts to himself and murmured curses under his breath.

"They don't believe me," Eric said.

"Why would they, Eric?" his mother asked. "It's not like you sound crazy or anything."

Her voice rose in pitch with each word.

"Mom, you know I'm right." Emotion clouded Eric's voice, causing it to squeak when he spoke.

"Eric, that's enough," his mother said. Anger was evident by the clenched fists, and her body shook. "Not one more word, not one. Not only are you grounded, but you will not leave this house until I have figured out how to get your ass back into school."

Eric slammed the door to his room, and restrained the urge to crank up the stereo. He knew if he encouraged his father's wrath, it would only get worse, much worse. Few things gathered attention in school like a black eye.

"Bitch." The word had slipped over his tongue and through his teeth, softly entering the room, too low to hear beyond his own tiny, shrinking world.

Eric had given up trying to get adults to listen. He felt nobody listened to him anymore, not even God.

He paced back and forth the length of his room, like a caged leopard, looking for a crack to slink through to the freedom of the jungle. The hard case of his cell phone finally earned a place in his consciousness.

Jamie, I have to call Jamie, was the first thing that implanted itself into his brain through the mists of rage.

Eric worked his way into his closet near the outer wall, hoping to muffle the call so his parents wouldn't hear.

"Eric!" Jamie shouted into his ear when she answered. "Are you ok? That ass didn't hurt you did he? Can I come over? Please tell me you're all right?"

The questions came fast, as though those might be the last words she ever spoke.

"I'm fine. No, he didn't, not this time. I'm grounded for life and sentenced to my room. They refuse to believe what I saw, just like everybody else."

"They will in the end," she stated, knowing the futility of trying to change the mind of an adult.

"Yeah, but by that time, it won't matter anymore," Eric returned. "Will you come with me? We can leave. Maybe we can make it to the cave"

His voice was almost pleading.

"Eric, my mom would kill me!"

"Not if she can't find us. You know what's coming,

and we have to go. Meet me at Finster's barn. Dress warm and bring extra clothes."

He hung up. If he had stayed on the phone, she probably would only have tried harder to talk him out of leaving.

Eric hid in the back of the barn when Jamie walked in, a bundle in her arms and a small backpack slung over her shoulder. He rushed to pick her and her burden off the floor in a massive hug.

"I didn't think you'd make it past your step-asshole," he quipped.

"That was the easy part. He was passed out in front of the tube as usual." Disgust filled her voice. She refused to relive the things that happened while her mother worked when her stepfather didn't pass out.

The last time her stepdad had tried to get overly friendly, he'd found his own .357 pointed at a very important part of the body, at least, a part of the body he would consider important. That was the last time he'd made that mistake, and it was the last time he had seen his own pistol. Jamie felt the pistol's comforting weight in the shoulder holster she had taken along with the gun.

"Let's get going before they come after us," was all she said.

Eric and Jamie climbed through the timber and crossed the creek. They followed the same path they had used many times before. That time was different though. That time they were not going to come back. They took extra care to hide their trail, walking in the creek, keeping on the rocks. Eric knew both of their lives depended on not being discovered.

"Do you think any of the people we told will try to hide?" Jamie asked.

"I don't think there is a chance in hell," Eric said, his voice flat. "Nobody ever did more than laugh at me."

"They won't be laughing much longer," she replied, her voice filled with conviction.

The trip to the cave was exhausting. After a couple of hours of climbing, jumping and crawling, they were both ready for a break. Eric crawled in first under the brush trying not to disturb the entrance, flashlight in hand. Although the entrance was small, the cave widened out enough to stand in after about ten feet, and a chamber opened up into an area large enough for twenty people. A smaller chamber the two had nicknamed *the pantry* opened off the back. They had sealed that off best they could. They had stored canned goods and other necessities. They hoped someday to make the caverns a home, or at least a long-term shelter.

<hr />

Earl Finnely was furious. He tore through his son's room to look for clues as to where he had run off.

"If I ever get my hands on that little shit," he repeated over and over.

Eric was gone. Along with him, Eric had taken clothes, a sleeping bag, some food and Earl's flashlight.

"I'll call the police," Eric's mother said.

"No," Earl erupted with a viciousness that made it clear his command was final. "Let him try to make it on his own. When he does comes crawlin' back—" Earl's fist smashed into the palm of his hand.

Tanya winced. Eric was not the only one to have felt Earl's anger.

"We just keep on livin', just like nothin' happened."

Tanya's tears were his only answer.

"That smart ass can starve before I go out and look for him. He's made us the laughin' stock of the town, tellin' everyone he met up with all about the invasion, an' how we was just cattle for the slaughter.

"Maybe I'll give him a dose of reality with the back of my hand."

Earl was sweating and shaking by the time he finished his rant. He kicked the back door and took his rage outside.

"Aliens, my ass!"

⋘⋙

Sarah Johnston was panicked. Jamie had been missing for nearly two days and not a soul had witnessed her leave, including Sarah's no good drunkard husband. She figured Bert was useless at everything but providing for his family. Plumbers made a decent living, even though he drank quite his fair share of that income.

"Jamie was trouble all right, with a capitol T!" Sarah told the sheriff when she had reported the missing teen the day before.

"She'd gotten worse once she got to know that Finnely kid. That boy is pure trouble, mind you. Pure trouble."

Sarah was not surprised when the sheriff told her Eric hadn't been to school either, or that his parents had not filed a missing persons report.

"That old son of a—" Sarah prided herself in being a good Christian woman and had cut the sentence off short.

"Jamie had never been an angel, but her behavior never got too far out of hand until she began hanging out with Eric. Eric got it into Jamie's head that the world was

• • •

gonna end and everybody was here just to feed some aliens or such.

"That boy should have been locked up long ago, if you ask me."

The sheriff held his tongue, not wanting to make any waves. After all, the sheriff's position was a political one, an elected position, so he made sure to keep the folks who voted happy when he could.

Sarah continued to speak, though, even without the sheriff encouraging her. "That child was just plain disturbed. He would scare the dickens outta ya with the things he would say. We was all being fattened up for the slaughter, and the aliens was commin' ta freeze us for later. Now where on earth would a boy go gettin' ideas like that?" she asked.

The sheriff could only shake his head and reply, "Video games, maybe. I hear he likes the really weird ones. When we catch that young'un—and we will—he is sure as hell goin' to the doc. I won't be one bit surprised if'n he don't end up with his sleeves sewed together."

Sarah brought the photo the sheriff had asked for and handed it to him.

"She's a pretty thing," John commented when he saw the photograph of Jamie, with her long blonde hair and sullen eyes.

"What color are her eyes?" he asked. "Height and weight?"

"Green. Five feet seven inches, and around a hundred and twenty-five," she answered.

The sheriff, promising to find the runaways, returned to his cruiser and headed back to the office.

The morning paper held a short blurb on the pair of

runaway teens, stating they had probably eloped and were sought by their parents. Even the paper had put the pair on the back page, and life in town had moved on without them.

⚬⚬⚬

Eric and Jamie's lives had changed a great deal over the past few days. Their time was spent gathering food and practicing skills they had read about in the survival books—books that had once only held a dream, a dream that was a reality they did not care to escape. Days were spent fishing and hunting, laughing and loving. Gone were the days of fear caused by circumstances beyond their control. Gone were the nightmares that called themselves parents.

Eric had trapped a rabbit and began to skin it when he realized he was in the same spot he had been in when he had seen the ship not so long ago, a memory he would much rather forget. If only he had not been the only witness, if only Jamie had been down there with him that day instead of up in the cave.

His memory played back as though misted by a thick haze. Nothing was clear, but more like remembering a dream. People and animals were herded inside, some frozen solid and carried on self-propelled carts. That dream had given him nightmares enough to last whole nights, and had awoken him nearly every night since the event took place. Only then, up there with Jamie, did he feel safe enough to sleep through the night. No more shaking, no more night sweats, and no more medication.

His parents had insisted on medication. They forced the doctors on Eric. They forced the pills on their son as well, always sure to watch him take them to make certain he swallowed.

Eric remembered the last few weeks' worth of pills he had hidden under his tongue before he'd spit them out and flushed them down the toilet. Those pills had taken away control over his life to point he felt he needed his parents' permission to breathe.

He and Jamie had made a pact back before his parents had their way and hurled him down the path of prescribed insanity, a pact they had made to end the pain and stop the suffering.

Instead, they were free, free to live, free to feel, free to breathe. The pact was a distant memory with no need of dredging it back up. It didn't matter that the sheriff couldn't find any missing people or livestock.

The sound of a .357 Magnum shot brought Eric back to the reality of the moment. He turned and ran for all he was worth.

"Jamie!" The word tore from his throat.

Eric crashed through the brush back up the hill to the cave entrance. Rounding the last twist in the trail, he nearly crashed into Jamie, who shook, her eyes loaded with tears. She pointed the gun at the ground. She was near hysterical.

"Snake!" she yelped.

"Did it bite you?" Eric inspected Jamie for wounds before she could reply.

"N-no," she sobbed.

He helped Jamie back into the cave and managed to calm her. He assured her he would be right back. He ducked outside and grabbed a large branch filled with leaves to work at erasing all traces of their presence from the ground and paths near the entrance to the cave. Retreating back into the cave, he erased his prints as he went.

Eric knew they had to stay in hiding, especially with the gunshot that would alert anyone nearby that people were close. Anyone who searched for the source of the sound would be a threat, and he did not want things to return to how they used to be when he lived with fear and hated each breath he took away from Jamie's side.

What if she had been bitten? he asked the silent question to himself.

❧

The sheriff stood over the corpse and squinted into the sunrise. He wished he were anyplace but there.

"A murder? Here?" he whispered.

It had been a robbery, and Jake McFarland had been shot dead in the process. It was the only robbery homicide the sheriff had ever seen in his town, in all the years he had held the office.

The coroner's office listed the cause of death as a single gunshot wound to the head, made by a large caliber weapon—a .357 Magnum at close range. The time of death was estimated at less than twenty-four hours prior.

The only fingerprints found were from a man who only owned a .38 special: the sheriff himself. Unfortunately, there were a lot of his fingerprints, due mostly to his ineptitude. The investigators found his prints on nearly every surface in the store where the robbery had occurred, as well as on the victim's personal effects.

The deputy's report showed little of consequence missing until a complete inventory was taken of the small convenience store at the edge of town. Bandages, two first aid kits, food items and several snake bite kits were taken.

Strangely enough to the investigators, the cash drawer had not been touched.

"Who the hell murders somebody for this kind of crap?" the deputy asked.

"No sign of a struggle or a fight."

"You think Jake knew the killer?"

The sheriff shrugged.

It had not taken Bert long to put two and two together after the news report about Jake's death. It took even less time to realize that if Jamie or her boyfriend had killed Jake over a robbery that they would not hesitate if they came across Bert.

"Besides, what better way to make sure that little bitch keeps her mouth shut about me?" he said under his breath.

It didn't take Bert long to make his way down to the sheriff's office and file the report on his missing pistol.

Jamie awoke and quietly watched Eric enter the cave. He slid in and began setting some bundles down inside the small room at the back. Jamie lay there admiring his handsome profile and wondered what he had found.

"Where were you?" she asked.

"I sneaked into town to grab some things." He smiled at her while he spoke. He reached for her and hugged her close.

"Is everything all right?" she asked. She gazed into his deep blue eyes.

"No worries," he said.

He smiled and then slipped the pistol back in its holster.

"I got some stuff from Jake, and he'll never tell anyone."

Eric showed Jamie the snakebite kits and the rest of
his goods, before he stored them inside the pantry.

"Jake let you have all of this?"

"It took all of my cash, but it will be worth it," he said.

Jamie knew something was wrong. Eric's eyes were
moist, and he kept looking away from her, not once looking into her eyes.

"Did someone see you?" Jamie asked.

"I'm not sure, but I think I saw someone follow me
until I made it to the creek. I took the long way back and
covered my tracks. I never saw them again"

Jamie relaxed a little at that.

"Any idea who it was?" she asked.

"Whoever it was, they were too far away, but I'm
pretty sure I lost 'em."

Eric finished putting the items away and headed for
the entrance. He told Jamie, "I'd better keep an eye out, for
a while, anyway."

Eric was more than happy to avoid any more questions. The image of Jake soaked in his own blood was
etched into Eric's mind and would live there forever. He
didn't want to add that to Jamie's memories too.

❧

Deputy Sheriff Daniel Barnes had listened to the chatter about the murder and had seen all of the evidence.

"It doesn't make a lick of sense," he said, finally giving his own opinion. "Jake would have given those kids
anything they asked for, and then some."

"Maybe they didn't bother to ask," the sheriff volunteered.

"Eric might have been a little weird, but murder?"

"According to the doc, he flipped his lid, completely lost it and kept on about aliens landing and gathering up people. No tellin' what somebody like that would do," the sheriff added.

Dan shook his head, trying to rid himself of the feeling that there were still some pieces missing from the puzzle.

"What about Mrs. McFarland? Any word on her yet?" Dan asked.

"All we know at this point is that she's missing."

"Put out an all points on her car," the sheriff ordered.

⚜

Bert had seen Eric the day of the murder and had tried to track him back into the hills. Eric had proved too resourceful and had lost Bert shortly into the jaunt. Bert had too many years of drinking and sitting in front of the TV to ever have had any chance of catching the teenager, but he had found out the general direction and knew the kids had to be hiding out in the mountains not too far from town.

Bert had every intention of turning Eric in right then and there, but Bert's own house got in his way. The liquor cabinet called his name.

"One drink won't hurt," he told himself.

Tired from his hike, it took more than one drink to regain his wind. Bert woke the next day in a pool of his own urine, and he staggered into the bathroom to get cleaned up. The hot shower worked wonders on Bert's foggy mind, at least until his foggy reflexes failed to respond to a dropped bar of soap.

Bert was still unconscious when Sarah found him. His

head had remained out of the water. The paramedics hauled him off to the hospital, and another day passed before he could give the sheriff his news.

In the meantime, the sheriff had visited the clinic where Eric had gone for treatment in hopes he could get insight into Eric's condition. The sheriff wanted to know if Eric was capable of committing murder. The good doctor had answered his questions, but he had left the sheriff with a problem that was still boring into the sheriff's mind even when Bert Johnston was wheeled into his office.

The doctor had said he did not believe Eric was dangerous.

Bert had unraveled his tale, including the lies, leaving the sheriff even more confused by the time he was done. The sheriff had no choice but to organize a search party. Once the party was rounded up, the sheriff addressed them.

"All right, quiet down!" he yelled to get everyone's attention.

"Eric was spotted in the mountains a couple of days ago, armed with a pistol. He has to be considered dangerous now that he took a shot at Bert. Stay in touch, pair up, nobody approach him alone."

With that, the sheriff led them to the spot Bert had described to get them started. Of course, Bert had declined the invitation to join the party, claiming he wasn't steady enough and would only get in the way.

"Let's get this over with," the sheriff said. "Dan, you stay in town and keep your eye on things until we get back."

⋙⊙⋘

The sheriff was livid. "I've about had a belly full of

Bert friggin' Johnston!"

"He was there." Bert's hands were clenched, his face was red and sweat poured off of him.

"Look, you little shit, we just spent two days searching all over that hill. He ain't there."

The sheriff's face was tight. His teeth showed, and the veins stood out on his temples.

"Not even one track," he said with finality.

"I'm tellin' you, he is!" Bert shouted.

He had let his temper escape, and there was no calling it back. Bert took a swing, aiming at the sheriff's jaw. He didn't realize just how bad his mistake was until he woke with a massive headache, looking out from behind the bars into an empty room. He slid back onto the cot, nursing his aching head in his hands.

Dan slipped a tray onto the feeding slot to the cell and added a cup of steaming coffee.

"Corn, fresh bread, Salisbury steak, and mashed tatters ought to make you feel better, along with these." Dan added a matching pair of aspirin to the tray.

Bert grabbed the coffee, slapped the aspirin into his mouth and washed it down with a sip.

The phone rang in the office, and Dan left to answer it. The phone barely disconnected before Dan was reaching for his hat and heading for the door.

"Sheriff needs to hear this," hissed past his teeth on his way out the door.

Dan fired up his cruiser and grabbed the mic. The sheriff answered within seconds. Dan filled him in on the matter at hand.

"You sure?" the sheriff asked.

"Yes, sir. She's in Marston sitting in county lock up,"

Dan added.

"Who would've thought?" It was more a statement, not a question, from the sheriff.

"Mrs. McFarland had the gun on her?"

"Yes, sir. She confessed when they pulled her over. Never even pulled her out of the car before she started in on how she wanted a divorce and he refused it," Dan added.

"Don't that beat all?" The sheriff muttered.

⁓⧉⧉⧉⁓

Eric neared town while he went over his mental list of everything he needed to do while there. He and Jamie had discussed it the previous evening. He had left near dawn, and headed down the hill.

He felt the fool, having left a map in his room that could lead his parents and anyone else straight to them. It was not very detailed but anyone who found it might figure it out and find them. He had made the map years ago when he had first found the cave, and he'd left the map on his bookshelf, tucked under the cover of a yearbook.

Good thing I told Jamie about it. It would have been bad if the ol' man had found it.

He also wanted to gather a few more things from his room while he was at it: a magnifying glass, camping pots, frying pans, and more camping supplies.

Eric reached the house and sneaked into the backyard. He felt lucky when his key still worked in the lock, having feared his father would change the lock. He slipped inside the door making an effort to be quiet. He crept down the hall to his room and checked inside; all was quiet.

Careful to remain quiet, he gathered all the items he

needed and turned for the door to find himself face to face with his mother.

"Eric!" she shrieked. "What did you forget to steal the first time?"

Eric was trapped. "This is all my stuff. I won't come back again."

"Damned right you won't," she said.

She tried to grab the pack out of his hands but he held fast to it.

"You ungrateful little thief!" she managed to get out through clenched teeth.

Eric pulled her around, aimed her at the bed, and pushed hard, sending her sprawling onto the bed in a heap. He yanked the pack out of her grip and ran for the back door.

∽⟨⟩∾

Dan responded to the 911 call, jumped in his cruiser and raced to head off Eric. Eric was nearly to the tree line when Dan spotted him heading into the trees at a dead run. Dan took the car nearly into the trees, sliding sideways to a stop and jumped out while the dust still boiled up from under the car and into the air. Eric wasn't too far ahead, and Dan was gaining on him. Eric knew the area well and leapt across the creek and dashed into the woods beyond.

Dan missed the spot Eric had used and hurled into the creek, landing solidly on his hind end, soaking him from head to foot. Dan jumped up and scrambled for the far bank just in time to see Eric disappear around a large rock. Through the chase, Dan would catch glimpses of Eric, like a ghost dancing a waltz with the pines that kept him on course. Dan tried to radio for help, but the radio had gotten wet in the creek and wouldn't transmit.

Through the trees, Dan managed to see Eric enter a small hole under some brush. He closed the distance between then and waited by the entrance, concealed by some brush like a hunter waiting out his rabbit.

Eric stopped only long enough to tell Jamie he had been followed, and turned around to head back out to watch.

Eric had hardly emerged when he heard, "Eric, put your hands on your head!"

Eric did as he was told.

"Tell Jamie to come on out, Eric. It's over."

"Jamie isn't here deputy; I'm all alone here."

"Nice try, kid, but I know better," Dan replied. "Jamie, come on out here, girl. It's over!"

Jamie emerged from the entrance and faced Dan.

"We can't go back, please," she begged.

"I'm sorry, Jamie, but you have no choice."

"Deputy, we couldn't walk out tonight if we had to. It will be dark before you even get halfway back," Eric said.

Dan realized Eric was right. There was no way around it. He had lost his flashlight and barely knew where he was at best. Wandering around in the dark would get somebody hurt, or worse.

Eric and Jamie spent a restless night handcuffed back to back while the deputy dozed off and on. When daylight came, he separated them, led them out and cuffed them together to keep them from running off. It took far longer to get back to his cruiser than it had taken to get up there.

Eric, Jamie and Dan walked in near silence. Even the forest seemed depressed at the outcome. Not a single bird had announced the dawn, not a squirrel scolded the humans in passing. The trip proved uneventful after the trio emerged from the forest and trekked toward the cruiser. Dan loaded the teens inside and started the car. Dan was irritated when dispatch ignored his call. The radio was silent, not even static sounded from the speakers.

Jamie was the first to speak after passing a few farms on the way in. "Where are all the cows?" she whispered.

She and Eric looked out the windows and saw that the fields were empty, the gates stood open, and not even a dog barked a greeting.

Dan pulled into town and stopped in the middle of the street. Doors stood open: house doors, car doors, even business doors all were open. Not a soul stirred. Dan gunned the car forward and slid to a stop in front of the sheriff's office. He jumped out and ran inside, not waiting to unload his passengers. After a few minutes, he returned to the car, opened the rear doors, uncuffed his prisoners, turned abruptly, and walked back in without saying a word.

Eric and Jamie looked at each other and followed the deputy inside. Paper was strewn all over the office, desks were tipped over, and chairs lay on their sides. The coffee pot sat full and untouched.

They found Dan staring blankly at a cell. The door had been torn off the hinges and the lock melted away. Blood covered the bars like paint, and everything inside was either broken or turned over. Blood washed the floor.

Dan sprinted for the office and grabbed a phone; it was dead.

Before long, the three of them were running from house to house, searching for any sign of life. All they found was emptiness. Water overran sinks, stoves had been left burning, doors left open, lights left on. It was a ghost town, where only the noise came from television sets tuned to nothing. No dogs ran up to greet them, no birds, nothing moved but the wind blowing the trees.

Eric's mother walked down the barren steel hallway with the others, but no one spoke. Like her, they could not stop walking or even turn their heads.

Words were no longer hers to speak, and nothing obeyed her will. The only sound was a cadence of footsteps and hooves beating. She had walked past row upon row of solidly packed rooms, their occupants quick frozen in garish poses and then stacked floor to ceiling.

Tears had frozen to her face once she had traversed the ramp, following a herd of people and animals deep inside the frozen bowels of the ship.

The only thought she had running through her mind besides sheer terror were the words of her son: *They're coming.*

THOMAS FORTHE

Thomas Forthe joined the Accentuate Writers Forum in October of 2008 and at that time he had very little idea of what it took to write correctly. The forum caused a long-forgotten longing to surface...a longing to put his imagination to work at writing, which had long been a passion subservient to life's little whims: eating, shelter and electricity.

Thomas learned new skills from the fabulous cast of fellow members at Accentuate, skills like reading what he wrote before, and not after he submitted his folly to the eyes of the world. Other skills were built; some are still under construction as it is a learning process in progress.

Thomas resides on the Gulf Coast in Florida, keeping a close eye on the huge body of water behind the house that holds such promise for a wanna-be-fisherman. Mrs. Forthe and their son keep close eye on Thomas to be sure he surfaces occasionally for food, air and the all necessary beverage.

Thomas has two sons, a wife and one perfect baby granddaughter. He's surrounded by the loving entourage of animals, one faithful dog, and five loving cats who love the food, the air conditioning and the bed... Thomas they're not so sure about, especially when he has the audacity to try to use the bed.

Thomas writes fantasy as a genre of choice, but may dabble in science fiction now and then with a sprinkling of horror for good measure. He reads a lot like he writes.

BOBBI LEDER

Bobbi Leder is a freelance writer who has earned her Bachelor of Arts degree in Journalism and Mass Media from Rutgers University. Leder's story "Being a Wife is Not Enough" has been published in the anthology WOMEN REINVENTED: True Stories of Empowerment and Change, and her story "Euri, the Miracle Worker" has been published in the anthology "Dogs and the Women Who Love Them".

Leder is a contributing writer for the Houston newspaper, "The Banner", and has been published with many print and web-based magazines including: K9; Dog Living; Urban Paws; Houston Pet Talk; Texas Cats and Dogs; Tails, Inc.; The Bellaire Buzz; Girlfriend 2 Girlfriend; and LifeScript.

Leder has also been published with a plethora of websites, including: Prevention, AOL, Dog Channel, OpEdNews, CNN, Travels, Made Man, The Daily Star, World News, Associated Content, eHow, Helium, Atlantic Publishing, Spot and Fido, Pet Friendly World, Daily Article, Examiner, Tails 'n' Trails, *and* Theatre Monkey.

When not writing, Leder's life revolves around her English Cocker Spaniel, Euri.

THE CALL

By Bobbi Leder

I answered the phone.
The ringing would not stop.
It pierced my ears as I lie half-asleep.
Who was calling so late?
The pick-up, disturbing
My parents: part-time relatives,
Bragging about their trip.
Las Vegas: Where gambling is a sport,
Green was the trophy.

Sunny, humid
Unlike our cold, damp weather.
Precipitation daily with chilled winds
Why do they leave me in this?
Hanging up, relieved.
The walk back to my room, dismal.

A pounce on my bed as the cotton protects my fear.
I close my eyes.
Darkness will ease disappointment.

LAURIE DARROCH-MEEKIS

Laurie Darroch-Meekis began writing stories, poetry and lyrics the moment she realized words had the power to move people. She is a freelance writer, poet and author.

She is eagerly trying to fill her published-works bookshelf. Her current works include multiple pieces in three books and short stories and poems in five future books in 2010 and 2011. The poems and stories in print now are included in Elements of the Soul, Elements of Time *and* Poetry Against Cancer. *Works scheduled for release in 2010 will appear in* Elements of Dimension, Best of Unsent Letters, *and a currently untitled horror anthology.*

Laurie received the 2009 Best Poem award from Preditors & Editors for her poem Mahingun. *The poem is included in* Elements of the Soul. *She is the featured poet in* Elements of the Soul *and* Elements of Time.

On inspiration for her writing Laurie says, "My mother gave me the love of the written word; the enjoyment of reading, writing and telling a good story. Being a poet herself, she taught me the texture, power and beauty of both the written and spoken word. I feel that good writing is often a pleasure to read aloud. Writing to me is much more than mere words put together. It is a symphony of letters, a painting in text. Words can take you to any dimension you choose to go."

Married with children, Laurie is also a traveler and explorer both by nature and nurture.

You can find Laurie online at:
www.darroch-meekis.webnode.com and various other sites.

INTO FAIRIELAND

By Laurie Darroch-Meekis

Carry me softly across moss-covered forest floors,
brightly lit by the full moon overhead, a lantern in the sky,
ground shadowed by low-hanging branches
and proud, tall trunks of ancient age,
centuries of life, stately beauty, mystical dark serenity.
No human footsteps make a sound in the sheltered wood.
In the clearing, a circle dance of life begins,
celebration of being, twirling and stepping
around a flame made of moonlight and fireflies.
Fur-covered creatures rustling through the dense undergrowth
come to join the dance, called by twinkling faerie song.
Bounding long-eared rabbits and graceful deer,
chattering squirrels, rolling hedgehogs,
one lively light-footed warthog.
A wise old owl perched above, watching the revelry,
the guardian, announcing his night watch.
The white gossamer wings of small delicate creatures,
with tiny pointed ears and silken cloth.
lightly brush across my exposed skin,
as they flit past me to join in dancing patterns,
woven through the cool night air,
acknowledging my presence there.
This wooded world visible,
but only to those who have not forgotten how to believe,
in the realms beyond their daily existence.
I am not dreaming. I see wide eyed into Fairieland.
I still hear the call to dance in joy at life.

SHONDA FOLSOM

Shonda Folsom has been practicing law for ten years but writing
stories for much longer.

Science Fiction and Fantasy
have been her favorite genres to read
for years – mostly because these
books have so many ways of answer-
ing the question "What if reality
were   slightly different?"

Shonda currently lives in West Texas and is an officer of
the West Texas Writers organization, where she learned about
Twin Trinity Media and their Accentuate Writers program.
Her story, Dead Brother, ELEMENTS OF DIMENSION is
her first published piece. She also writes a book review blog:
TexasRed Books http://www.texasredbooks.com/.

DEAD BROTHER

By Shonda Folsom

When the timer on my cell phone beeps, I realize I've forgotten to turn my brother Eric over during the past hour. I can already see the pink starting to show in his skin. Eric warned me that there would be no more sun-bathing after the last time I left him out with a Playboy bunny sticker on his chest.

He'll kill me later tonight when he realizes I didn't pay any attention to his note. Oh well, I'll be dead by then, anyway, so it's not like there's much he can do to me. Plus, I know he needs vitamin D or whatever the sun is sup-posed to give, even if he doesn't like being out in the sun all day.

I put down my newspaper and get up to drag one of the pool umbrellas over to shade Eric's lounge chair. He looks so peaceful lying there, like he really could just be asleep in the sun. Hope the pink cheeks don't get in the way of his dark, brooding creature-of-the-night persona. Guess he'll let me know if it does.

I settle back into my chair to finish flipping through the newspaper, a task that is hard to concentrate on with my wife doing laps in in the pool while wearing her bikini. Good thing we have a romantic lunch planned this afternoon, and I've officially taken the after-noon off work.

Of course, Anderson Brothers Investigations is still open for business all day, and all night too, from what I understand. My taking the day off just means Judi, my secretary, would have to contact me by cell if anything new came in or shook loose on one of our cases. This month's been relatively quiet. We've had enough unfaithful spouses and teen runaways to meet budget for the month already, but nothing that really calls for our particular talents.

"Find anything good in that paper of yours?" Suzi asks from the edge of the pool.

"Nothing Eric needs to look into, why?"

"Well, the sun sets early tonight, but we still have lots of time between now and lunch to enjoy your day off..."

Suddenly, I couldn't care less if my brother turns neon red in the sun. I scoop Suzi up and we head into the house. If there's anything I've learned from my crazy life, it's that the days are too short to waste.

⋙⋘

The pool by moonlight would be a beautiful sight if my waking up here didn't mean one thing. I've been left out all day... again. I push myself up off the lounge chair stiffly, grimacing at the striped speedo that I seem to be wearing. God, who picks these things out, Suzi or Jon? Either way, someone's going to have to quit playing dress up doll with the dead brother, or Jon's going to wake up bald one morning.

I wander into the house and get momentarily distracted by my sun-kissed appearance in the hall mirror. No, sun-kissed is a major understatement. More like sunblasted. What am I, the Coppertone kid? Who respects a private investigator with a sunburn? Do freckles instill trust in some bizarre daytime world my brother lives in? Asshole.

I'd make shaving his head my first order of business if he didn't have Suzi watching over him while he was dead to the world. Who knew a guy could successfully romance an exotic beauty without ever staying out past curfew.

I can't believe she's okay with our freak-show life. I can't deny that she's helpful, even when she keeps me from exacting revenge against my twin brother.

"Forgot me by the pool again, huh?" I ask, when I enter the lounge. Suzi is doing something on the computer–probably tidying up our financial records–and looks up at me, guilt evident on her face.

"Sorry, Eric. It was our anniversary, and I guess we kind of lost track of time. You didn't burn too badly, did you? Jon thought you needed sun."

"I skulk around in dark bars and tail shady characters. Would you please convince him that I don't need to look like a lifeguard just because we live in Florida? Remind him about skin cancer or something."

"I'll let him know," she replies. "He left your memo on the desk over there. Nothing much on tap today."

I walk into the office and pick up the memo off of the desk Jon and I share, like we share so much else in this life.

"Looks like he didn't even make it through the paper today," I say, while I walk back toward Suzi. "Doesn't matter, I'm headed out to the clubs. Things seemed a little off last night, and I'm not sure if something new is blowing into town. I'll just go up and say hi to Jon before I head out."

Suzi finally looks up at me.

"You know I'm not going to let you go in there alone, right?"

"What? I'm not going to do anything."

"He didn't mean to leave you by the pool all day, Eric."

"Whatever did he do before he had you to protect him?"

"I got some idea of that when he showed up at our wedding without eyebrows because you got cranky the night before. I'm amazed you guys made it to adulthood."

"Number one, I wasn't cranky. I was just helping him enjoy his bachelor party. You're not allowed to see those pictures. Number two, *he* only made it to adulthood because he had me here to watch his ass all night and, don't you forget it, sister."

"Well, now he has me to help watch over him," she replies, "and I'll try to blank out the comment about you watching your brother's ass for years and years."

Heh. Well played. Can't say my sunshine-loving brother didn't settle down with a good woman.

I give one more glance to the nightly memo and then toss it in the basket as I head up to my room to get dressed for another evening out.

⋘⋙

I yawn and stretch as the first rays of morning come through the window and warm my face. Looks like another lovely Orlando morning. I'm still not convinced the folks with mouse ears haven't found a way to control the weather, but I'll take whatever they've arranged for today.

I head into the bathroom and jump. Some sort of modern art painting is looking back at me from the mirror. Crap. Looks like Eric was pissed about the sunburn and found Suzi's eyeliner pen.

I take care of business and try to wash the marks off my chest. Okay, so he was more upset than I thought. It's not eyeliner but permanent marker. Still, he kept it all below the shirt-collar. Either he's holding back, or he needs me to do something for him.

Not surprisingly, it's the latter. It's amazing how many things can only be handled from nine to five. I pick up the morning memo while I drink my coffee.

Hmmm, looks like he actually wants me to do something work-related. That's different. Usually his memo includes notes like, "Appear at traffic court" or "Return underwear to Bambi."

Granted, this morning's memo involves a woman named Candy, who is a stripper, but she seems to actually have a case. I seem to have an appointment with her at nine o'clock.

I spend a couple of hours exercising and taking care of paperwork before Suzi shows her face downstairs. Not everyone in our side of the house has to be up at dawn.

"Hi, sweetheart," she says when she walks into the lounge on her way to get her morning tea. I immediately think how unfair it is that I have to spend my morning with my brother's stripper when my wife's barely wearing one of my t-shirts and looking ready to tumble back into bed.

"Anything interesting happen last night?" I ask.

"Not much. Eric seemed upset about the sunburn, but he got over it and went out stalking the city's underbelly again."

"Who knew America's vacation play land had such a vast underworld. I really thought when we moved here that he'd just be watching fireworks and sipping Mai Tais all night."

"You should know your brother better than that, sweetie," she replies. "He'd be drawn to the dark side even if it was just one Goth teen hanging out in his parents' basement. What does he want you to do today?"

"He's got some stripper he wants me to meet with."

Suzi's eyebrow raises and she stops mid-sip of tea.

"Not that I want to, of course." I cough. "But he thinks she has a case for us."

"I bet," she says with a sniff, sarcasm lacing her tone. "When should I expect you home?"

"I'll see you at least by lunchtime," I assure her. Then I gather up the paperwork Eric started and head out toward the office.

Candy is everything I expected her to be. She is blonde, busty, and beautiful–the three characteristics important to my brother. She also speaks with an Eastern European accent. That isn't a surprise in itself—my brother has certainly hooked up with his share of international night-life—but his notes said she had a family problem, so I am slightly surprised. Orlando certainly has a fair amount of immigrants, especially with the Kingdom's guest-worker program, but for the most part, the various communities take care of their own and don't look to outsiders for help.

Eric's notes say that he'd been talking with Candy for at least a week before she agreed to meet with me. She's clearly not comfortable talking with someone who looks like her friend, but is in every other way a completely different person. I experience this often with Eric's acquaintances.

"Please come in and sit down. My brother told me all about you. It sounds like you could use our help."

"It's my sisters, Mr. Anderson," she begins.

"Please, call me Jon," I reply. "I even answer to Eric from time to time."

No smile from the curvy blonde, just an eyebrow raise.

"It's my sisters," she continues. "They've disappeared. I'm afraid that when they heard how successful I've become, they fell into the same trap I did."

Now it's my turn to raise an eyebrow. She stares back at me. Okay, this is not a woman I want to argue with about the meaning of the word success. Of course, even I know there are worse things in this life than dancing at The Paradise in a g-string. I wonder how many of them she's seen and what, exactly, her sisters might have gotten themselves into.

Although I've had some training, I'm rarely our operation's field operative. Instead, I specialize in maintaining the legitimate face of our agency and creating paperwork. That's what I turn to now. Names, birthdates, correspondence records, personality descriptions, I get it all down. I've seen too many next-day notes with messages like, "You forgot to ask about known hangouts" to rush the process.

There's nothing like knowing someone else is going to have to follow up on your files to motivate you to do a thorough job.

Apparently, Candy — or Bohuslava, as she was known

at home—had been brought into the United States by someone claiming to work for one of the big theme parks. When she'd arrived in Florida, she found her passport had been confiscated by her erstwhile boss until she paid off her so-called incidental travel expenses by working in his brothel. Candy survived with her sanity intact—which was more than most of the girls there—and eventually bought back her freedom and the right to walk away.

In the year since, she'd been working at The Paradise, and she'd managed to send back regular checks to her family.

"Last week, I got a letter from our neighbors in our small town in the outskirts of Kovel, reminding me to take care of my sisters when they arrived in Orlando.

"I had no idea they were thinking of coming here. Vira is only sixteen, and Daryna is thirteen. The last anyone saw of them, they left town, talking about catching the Autolux bus to Kyiv.

"Eric said human traffickers will some-times use family support checks as evidence that their program is working to lure new victims away from home. Please, can you help me find them?"

"Absolutely. We'll do everything we can," I reply. "What else can you tell me about the people who brought you here? Do you know anything about their business? Who else they might work with? What banks or computers they might use?"

Okay, that last question is a long shot, but it's my other specialty, so I have to ask. Usually it takes at least one night of Eric skulking around dark buildings before I have anything to work with, but it's worth asking.

Ahh....waking up in my own bed is so much nicer than having to figure out where I am in my first few moments of the evening. When I start to rummage for coffee, I notice my new manicure: bubblegum pink. Nice, tidy edges. If Suzi's done this, she's also probably hidden her polish remover in a vault some-where. Hell, looks like a trip to the drugstore's in order before I head to Candy's former place of employment.

I drive down the East-West Expressway to the industrial district and park the car at a local drugstore. It's a busy, well-lit parking lot. A perfect place to leave the car while I'm working. I text the location to Jon, just in case, and head in to take care of my pink fingertips.

When I leave, I walk past the car and in the general direction of the Executive Airport. It's easy to blend into the shadows.

I clutch the bottle of rum I brought with me to fit into the scene, with its purposely crumpled paper bag and watch for anyone paying attention to me. I slide along in the shadows of buildings.

Not a lot of people out in this neighbor-hood of warehouses. I would have started in the showier front house of the prostitution operation, but Jon's note says it's fairly legit. Well, obviously illegal, but otherwise just what it seems to be.

Candy's memory, which Jon confirmed, is that there's no office or any other record room at the building in Celebration. I'd love to know how he confirmed that. I know how I would have investigated it, but knowing my brother, and his wife, I'm pretty sure he pulled the blueprints from somewhere or something equally boring.

The other place on this end of town operated by these

people is the warehouse I'm approaching now. It looks like every other warehouse, and for good reason. According to Jon's memo, the bordello operators, Smith and Jun Chi, don't own this place. They lease it through a series of affiliated shell companies. That's the legwork that impresses me most. I don't know how Jon managed to trace all of them back so easily.

He's also provided me with a blueprint of the basic warehouse layout. Of course, that's the blueprint from the building's actual owners. There's no way to know what they have set up inside that big concrete box. At least I know where all the entrances and exits are, and it looks like either my lock picks or bolt cutters will get those open for me.

I'm able to stay under the radar and slide in through a door in the back of the warehouse. I guess they think they can stay under the radar by investing in front companies instead of high tech security systems. I'm thankful for small favors.

I'm also thankful that the place seems dark and deserted. Should be easier to use the pen light to find what passes for an office around here and make copies of their records. It would be nice if they had a book nicely labeled "Human Trafficking Records" right next to one labeled "Bank Records". I'm not holding my breath. People with a penchant for organization and right living usually don't smuggle thirteen-year-olds across international borders to serve up to businessmen in Orlando.

The inside of the warehouse is more built up than I'd expected. For the most part, it's been partitioned into little felt-walled cubicles with desks and computers. If it wasn't in the worst part of town and a building with no ground-level windows, I'd think we were in some suburban cube farm. This must be where they've been doing research about their recruits and making calls back home on their behalf.

I see a cubicle set up with a framed diploma on the wall and a fake potted plant in the corner. It has all the appearances of a successful office cube, but I can't read the name on the diploma or see anything actually personal around the computer. There's also a tripod set up by the doorway, so I can imagine what this cube's for. The camera's gone, though.

The file cabinet in this cube doesn't have a lock, so I'm guessing there's some room around here that does.

Eventually the rows of cubicles stop and the warehouse floor opens up. Toward what I'm thinking of as the front, right corner of the space, I see the chain-link walls of the room I bet I'm looking for. Interesting choice. There's no secure space in the warehouse, so they built one. Looks like it started out as a dog-run designed to hold in Dobermans. They've sunk it into a slab of concrete that rests on top of the warehouse floor. I wonder if they actually poured a new slab section on top of the floor or if they brought the whole contraption in somehow by forklift or something.

The door is hidden near the outer wall of the warehouse. The chain link fence has been lined with some sort of black fabric all the way around. It's clearly designed for privacy from peeping eyes while allowing the people inside to listen to their workers in the cubicles.

This lock's harder to work loose. It takes me some time before it springs open so I can quietly swing the door out enough to move through into the little room. The light from the windows at the top of the warehouse still shines into this room, but the cloth on the fence wall throws most of the space into shadow. As expected, everything's locked up. The few papers I see out are all written in Chinese. Great. Here's hoping the Rosetta Stone program taught me the words for "illegal slave trade." I turn on the pen light and get to work.

＊＊＊＊

Ah, a morning without surprises from Eric. He must be in a good mood after his skullduggery last night. I slide away from my sleeping wife and head downstairs to see how his nightly foray turned out.

A minute later, I'm back upstairs shaking Suzi's shoulder.

"There's no memo, and Eric's not in bed," I say, as calmly as I can.

Suzi usually takes a cup of Earl Grey or two to wake in the mornings, but today, my announcement is all it takes.

We throw on clothes and start making phone calls. First stop will be the location of the car at the drugstore that Eric texted to me. Assuming it's there, we'll head to the warehouse address I sent Eric. I'm on the phone with our friend Mike in the Orlando Police Department by the time Suzi's thrown on jeans and a t-shirt and pulled her dark hair into a ponytail. He'll be unofficially on call.

"Let's go."

The car's still where Eric left it. While I pull out the warehouse information, Suzi calls Mike to let him know we'll need his help. If there's ever a time to call in a few favors, this is it. Unfortunately, today he's unable to shake his new partner, Rick. Instead of being able to spring into action as soon as the squad car arrives, I have to go into my backstory, again. Cops, even rookie cops, aren't nearly as easy to pacify with half-truths and vague comments as are damsels in distress who readily believe or accept our excuses.

For the most part, I sum it up that we're identical twins, not so uncommon an occurrence, with a very unique genetic mutation. There are enough people with rare genetic abnormalities out there these days that it's almost believable, at least for Rick.

It's actually more believable, I think, than the truth. I don't think there's a cop in Florida who would buy the idea that my brother and I were pretty normal until we were about six months old, got the flu, and one of us died.

Well, that part is unfortunately common; twins aren't known for their hardiness. What would be impossible to swallow would be the part of the story about our great aunt not taking too kindly to losing one of her great-nephews so early and somehow splitting whichever one of us was still around, giving half of his life to the other.

'Splitting the baby' is supposed to be just an expression, but I guess half a life is better than none, right?

I was worried enough about losing my brother as a friend and business partner. There was no need to explain to either Mike or Rick that I had the added motivation of not knowing what would happen to my half of our life if his ended... permanently. I'm planning not to find out for another fifty or sixty years, at least.

Finally, I've answered or parried all of Rick's questions, and we can get down to business. I got some training at the police academy once Eric and I decided on this line of work, so I have a shared background to draw on when working with official backup. The plan is for Mike and Rick to cover the back door and Suzi to stay outside of the front door while I go inside and investigate.

The bright sunshine makes it seem like a more appropriate day to be riding roller-coasters or sipping Mai Tais in-stead of getting ready to break into a human trafficker's ware-house to find my brother. When we separate to surround the building and cover both doors, a cloud briefly covers the sun. That doesn't really make it any better. This is definitely Eric's area of expertise. I just hope I don't let him down.

It takes my eyes a minute to adjust to the darkness once I'm inside the door. The light from the windows filters down into the warehouse, but the overhead lights are still off. I see what appears to be a dog run lined with black to my immediate left, but the only light I see is in the first row of cubicles that have been installed in the middle of the open warehouse space. Two men and a woman are arguing.

I have approximately fifteen minutes to find my brother's body, get the records showing where Candy's sisters are, and hopefully incriminate the Chi family enough to justify Mike and Rick getting officially involve-ed, and get out before the cavalry comes charging in. The survival odds for Vira and Daryna, and any other girls being held with them, would go down dramatically as soon as the police were involved.

I creep over to the converted dog pen to begin my research, keeping an ear open to the argument in progress on the other side of the room.

"What did you do to him?" I hear screeched while I slide in through the chain-link door.

"We didn't do anything! We tied him up to the chair and called you. By the time you got here, he was just dead. I swear we didn't do it."

Ah, leave it to Eric to provide a handy diversion, even without being conscious. Now that I know the situation with him, I can concentrate on the paperwork in front of me. Chinese... Chinese... Chinese... Bingo: Cyrillic lettering. I believe I have here some Ukrainian work applications. A few more seconds, and I find papers with names matching Candy's sisters, which I had her write out for me during our meeting so I would be able to recognize them if I saw them.

I grab the entire folder with their records, as well as three other folders that were on the same shelf, and stuff them into my knapsack. Never hurts to have *more* information than required, especially considering I speak neither Chinese nor Ukrainian. I hope Candy or one of our other resources can translate these documents.

I make it back out of the make-shift room without rousing suspicion. The argument about who caused my brother's death continues unabated in the front of the cubicle block. If there were something other than open space between me and the cubicles, I could try to distract the Chis and whoever they're arguing with by a phone call to the number listed on the rental form for the warehouse. I'm pretty sure, though, that the phone would either ring to a mobile phone in the cubicle or the office phone in the room I just exited. Guess I'll have to rely on a more low-tech diversion.

I sneak back into the room I had just left and grab a couple of pens from the desk. I shove them in my pockets and then carefully and quietly sneak back to my previous position. Nobody seems to notice when I skip the first pen down the hallway between the makeshift cubes. The second one gets Mrs. Chi's attention, and the third is heard is by everyone.

Mrs. Chi and two men leave the cube to investigate the sounds. From what I can tell, no one stays behind to watch my brother. I guess they figure there's not much need to guard a dead guy. There's some general kafuffle while they argue over who should turn on the lights and how many they'll need.

Suits my purposes perfectly. The more time they spend arguing, the longer it'll take them to figure out there's nothing to see in the back of the warehouse. Meanwhile, I walk in a crouch into the cubicle and use my Boy Scout knife to cut the plastic strips binding Eric to the office chair. I wish I could wheel him out of here without causing any extra noise, but decide that carrying him over my shoulder is a better bet for stealth at this point. I do stop to collect the plastic pieces, just to, hopefully, cause an extra argument over the dead guy's vanishing act, and then hoist Eric up.

I've got one shot at making it back through the front door. Here's hoping my luck holds out just a little longer.

I'm sure they can hear every squeak of my tennis shoes on my way out, but apparently there's some fuse box in the back that controls the overhead lights, and Eric thought ahead to flip it off the night before. There's more arguing about how the switch got flipped and whether or not it's safe to turn it back on.

The Chis and henchman seem oblivious to the fact that if there was someone skulking in the back, he'd have surely attacked them by now. I manage to make it out the front door and find that Suzi had the presence of mind to pull the car around.

I swear that woman's a mind reader sometimes. One of the many, many reasons I fell in love with her.

I load Eric into the back and slide in the front. Then I call Mike and Rick while Suzi pulls the car away as quietly as possible. We'll reconvene at our house to look over my haul. I want to check Eric out as soon as possible to be sure the scenario I overheard during the argument is what actually happened. Then we need to get to those girls as soon as possible.

⚬⚬⚬⚬

It's always disorienting to wake up in a different place than where I died, but tonight I'm grateful as hell. The fact I recognize my own room means my brother did whatever was necessary to pull me out of that ware-house. I'm hopeful he took care of the rest of cleaning up my shit and we actually have some information to go on. Otherwise, our traffickers are likely to be too spooked to take care of their possessions, and my stupidity will have caused the death of God knows how many girls.

Mike's sitting with Suzi at the kitchen table, which is covered with papers, when I get up.

"Eric, good. You're okay," Suzi says, coming over to hug me.

Even while I have my arm around her, I'm looking to Mike for an explanation of what we do next.

"Jon got the application and lodging records when he got you out," Mike began, making my night a little brighter. "We've spent the afternoon having them translated and putting half a dozen motels under surveillance."

"Jon figured you'd be upset if you missed out on all

the action," Suzi piped up, "so we took care of all the official paperwork and got the team together while you were knocked out. Everyone's ready to go as soon as you're ready to lead the raid on the motel where Candy's sisters are being held."

I'd rather be taking out the bastards who tied me to a chair, but this is a great way to start the night. Maybe that other part will come around later.

"Let's go," I say. I grab a jacket from the hall.

I guess if someone ends up owning a falling-down roach motel, they have a couple of choices. They can pay to fix the dump up, or they can rent to the scum of the earth and not ask too many questions about why they consistently need long-term housing in such a crap hole. Looks like the proprietor of the Golden Rose Inn chose the second of those options. The place looks like the set of some 1980s movie, and I'm here to supply the police raid to complete the scene.

The Chis were good enough to supply the girls' room numbers, so all we have to do is spread out and cover those doors and the main office. Not surprisingly, those rooms are the only rooms with any signs of life inside.

I'm on the team that crashes open the door to Candy's sisters' room. Once we're sure there's no one else in the room, it's great to be able to tell them that they're safe and that Candy–or rather, Bohuslava–is waiting for them.

While I'm helping the girls get their stuff together, we hear that the rest of the raids went just as smoothly and that the Chis are in custody. Several flea-bag motel owners have already given incriminating statements against them, to save their own skins.

Looks like the good guys have pulled through for one

more night. I remember to stop by the all-night grocery store to grab a bottle of cheap champagne to leave beside my nightly memo as a thank-you to my daylight-loving brother before I let the cops drop me off at home.

It's not the ideal situation for either of us, each being dead half the time. Sure, I miss not truly being able to know my brother, and I'm sure he feels the same sometimes. But at least tonight, we have found a way, together, to bring justice and reunite a family.

It's a damned shame we can't do the same for our family, so my brother and I can both be alive at the same time.

I finish writing the memo to my brother and place the bottle of champagne next to it. I start to head down the hallway to my room, where I will wait to die, like I do every morning.

I stop and turn back to the memo, grab up the pen again, and write:

Thanks, bro.
Love,
Your dead brother

LINDSAY MADDOX

Born and raised in the Pacific Northwest, Lindsay Maddox has always been a writer at heart. Growing up, many rainy days were spent reading and writing. From composing and performing plays with her brother or jotting down short stories in her diaries, writing has always been an integral part of her life.

Writing took on a whole new meaning when her oldest son was born. It became an outlet; a way for her to find humor in parenting and share with others the trials and joys of parenthood. Since then, Lindsay and her husband have welcomed a daughter and twin boys to their brood, each child offering even more inspiration for stories and blogs.

When she isn't chasing kids around the house and blowing kisses on chubby little bellies, Lindsay can be found at her computer writing for her Silly Mom Thoughts blog, chipping away at her young adult novel, or writing short stories to compete in the Accentuate Writers Anthology contests. This past year, she has seen her name in print in Accentuate's anthologies, Elements of the Soul, Elements of Time and now Elements of Dimension and is excited to see her writing dreams become a reality.

You can visit her website here:
http://site.lindsaymaddox.com

THE ROOMMATES

By Lindsay Maddox

For the record, I am so not okay with this. This whole situation is entirely out of my control, and for that, I am exceedingly resentful. Imagine having to move from one place into a new one with no warning, no preparation, nothing. It's stressful, to say the least. I'm wading blindly through this foreign new place, unsure of where exactly I fit in.

My last home was perfect. Sure, it wasn't the roomiest abode, but it was all mine. I took pride in the warm coziness of it. I lived by my own rules. I slept when I wanted and was quiet by myself whenever I pleased. It was sheer freedom. Plus, I had a waterfront view.

It hadn't only been the view I loved. Sometimes, late at night when I find myself tearfully remembering my old home, I try to remember the sound of the waves. I took immense comfort in that steady, predictable sound resonating in my ears. Here, I look out the window and see nothing but haze and fog and hear nothing but the deafening shrieks and honks that often accompany living in

* * *

167

the midst of an enormous city.

So, how did I get here? you wonder. To be frank, I was forced from my home. The entire situation was frantic and traumatizing, all a blur of heartache in my memory. I barely had a chance to steal a glance back at the home I had known for so long before I was forced to turn away. Almost immediately, I was placed in the sterile, unfamiliar surroundings of a temporary holding facility.

Fortunately, the stay was short.

Unfortunately, it meant being placed in a more permanent residence that is equally as unfamiliar to me.

Worst of all, I have roommates I have never met before being forced to live with them.

Can you imagine what it's like going from a life as a bachelor, doing what I want when I want, to sharing a home with two roommates? As if that weren't bad enough, here's the icing on the cake: we don't speak the same language.

Take last night for example:

They, a male and a female, roughly the same age, were standing in the kitchen and, I assume, discussing dinner plans.

"I'd really like Pad Thai," I said.

She looked at me sympathetically, and for a moment I thought she had understood what I had said. To my disappointment, she merely patted my hand and went back to the conversation with the other roommate. At that point, I was frustrated. Thai-type food sounded comforting and familiar to me, and I wanted some say in what we would be eating that night.

"I want pad Thai, wonton soup and roti canai!" I

screamed.

The male roommate looked over at me, apparently startled by my sudden outburst. But, that was the only reaction I got from either of them. In the end, I didn't get the cuisine I had so badly wanted.

It has taken me a month of living here to even be able to talk this much about my move. Right now, I'm actually pretty exhausted remembering the inklings of emotional turmoil I have been subjected to. I think it may be best if I nod off for a bit and let myself mentally recover.

⁓∞⁓

I think I have finally figured out my roommates' names. He calls her Simone, and she calls him Jacque. It's nice to finally be able to understand that much, at any rate.

Simone seems to be making a greater attempt at communicating with me. Each time she walks by, she steals a quick smile in my direction. Thankfully, the language of a smile is universal, and I know that, at the very least, she enjoys my presence. Though I haven't yet mastered her language, I know my return smile is sufficient for the time being.

It has been four months, and though I still mourn my former home, this one is growing on me. I'm not sure what it is, but suddenly I am noticing the blue sky outside my window more often, where once I saw merely fog and haze. I wonder if my improved attitude and acceptance of my fate has allowed me to see the brighter side of my living situation.

⁓∞⁓

Okay, that's it. Everything *was* going well, but the habits of my roommates are beginning to thoroughly grate on my nerves. Who passes gas that frequently? Not me, that's for sure. I want to scream to Jacque that I'd rather not see him towel-clad every single morning. The towel isn't the issue; it's the paltry coverage it provides, especially when he bends over.

If that isn't inappropriate enough, my brain is bursting to scream at them, "Please, for the love of all things holy, if you two are going to get touchy-feely with each other, do it in your own room!"

They don't see me bringing chicks over to our house, do they? No. Do you know why? Well, to be honest, I am still too terrified to leave the house by myself. I have been out with the roommates to the occasional dinner, the market, other short errands, and even those short expeditions left me feeling overwhelmed and mentally and emotionally exhausted. I have a significant amount of learning to do about this place before I'll feel comfortable venturing out on my own.

But that's all beside the point. If I were to bring a girl over, you can bet I wouldn't be behaving so inappropriately in front of them. I have a private room, at least. So do they, so they can take it in there.

On a more positive note, I believe I am beginning to finally understand their language. Compared to my own, it is quite complex, so it is no wonder I have had such a difficult time. My understanding is broken up into bits, but I believe I'm getting the gist of what I hear. I have even tried my hand at a few of the more simple words, but my roommates mostly smile and nod when I speak. I can tell I have a while yet before I am solidly able to communicate.

In the time I have spent at home, I have focused on

my body by strengthening my muscles. To my chagrin, in the months I have lived here, I have put on a few pounds. When I do eventually go out on my own, I want to make sure I'm fit enough to protect myself. Or at least run away quickly.

❧❧❧

A little over half a year here and things have taken an awkward turn. Yesterday, I was alone with Jacque, an unusual occurrence since he seems to work constantly. We were sitting silently, not making eye contact. It was one of those situations where he would look across at me, I would meet his eyes, and we'd both look quickly away. Awkward in itself, without what happened next.

This charade goes on for what seems like hours, though in actuality, it is probably merely minutes. Bored with the silence, I reach toward my drink that happens to be sitting closer to Jacque than me. He mistakes my reach as an opening up for a hug and before I know it, he pulls me in tightly and kisses both of my cheeks. I'm still trying to convince myself his actions are simply foreign to me, something from his culture. But at that point, I simply want to go back to my room. Alone.

❧❧❧

"I wonder if there's something wrong with him," I overhear Simone whispering to Jacque today, the ten month anniversary of when I moved in.

She looks over at me apprehensively and I reciprocate with a smile. Apparently, the once-comforting universal language of smiling has worn out its usefulness, because she barely offers a grin in return. It is infuriating to me that I understand them, but I can't quite bring myself to try to repeat those same words. I think it may be the perfectionist in me, the side of me that doesn't want to truly attempt something until I can do it well.

After my useless grin attempt, I struggle to give them some sign that I am not an idiot and my brain is, in fact, working inside this head of mine.

So, I wave.

It proves fruitless, because Simone has turned back to Jacque, and neither see my attempt at nonverbal communication.

This has to end. Soon. I absolutely must break this language barrier. Simone looks distressed, and I worry they may ship me off to some institution if I don't give them some inkling of communication.

✣

Today is the day. My heart is beating excitedly, and I cannot wait to show my roommates that I can finally talk to them. They have been immensely patient with me this past year; it's the least I can do. After all, they brought me—a complete stranger—into their home. They kept me well fed, didn't push me to venture outside when I wasn't ready, and were never frustrated when I showed my distaste for them and being forced to live in this new place. They offered condolences for my tears, and put up with my outbursts. They have been more of a family to me than anyone, and honestly, I have grown enormously fond of them.

Okay, Simone is walking toward me, and Jacque is directly behind her. I can't believe I'm really about to do this. I practiced all last night in my room so I could be sure I was going to say this the right way.

They're close to me now. This is it. I'm opening my mouth, waiting for my brain to catch up with my voice

box, and—

"Mah-ma," I hear my tiny voice coo.

Tears erupt from Simone's eyes, and she smiles wider than I have seen her smile in a long time. Jacque scoops me into his arms, an equally wide grin on his own face.

Awh, heck, why not? I didn't rehearse this, but I know what I'm doing now.

"Dah-da."

I smile and open mouth kiss his face. I can feel my own slobber running between my chin and the roughness of his cheek.

"About time, champ," he says, chuckling and then kissing both of my cheeks in return.

Eureka. Communication established.

"Honey, what do you say we go out for dinner and celebrate?" Jacque suggests. "We haven't had Thai food in a while."

I look over at Simone and excitedly clap my hands.

"I lived off of that stuff when I was pregnant, remember?" She laughs. "I was certain our little boy was going to come out demanding pad Thai and wonton soup!"

I grin, baring my two front teeth. If only she knew.

THE TALE OF THE
SUBURBAN DUNGEON

By M. Lori Motley

Hands clutch cloaks 'round bob-apple necks
A quatro of teens who will never have sex.
Weapons... err pencils... grasped tight in sweaty fists
The storyteller spins his tale, checking charts and lists.

There's Mannwin the Brave. His eyes flash behind glasses.
Counter to real life, his strength it surpasses
all other die rolls on his character sheet.
In the suburban dungeon, and in dreams, he is 'leet.'

Cyyr the Fireballin' speaks, for the first time that night,
"Can we get on with it? I have math, and an essay to write."
The DM nods and says, "You step into Ghraa's cave."
And they're off, those adventurers, to glory or grave.

"Um.. I attack with my sword," Mannwin bravely mumbles.
His decision is met with rolled eyes and mad grumbles.
Agrril the Token Female cuts in with, "OMG, WTF?"
"You always rush in without us, you shmuck."

"I can take him!" he cries, full of RPing teen guts.
Agrril snaps her notebook closed and calls him a putz.
"I don't know why I bother!" she says, as she storms out of the room.
The two left just stare blankly, knowing they face a sure doom.

"Without a healer, you have no chance," the DM begins,
"Your sword does 5D10 damage, but Ghraa's lightning breath wins."
A sudden Mom call from above, "Your ride is here, Josh!"
They groan, then pack quickly. "Well, that was a wash."

* * *

"Kim won't stay mad long and she'll heal us next week."
Mannwin...err... Josh doesn't get girls. He's a geek.
They tuck rule books and dice out of sight in sad shame.
They'd get beat up at school for even playing the game.

But they like the pretending, and plotting campaigns.
Deep inside, through the week, the magic remains.
The mundane interrupts just when things are getting fun
They go back to their lives; their hearts stay in the dungeon.

DEREK ODOM

Derek Odom is a full-time freelance writer and author who lives in Southern California. He has a degree in Administration of Justice and is working on a creative writing degree. He has a fantasy novel in the works, and he enjoys writing short stories. Influences include: Lovecraft, King and Bradbury, to name only a few. Accentuate Writers pushed him back into writing after a long hiatus, and it lit a fire under him that will burn forever.

Besides writing, he enjoys camping, off-road vehicles, classic Chrysler cars, R/C rock crawlers and working in the shop. He is also addicted to chess and competes both on the Internet and at live tournaments. He sends special thanks to his long-time girlfriend, Eliza Bishop, for putting up with him and supporting him in whatever he does. She has been an instrumental part of his writing journey. Steve King has Tabitha; he has Eliza.

I MISS YOU

By Derek Odom

When the fog is thick,
And the moon hangs low,
My old heart races,
And my mind is slow.

I hear beasts walking,
Growling and snarling,
I feel so alone,
I miss you, darling.

Lying in my bed,
The shadows grow long.
I reach out my arm,
Forgetting you're gone.

With my eyes shut tight,
I whisper your name.
But no one responds,
Nothing is the same.

I want to let go,
Of you and this place.
Each spot has your scent,
Each room has your face.

I wander outside,
And lay in the dirt.
Offering the beasts,

My body, my hurt.

I weep when I see,
That no beasts have come.
It's only me there,
Just me and the glum.

Trapped in memory,
With unblinking eyes.
There is no more life,
There is no surprise.

Deliver me, please,
Away from this world!
The edges of it,
Are burnt up and curled.

These thoughts are broken,
When I hear the door.
And soft feet walking,
Across the wood floor.

You enter the room,
My eyes fill with tears.
How long has it been?
Surely many years.

"Oh, honey, don't cry,"
You say with a smile.
And stroke my old cheeks,
I feel like a child.

"I don't understand,"
Say my shaking lips.
While you hold my head,
Rotating your hips.

"There, there, my sweet man,
It's you who's been gone.
Sitting and staring,
At nothing so long."

I hug you so close,
And whisper your name.
You whisper mine back,
My heart is aflame.

Then the room is dark,
The wind roars outside.
I pull up the sheet,
Trying hard to hide.

Now I hear the beasts,
Leaves crunch under feet.
Closer, closer now,
I can feel their heat.

I wish you were here,
My angel-white dove.
Can't do this alone;
I miss you, my love.

CHRIS WILLIAMSON

Chris Williamson lives near the beautiful wine region, McLaren Vale, in South Australia, with her wonderful partner and two children. She grew up in a small tourist town in the South West of England and travelled for a few years before settling.

Chris writes with aspirations for completing a novel in the future. She has kept her writing personal until she found the courage to go public, and hence have her first short story published. She continues to write in the comfort of her home, when she can, around the distractions of family life.

NIGHTLIFE

By Chris Williamson

I woke with a jolt at 4:27, according to the alarm clock. I lay still while I waited for the shuddering to stop. It felt like electricity travelling through my veins. Though it felt like minutes passed, I checked the clock by my bedside to see it still read 4:27. My skin felt clammy. I scanned the room to see the usual shadows were in place.

While the feeling settled, I tried to recall the actions of what had already begun to feel like a distant memory. I wasn't going to let that one go. I grabbed my notebook and pen from the bedside table and flicked through the pages of scribbled notes before I came to a blank page.

It was not unusual for me to have vivid dreams. I have seen doctors, therapists and specialists. Been pre-scribed sleeping pill after sleeping pill. Nothing has stopped the dreams. When I am asleep, it's like I enter an-other realm, another world. The people I meet in my dreams on a nightly basis are always the same, to the ex-tent that I have better relationships with them than people in my physical world. I say people because they aren't just faces. These are people that I interact with in different scenarios. It is exactly the same as any normal interaction one might have with friends, family, work colleagues or even strangers. What you would say is normal for you in your day-to-day life I would say is abnormal for me, because it happens in my dreams. They are the ones I interact with on a daily basis. My physical world has indeed suffered because of this.

I remember one dream where I went to a movie. When I left the theatre, I bumped into a friend of mine named Jenna. After chatting briefly, we arranged to meet for coffee the following night. Sure enough, the next night I closed my eyes, and I walked into a coffee shop to meet Jenna. She was waiting for me just as we had planned in my dream the night before. You see, the people in my dreams are my friends. They hold no significance to my waking life. Neither do I even know if they exist in the physical world.

Not one expert has ever shed light on what is going on. Only one neurological and dream specialist had come up with a theory for me. They had an explanation for what could possibly be happening, but no scientific proof existed. Maybe the people in my dreams were experiencing the exact same realities as me. In the sense that there really could be a lady named Jenna, who also had the same dream as me, that each person in my dream was actually there, in their own dream. Or maybe everything was just me.

I mean, is it possible we can connect on a different level? I don't know. All I know is, each time I close my eyes, a different life begins for me.

The dream I woke from that particular morning was different. Aside from the usual people milling around, there was a new person. A man. Only, I couldn't see his face. It was almost like a blurred vision. I was at the airport, waiting to meet a friend. I walked through the main entrance toward the arrivals. The mysterious man stood there, checking the screens.

He tried to speak to me, but I couldn't hear him. All I could see through the blurriness of his face was his mouth moving with no sound coming out. It frightened me. I have never been frightened in any of my dreams before. I moved away. As I walked toward the gate, I spotted a friendly face. It was Gerade, another of my nightlife friends. He was wearing a flight crew uniform and looking as handsome as ever. He saw me and waved me over, and I was glad for the invitation. He greeted me with a kiss on the cheek.

"Do you know the guy standing over by the arrivals screens?"

Gerade looked over my shoulder. "I don't see anyone in particular. What does he look like? There are quite a few people here, you know." His sarcasm shined through his smile.

"I guess you're right. It doesn't matter."

"Are you flying somewhere tonight?"

"No, I am supposed to be meeting a friend, but I'm not sure who at this stage."

"Ah, one of those, eh?"

"Hmm... yes, one of those. I'd better go. I'm holding up the queue. Maybe I'll see you again soon?"

"In your dreams!" He laughed and turned his attention to the passengers waiting behind me.

I walked aimlessly through the terminal. I couldn't help but think about the stranger without a face. Just as I turned a corner, there he was again. He appeared to be looking for someone or something. His face was no clearer than before. Almost featureless, blurry again. As he searched in all directions, I froze, praying he didn't see me. I couldn't move; the fear had me weighted to the ground. Then he was facing me, maybe twenty meters away.

He paused for a second and then moved toward me. I turned and walked away from him. I increased my pace as I weaved through the hordes of passengers and their luggage. I looked back in his direction. He walked behind me, following my trail. Before I knew it, I was speed-walking as fast as I could without breaking into an obvious run. I could sense him behind me. I had picked up on his anxiety. The quicker I moved, the stronger his emotion became.

Wake up! Wake up! I was screaming at myself, but still, I kept moving. I could see an arrival gate ahead of me. Apart from that, all I could see were the huge walls of glass that provided a view of the runway.

OK, just calm down and stop. Maybe he won't hurt you. But what if he does? You're asleep, stupid. What's the worst that can happen?

I came to a halt, and I could still feel him behind me. When I turned, I could see his figure slow down to a walking pace. My heart pounded harder and heavier the closer he moved to me. He held his hand out toward me, clutching what looked like a piece of paper. I could see it had writing on it. When it came into focus, I read aloud, "I need to speak with you."

Because I concentrated on the words, I did not realize he had stopped less than a meter in front of me.

What does it mean? Why can't I see or hear him?

When I looked up from the script, his hand reached

out toward me; he was too close. Before I could back away, he placed his hand on my shoulder. A sudden bolt shot through my body, and then I was awake. Soon after, I found myself scribbling away in my notebook.

My hand finally stopped shaking. I glanced back at my notes. At least they were readable. The clock read 4:48. I couldn't call anyone. Besides, who would I call? My therapist most likely, but he was still on vacation. I hadn't explained my bizarre dreams to any of my friends. I had learned the hard way with not to do that. In reality, I was lonely. I hadn't had a boyfriend for two years, and as long as my nightlife existed, I doubted I ever would.

The last guy I was with, Marko, had been understanding, in the beginning. After about nine months, he started to distance himself. We argued a lot. I knew why. I had been there many times before with both lovers and friends. My dreams and the people in them were too real for me to ignore. I sometimes got confused and would discuss people from my nightlife with people who surrounded me in daylight. They couldn't understand.

Marko found it funny to begin with and would mock me. Until he'd had enough.

"These people don't even exist. They're not even people we can see as a couple, and yet you are more involved with them and their lives than you are with ours. I just can't compete anymore."

It was always the same words in a different sequence. They were the last words Marko ever said to me. I went home from work, and he was gone. So, for the next two years I trained myself to keep my nightlife to myself. At first, it was hard, but I did it. The only sacrifice was that I don't let myself get close to anyone anymore. Fear of rejection, I guess you can say.

When the sun finally decided to show itself, I got out of bed, shuffled my way to the kitchen and grabbed a juice from the fridge. Aden curled his way through my legs.

"Good Morning, Aden. You want some too, huh?"

He purred enthusiastically while I poured some juice into a saucer for him. My bizarre world. Even my cat was bizarre.

My day at work dragged. Data entry wasn't the most exciting experience, yet it paid the bills. It was especially mind numbing when I had to listen to the two girls I shared a desk with in the hub, Lauren and Claire, discuss their most recent retail therapy session. I participated in the chatter as much as my concentration allowed.

The man with the note in my dream disturbed me all day. *Why on earth would he go to me?* Maybe no one else could see him. *Why did he need to speak to me? Why did his touch electrify my body so intensely?* The questions were endless. At the end of the day, as much as all I wanted to do was get through the traffic and get home, the last thing I really wanted to do was sleep—but it was inevitable.

Later, when the lights were off, my eyes slowly closed. It was a fight I could never win.

###

I sat in a taxi. I could see the airport in the distance.

"Where are we going please?"

"The a-airport, ma'am," the driver stammered. His eyes in the mirror reflected his internal question of my sanity.

"Ah, I did tell you then?"

As we pulled into the waiting bay, I dropped some

cash on the passenger seat and opened the door. I felt anxious, and not in a good way. I looked toward the sliding doors of the terminal. My heart thumped. As much as I didn't want to go in, something nagged me in the opposite direction of my feelings.

I didn't know who I was supposed to meet again, but nonetheless, it was someone. One deep breath and I took a step forward, and the doors opened on my command. I walked toward the arrivals screen, wary of the people around me. I looked up at the screen, starring at it but not actually seeing anything. I didn't really know what I was looking for anyway. It was all a guessing game from there on.

"Clara? Clara?"

I turned around at the sound of the familiar voice. "God, you made me jump, Jenna! What are you doing here? Am I here to meet you?"

"Oh, not tonight, I'm afraid. I'm meeting--"

"Hello, ladies! Fancy seeing the both of you in one night." David appeared, wrapped his arms around us both and pushed his way between us. We all laughed.

"As I was saying, I am meeting David for midnight snacks. Shall we?" Jenna offered her arm to David, and he accepted.

"I'll catch you another time then, Jenna. It was good to see you again."

"Sure will, and you."

They talked intensely about something while they walked away. I was envious that my dream did not take me with them. I returned to my vacant stare at the screen, but something in my peripheral vision distracted me. My pulse gained strength. He was there. I could feel him again, watching me. The man with no face. Without a second thought, I turned and walked through the terminal.

Perhaps he hasn't seen me. Maybe he is on his own journey tonight.

But then I looked at the wall of glass that separated me from the runway, and I could see his reflection behind my own. My throat tightened. My breathing became shallow and quick. I never felt this way when I first met any of the others.

I have to make a decision. Do I stop, or do I run?

I picked up my pace. I looked at the people around me, and no one seemed to notice my panic. I guess everyone else was there for their own reasons. I stopped, and when I turned to face the man with no face, he stopped, too. We are faced each other. His features became clearer. He had a square face, with an incredibly chiseled jaw. His lips were full but set in a solemn line. I still couldn't see his eyes clearly, except that they were green. His hair was dark, medium length and slightly lifted on top. Maybe it made him appear taller.

From what I could see, he was distinctively handsome. Without seeing his eyes clearly, it was impossible to tell what he was feeling. I stood still, frozen again. He slowly walked toward me, his hand held out in my direction. A repeat of what happened the previous night. The fear returned. His presence made me feel uneasy. My fear was the unknown. Without my realizing it, my hand stretched toward his. He was a millisecond away from touching me.

With a gasp, my mouth opened. "What do you want? Why are you here, and why are you following me?"

Again, there were no words. He reached out toward

me, and he held another piece of paper. Another note, but I didn't get to read it. As he placed the paper in my hand, our fingertips touched. There it was again, that sudden jolt shot through my body. I felt the power of his touch had thrown me back. When I opened my eyes, it was dark. I was in my bedroom again, the comfort of my bed beneath me.

The clock read 4:27, the exact same time I had woken the previous morning. I didn't know what the hell was going on, but there had to be some meaning in it. I grabbed my notepad and jotted down the date, time and details of what happened, even the features I was able to discern of the almost faceless man. I was beginning to wonder if he was the reason my dreams were sending me to the airport. But why the airport? Maybe I was the one he was searching for, which brought me to the conclusion that there was something to the dream.

There were too many reasons for me not to think that. I had been to the airport two nights in a row. I have never been to the same place night after night. Technically, I still hadn't met the person I was there to meet; unless, of course, it was him. I was only assuming that I was meeting someone off a flight, because I was at the airport. I let out an exasperated sigh. I really didn't know what to make of it. I needed to go back to sleep. I needed to see if I would return to the airport.

I jumped out of bed, went to the fridge, grabbed a cup of milk and drank it fast. Aden had obviously woken up with the sound of the fridge and meowed incessantly at me.

"Not now, Aden. It's time to go back to sleep."

He didn't like it, but he followed me back into the

bedroom and jumped up on the bed. I felt tired. I lay my head on the pillow and let my thoughts wander. Not that they wandered far. The man seemed to consume my every waking moment. It was all too unknown for my liking. While my thoughts travelled, the sun began to say good morning through my window. It was time to get up.

Later, after battling through traffic to get home after work, I walked into my apartment. Aden greeted me like he always did, along with a nagging beeping coming from my answer machine. I pushed play and headed to the fridge to feed Aden. Mum's voice was loud and clear.

"Hi, Carla, it's your mum." Like I didn't know that from the sound of her voice. "Just thought I would call to let you know I will be coming up a week today. I am flying in this time; I can't do that drive again. Anyway, the firm is paying, and they can afford it. My flight gets in at 5:30 in the morning. Give me a call when you get this."

Great! That's all I need, I thought. *Ah well, maybe some company will do me good. I just know that it will be shopping and lunches for the duration of her stay.*

I called mum back and agreed to not only put her up, but to pick her up from the airport. I would take a couple of extra days off work to accommodate her, at her request.

After dinner, I sat down to read my book. I couldn't concentrate, but I read until my eyes closed.

I was at the airport again, and he wasn't there. I felt calm, but I couldn't help looking all around me. If only Jenna, Gerade or anyone else were there, maybe I could find some normality. I doubted it. I knew, deep down, I was actually looking for the faceless man.

I was more intrigued than anything. The man had kept my mind occupied for the previous couple of days. I had to find out why. As much as I didn't want to see him again, I also desperately wanted to. I didn't know if that made any sense. While I looked around, I saw a couple of faces I knew, which was a relief. Gerade was a businessman that night. He looked like he was in a rush. He caught my eye and gave a wave in recognition.

Then there was David, struggling to help an elderly couple with some bags. He didn't look like he was enjoying himself so much as the night before. I often wondered: if my nightlife friends did actually exist, what would they do for a living? Would we even know each other?

Seeing them had distracted me for a moment. When I turned around, I jumped. There was the man. I felt myself weaken. I was stunned. For the first time, I could clearly see his face through the crowds of people. He was gorgeous. I saw his eyes, the brightest green I had ever seen, and in contrast to his olive skin, they really shone.

The look of concern on his face was what caused my fear. Not to mention the fact that each time he noticed me, he made a beeline in my direction. Before I knew it, we had both stopped again. His hand moved toward me.

That jolt got me every time. I looked at the clock: 4:27. The mystery was driving me insane. I got up and flicked the TV on so I wouldn't fall asleep again. I jotted down some brief notes. I didn't go into too much detail, because I couldn't be bothered, quite honestly.

The next few nights were pretty much the same. I found myself doing anything I could to keep myself from falling asleep. But, each time I closed my eyes, I was at the airport again. However, the reason became apparent: I was there was to meet my mum, and she was never there.

Each time, the man clocked me; he came toward me

and reached out. It became too predictable—I knew it was coming. One night, I stood still and just waited for it. Then the next, I tried to dodge it. Like trying to free oneself from one's defense player in a game of netball or something. It became quite amusing. I laughed in my dream, trying not to take it seriously, I guess. Each time, he didn't speak, his face serious. I was just over it. It really did get boring. There was obviously some meaning to it, but if I couldn't communicate with the man, and every time he touched me I woke up having convulsions like an electric shock. What was I supposed to do? The only thing that held any apparent significance was that I woke at 4:27 every time. It's like I was stuck in some sort of time warp or *Groundhog Day.*

So, life went on, only by that time, my nightlife was not much different than my day life. I got up, went to work, went home, went to sleep and dreamed the same thing over and over. I suffered sleep deprivation from waking so bloody early every day.

The night I had to pick mum up from the airport, I thought it might be different. I had to leave the house at 4:00 in the morning. After dinner, I sat on the couch and had a read, and I drifted into a sleep before I knew it. It was a disturbed sleep. I kept waking and drifting without actually entering my nightlife. For the first time in years, I didn't actually dream. If I did, I didn't remember. It was total bliss, with the downside of being exhausted by the time I had to get in the car and drive for a half hour or so.

I'm not sure if I fell asleep at the wheel or what. All I know is that I was driving to the airport, listening to the radio with the window down to feel the breeze on my face. I could see the airport tower lights not far from where I had to turn off. Once I turned, I don't know what happened. All I could see were bright lights coming toward me. I heard a loud noise.

I remember lying on a cold surface with people all around me. Lots of noise and screaming. I didn't feel anything. I could see figures above me. Arms reached in to do things to me, but I couldn't feel a thing. I didn't blink. Slowly, the sounds around me faded away. I could barely hear voices.

"We're losing her. We're losing her!"

"Jimmy, how's the guy doing?"

"It's too late. How is sh-she? Oh, my God. I don't believe it."

"Jimmy, focus. What's wrong? Do you know her?"

"I—I—I'm not sure. I think I do." His voice rose questioningly at the end, obviously unsure of himself.

"Whether you think you do or not, we're losing her. Get the paddles ready. Come on, lady!"

"Carla. Her name is Carla."

"If you know her family, you need to let someone know. She's gone."

No! No! I am not gone. Wait — don't give up, please! Just try one more time, please!

Is this a dream? Any minute now, Jenna or David will come on the scene and confirm this is nightlife.

They never came. A shimmer of light flashed past the men whose voices I could hear. It was him. The man. My irritating dream man was there again. I was sure it had to be a dream, but something was off.

His beautiful eyes were looking down at me. This time, it was he who looked fearful.

"Time of death: 4:26."

● ● ●

What? What did he just say?

"Shit! Shit! Shit! C'mon, fire up, fire up!"

"Jimmy, what are you doing? It's too late."

"What time is it?" I heard Jimmy say.

"What?"

"I said, What time is it goddamn it?"

That's when realization hit me.

Please, Jimmy, do it. You're thinking what I am thinking. Please just do it! It will work. I know it will.

"Just turned 4:27. Seriously, what are you doing?"

"Clear!"

I felt it. The jolt of electricity pulsated through the core of my body. I took in a huge gasp of air. I could feel my heart beat again. Funny, I hadn't noticed when it stopped.

"Jesus, Jimmy! You did it? You bloody well did it! Well done!" I heard the hand slapping noise of a high five. I could hear people cheering and clapping.

Jimmy leaned in toward me with an oxygen mask. "Hey. It's Carla, isn't it? I don't know how I know, but I know! Blink twice if you know who I am."

I blinked twice as he placed the mask over my nose and mouth.

"4:27 on the dot, eh?" he said. Then he smiled.

IMP

By Lucinda Gunnin

Tiny little imp steals my days away
Just one second at a time.
Disguised as distraction, games and telephone calls,
He worries away a minute, then an hour.

Such an innocent looking imp,
Stealing the day away.
Once I notice his presence
Chores are undone, work is late, dinner is burned.

Joyful imp, with shining trinkets
He grabs my attention
Hides my dedication
Begs me to play.

Be gone time-stealing imp
Work calls my name
You can have my tomorrow
Or possibly, my yesterday.

GILLIAN TABER

 *Gillian Dawn Taber, known to many as Mojo, knew she'd found her calling the moment she opened her mouth and words tumbled out. From the first story she can remember clearly, written around age six, called 'The Blob' to the tentatively titled 'Shadowbeast' that aims to be her next novel, writing has defined every age and event in her life.*

Ask her who she is and she will answer, 'I am a writer. It's simply who I am.' Gillian often she writes rubbish; she acknowledges this, but writing rubbish is better than not writing. A day without writing is like a day without breathing. Fortunately, the magic happens more often than not and stories tumble out of her head, eager to see the light and find an audience.

There are two other great passions in Gillian's life. Music is the first. Life without music would be unbearable. Her second passion is her belief in a pagan path. She has been walking that path since her early teens and loves her status as a hedgewitch.

Gillian lives for her writing and for her love of the unique and wonderful people around her, people who provide constant inspiration and love.

A LIFE IN A MIND

By Gillian Faber

She rested her elbows on the desk, leaned her chin on the bridge of her interlocked fingers and stared at the monitor. She wondered what she would unlock with a single click. Whatever it was, it had to be better than the confusion in her mind. She sat back and let her finger hover over the mouse. In her mind's eye, she saw the chain begin to form. A single message posted on a reunited friends site connected to a name from her past. That name entwined with another, and the second name locked onto a memory. From there the chain steadily grew.

The quiet click in the still room tolled deep in her head. The movement had appeared involuntary, yet she was sure it had been under her control. Not consciously, but an action by the part of her that knew she had to find the truth. The screen flickered and refreshed.

MESSAGE SENT

She wondered if she should sit and wait and see if he

was online. She pushed the chair back and wandered to the window. The pampas grass swamping the lawn swayed. A car took the corner a little faster than was safe on a family street. Her neighbor was cutting the grass. Everything was normal, but that was a lie. Nothing had been right from the moment she had begun to write her memoirs.

It had been her therapist's idea. "Write it down. Get it clear in your mind," he'd said.

Easy for him to say, she thought, but she suspected he'd never experienced a day of depression in his life. She knew from experience, it didn't matter how much someone read or how many lectures someone took. It was impossible to understand depression unless someone has been there, faced the pit and crawled up into the light.

Writing was her job and who she was. If she couldn't write, she had no way to express herself. Talking to people face-to-face made her nervous. If the phone rang, she was likely to ignore it rather than face talking to a stranger.

Taken with the idea of transferring the traumas in her head to the safe confines of a computer screen, she'd made a start. She'd been surprised at the ready flow of words. They poured from her fingers, filling the screen for page after agonizing page. Easy as the physical process had proved, the mental torment had constantly reduced her to tears. Recalling the horrors of her childhood, seeing herself reeling from one abusive verbal beating to another while the page count grew had been difficult. However, the thread that had emerged was the cause of her uneasy but necessary deal with the devil. Send the email and find the truth or live the rest of her life in vaguely unfocussed

• • •

ignorance.

The incident with Jack had brought her up short. Juxtaposed against her clear image of playing King of the Castle with a scab-kneed, tousle-headed boy of six was the thought that she knew those details to be wrong as an adult. In her mind, she had played with Jack, crawled under the fence of her backyard and clambered up the pile of bricks on the building site, scared but exhilarated by her daring. She had reread the entire episode on the screen and sensed the jarring deep in her mind. It had taken her two days of staring at the paragraph on and off to realize the glaringly obvious: There had never been a building site behind the house where she had spent her first five years.

There had been a pair of garages which connected to the next row of houses. No building site, no clambering up bricks, no Jack. She was sure of that final fact. Jack had been the male half of twins in her nursery class.

Was the other really called Jill? she tried to remember.

The problem she had to face was that of not knowing. Her memories were becoming less reliable. The more she wrote, the less certainty remained. The girl in the mirror and the incident with the magazines had frozen her fingers while she read the screen. Disbelief had pervaded her mind as the memory played out in Courier twelve point.

Talking to the girl in the mirror had appeared normal enough. Many children had imaginary friends. A lonely child, isolated in an abusive world, she couldn't understand. Naturally, she had made up a better self who was stronger, wiser, better able to stem her tears and be all the things she wasn't. She recalled spending hours sitting cross-legged before the floor-length wardrobe mirror, facing herself but convinced of the world behind the glass. She remembered thinking that the girl could step through, if she wished, and change places with her.

The magazine day was a clear moment in time. She remembered walking to the newsstand to collect her weekly magazines and being told that she'd already picked them up. Despite her eight-year-old vehemence, the woman behind the counter had insisted that she'd been in the day before and picked up her magazines. Unable to fight an adult, lacking the knowledge to explain how wrong the woman was, she had walked home and found the magazines on her bed.

Back then, she had convinced herself that the girl in the mirror had stepped through and gone to get the magazines because she was impatient to read them. With adult eyes, she saw a traumatized child making up stories, convincing herself that her alter ego had done the deed and accepting it because the alternative was beyond her understanding. The thought that she might have a split personality was too difficult to verbalize.

Reaching that age in the memoirs had kicked open a chest of horrors, memory after memory that appeared suspect at best, impossible at worst. The day before, she had reached the big one: The series of memories that had haunted her for close to twenty years.

The ghost memories.

She'd written it exactly as she remembered, fighting not to alter it to fit her need for the truth. Reading it back, she had realized that there was a way to verify a memory. With a little research and luck, she could learn what had really happened.

Back in the present, she turned from the window and

stared at the computer. It purred quietly, the screen flickering occasionally as it refreshed, but there was no ping. No sign that an email had arrived, that her chain of answers was being forged. She glanced at her watch. Five-thirty, which meant he was probably at work. She needed a distraction. She turned on the television and aimlessly flicked through the channels, the hypnotic repetition lulling her into a doze. An image flashed across her mind's eye, and she bolted upright, shivering. Vincent's face, ashen white, his dark eyes filled with fear. She knew that moment, knew when it had happened. No, she thought she knew, and only the chain of answers would tell her the truth.

She glanced at the computer and saw the flashing envelope in the lower right-hand corner of the screen. Her heart lurched, and she felt swimmy and sick. Her body felt incredibly heavy when she forced herself to her feet and crossed the dozen paces to the desk. She blinked rapidly, took a couple of slow, deep breaths and clicked the icon. A single email sent from a familiar name, V. Harris. Vincent Harris of the huge brown eyes, crazy mop of dark curls and the goofiest grin she'd ever seen.

You never really forget that first crush, that exhilarating rush of blood that you don't know what to do with but feels like heaven, she thought.

She opened the email before she could change her mind and delete it. Vincent's style was the same: brief sentences filled with his humor.

    Hey!
    Is it really the little bookworm?
    How ya been, kiddo? Drop me a line
    and tell me all the juicy bits.
    Vince

She read it twice before hitting the reply button. Her original message had been a brief:

Hi, is this the Vincent from my class in '74?

She had to consider what to say in the next message. She knew she had a habit of coming on too strong, too eager. It took her four tries before she had something she was happy with. She told him about her work as a journalist, about her divorce, that there were no kids to muddy those waters. She asked him what he'd ended up doing and said she hoped he'd reply soon. She signed it *"Bookworm"* and sent it.

The nickname set the ghost memories pouring out of her personal Pandora's Box, and she knew she needed to get a handle on her emotions. Fear was creeping around the edges of her mind, leaving her edgy and unable to concentrate. She had a deadline, a major piece due in three days. She spent an hour pretending to work, her eyes flicking to the silent email icon every couple of minutes. Looking at the depressing amount of errors in the single paragraph she had managed to produce, she experienced a flash of anger at Vincent for not replying instantly and switched the machine off.

The following morning found her tackling any task that kept her away from the computer. Her mind whirled with possibilities that she wasn't ready to face. Her therapist constantly talked about "...getting it all out in the open," but she couldn't grasp the necessity.

She left each session drained in mind and body and frequently spent the following couple of days in black moods interspersed with uncontrollable weeping. How that could be good for her was beyond her understanding. She trailed back from the shops with groceries she didn't need and dumped them to lie unheeded on the kitchen table. Then, she gave herself a mental shake and insisted that she stop procrastinating and turn on the computer.

As soon as she opened her mail, his name popped up. She didn't give herself any options, hitting the button to open the email before her mind could send out objections. He was so pleased to be in touch after so long, his email read.

"Isn't the internet a wonderful thing?" he wrote. He was a firefighter, still the clown and married to a great girl named Tracey. He had a couple of kids, a dog and holidays in Spain. Did she remember Mr. Lewis? Did she remember the playground and the "banned stairs"?

Her eyes lost their focus, and her mind drifted back to the day it had started. The school had been a converted Victorian house with stone flights of stairs leading to the first floor. Those on the junior playground had been used as a fire escape, and the kids were under strict orders never to play up there. She recalled the game of tag, how Vincent had hidden in the recessed doorway at the head of those stairs, waiting for her and Tanya to find him. Already in awe of his confidence, she'd been further entranced by that act of daring.

It was Tanya who'd pointed out the anomaly on the top window, visible from the foot of the stairs. A double row of narrow eight-paned windows were set at the level of each floor, three sets high. Tanya had pointed to a white X on the bottom pane of the third floor windows. It had dripped, reminding her of runny paint. Intrigued as to the reason for it, Vincent had indulged in another bout of daring, creeping past the dinner nannies and racing up the internal stairs until he stood at the window waving down at them.

Despite the hammering of her heart, her fear that he would get caught, everything had been normal—aside from having to restrain herself from hugging him when he returned unscathed by the sharp tongues of the nannies. It was the puzzled frown on his usually open face that tipped her off that something was wrong. The frown had been mirrored on the girls' faces too whilst Vincent explained that he couldn't see the X when he was up there. They accused him of teasing, but he couldn't be shaken from his story.

She snapped into the present, catapulted forward by a new question. What had they done next? She frantically rummaged through her memories but could find nothing connected to the incident. Had they asked anyone, a teacher maybe, about the strange mark? She didn't know. The memory ended with her looking at Vincent's puzzled frown. Why couldn't she remember what came next?

She hurriedly fired off another email, rushing through the pleasantries to get to the question that mattered.

She paused, considering her choice of words. She decided, "Yes, I remember the stairs. Do you remember the X?" was innocent enough and clicked send. Her nerves were so taut that she almost jumped out of her skin when her mail notifier went off a couple of minutes later. She clicked the mail open button but wished she hadn't when she read the brief note.

I'm off today. It's nice to talk to you in what passes for real

```
time. Can't say I remember any-
thing about the X right now. Care
to expand? Vince
```

"You have to remember, Vincent. You have to re-member."

Shocked by finding herself talking to the screen, she stood and paced the room for several minutes. Something was nagging at her, an itch that she couldn't scratch, bur-ied deep in her mind. She stalked to the computer and scanned the last two messages, certain the answer lay there. She gave a chuckle, more hysteria than amusement, as Mr. Lewis's name virtually jumped off the screen. He was the best teacher she'd ever had, and he was etched forever in her mind in his tweed jacket, standing at his desk with smoke wreathing his head from his ever-present pipe.

Her mind whirled back to the day they had been ap-pointed monitors. She hadn't really been surprised when her name wasn't called for any of the monitoring posi-tions at the beginning of the autumn term. Shock had glued her to her chair when Mr. Lewis had named Vin-cent, Tanya and herself as the monitors for the positions in the library. If there had been a dream job for her, that was it. It had kept her in at break times, away from the teasing of the playground and amongst her favorite com-panions: books. She recalled weeks of peacefully filing books on shelves, stamping date slips, filling out index cards and reading during the lulls, safe behind the enor-mous library desk.

The itch ceased as the memory was hauled into the light. Vincent had pelted into the library, scaring the hell out of her and Tanya. He'd been white as a sheet, his eyes black holes in the pallor of his skin. He stumbled over his words as he told them that he'd seen a ghost. Tanya had been openly skeptical of his tale of a woman wearing a long black dress, hair done up in a severe bun. He had said she'd walked across the upper hall, which was used for assemblies and gym class. The "ghost" had walked up to the stage and continued straight through it. That seemed to freak Vincent out more than actually seeing something supernatural.

Snapping back to the present, another question hounded her. Her memories were fragmentary at best. She knew she'd felt what the supernatural shows liked to call a "cold spot" when she'd walked between the junior and infant libraries. She knew she'd been terrified, but she had no idea why. She was certain it had happened on another day, but then a void opened up. There was no trace of a timeline between the incidents.

She sat down, grabbed a pen and pad from the table and started to write. Ten minutes later, she had a list of memories. She knew they were all connected, but her attempts to place them in a timescale were futile. The X incident was the first in what she thought of as the ghost memories, but how much time passed between that and getting the library monitor position? In her mind, she was the same age throughout. And yet...

If the X memory was the first, the only way it could have happened before the monitor memory was if it had occurred prior to the summer holidays. Monitor positions were always given out on the first day back after summer. How could she have been made a monitor after seeing the X? In theory, it was possible that it had happened before the end of term, but it didn't feel right. Her gut told her that the incidents had happened close together. If the X happened before the summer and the ghost memory began during the autumn term, why would she connect them?

Her eyes fell to the list, and she considered the next series of memories. Vincent being scared by the ghost had been followed by the cold spot, and lastly, the whispered discussion between the three of them in the library. Tanya had written the word "witch" on a piece of paper and stuck it in the library desk drawer. That much was clear in her memory. Had it been the same day or the next?

Another thought struck her whilst she chewed on the pen—a childhood habit returning to haunt her along with the memories. Where had the witch idea come from? How did the ghost woman suddenly turn into a witch? There was no memory of a discussion about the ghost or the witch, if they were indeed one and the same. The two being one felt right, but she had nothing more than her gut to work with. Why a witch?

Worrying at the question, she felt a shudder of fear run through her as another memory surfaced, a memory of clawed hands and tangled hair. Vincent was in this memory again, but this time, she was there after school and the boys were shooting hoops. The ball had gone flying over the fence into the knee-high weeds and grass of the abandoned house next to the playground. Being the lightest, she'd been boosted onto the fence to climb over and retrieve it. The pleasantly musty smell of trampled weeds floated around her whilst she moved closer to the house in search of the elusive ball.

There was a sound, a creak of hinges like one would hear in a horror house, and then she trembled in abject terror when something came out of the house and started toward her. She could remember the clawed hands with ragged brown fingernails that extended from grubby white sleeves. Above them, a mass of tangled graying hair whipped about a face that was mercifully lost to time. She recalled Vincent and the others yelling for her to get back, remembered running through the grass, stumbling in blind terror, crying as the boys reached down and grabbed her wrists and yanked her back over to the playground.

The memory ended abruptly, and she hurled the pad to the floor, spitting out the ink that had filled her mouth when she bit through the pen in frustration. Why didn't she know what happened next? Surely someone had confessed to setting her up, a prank by the boys on the mousey girl? At the very least, they had to have talked about it, but the void had opened up and left her with nothing but more questions.

How could she have been at the playground, least of all in the company of boys? Her mother had always picked her up when school let out, marched her home and made sure she was in bed by eight, come hell or high water. If the fence was so high that the boys had to boost her over, how had they managed to lean over it to pull her back? None of it made any sense, and her head was beginning to pound with the certainty of a migraine to come.

The computer blinked, refreshed and beckoned the part of her that desperately wanted answers. She forced herself back to the keyboard, hit reply and froze. There seemed no simple way to ask the questions.

How do you ask someone that you hadn't seen in decades if

they remembered ghosts and ghouls without sounding like a freak? she wondered.

Vincent didn't remember the X. Shouldn't that be cause enough to tell her that her memories were suspect? His memory might simply need another nudge, but resignation was beginning to settle in. Somewhere in her past, it was possible that she had lost the ability to differentiate between reality and fantasy.

It was the word "possible" that continued to nag at her. Possible left room for doubt, and doubt was something she could not live with. If she ever wanted to move forward and put the traumas of a fractured childhood firmly in the past, she had to know the truth. However, could Vincent provide it? A flash of inspiration hit her and her fingers flew over the keyboard.

Hi, Vincent,
Have you heard from Tanya? We were good mates, and I can't find her on the site. I'd love to talk to her again but she appears to have dropped off of the face of the earth! Do you still like to shoot hoops?

She watched the email float into the invisible network, something she always mentally envisaged as a flickering river a few feet above the heads of humanity. She sat back to wait, but his response was almost immediate.

Yeah, I still dunk a basket from time to time. Funny how you remember that when it was the boys' territory. Did you watch us maybe? I seem to remember girls were

banned from such masculine pastimes (ha-
ha). No, haven't seen Tanya since we left
school. No idea where is these days. She
was a cool kid though, wise beyond her
years as I recall. V

She silently castigated herself as the words sunk in.
How much truth did she need to convince herself that she
was chasing a child's fantasy?

The phone rang, and she startled badly, shaken out of
her fearful musing by its shrill scream. She hurried to answer it, hoping to be distracted from the task she knew
she had to complete. A rich, masculine voice floated
down the line and she felt her knees weaken. She sank
down, sitting with her back to the wall and a death grip
on the receiver.

"Hey, bookworm."

"Vincent?"

"The one and only."

"How did you get my number?"

"You forget you're a famous writer these days."

"Hardly famous." She took a deep breath, trying to
swallow the quaver in her voice. "Just a local hack."

"Famous from where I'm standing. I don't have my
name in print. I rang the paper, told them I had a story for
you, and they gave me your number."

"They're not supposed to do that. Someone's going to
get in serious trouble for handing out my home number."

"I told them I was the local flasher and wanted to put
myself in your hands."

She could hear the humor in his voice and regressed
to her ten-year-old self, her face flushing and a soppy grin
tilting her lips.

"Yeah, right, you got me." She giggled and felt the tension ease in her muscles.

"You left your number on the site. Did you forget?"

"I guess so. Don't remember doing that. It's not something I usually do."

"Still a mystery, huh?"

"Sorry?"

"We didn't really know anything about you when we were at school. You were just the bookworm. You even had the library monitor job."

Her heart hammered twice in rapid succession, a flush of hope making her stammer over her words in her rush.

"You remember that?"

"Yeah, 'course I do. I was the one that had to lug the stupid returns trolley from class to class and then turn it over to you for filing. Dunno how you managed all those books every day."

"I had Tanya to help me, and you."

The words were out before she had considered the consequences and the silence that followed held a puzzled quality that had her heart skipping for the wrong reasons.

"I only hauled the books. Not much help, huh? I didn't know Tanya used to help you."

For a second, her brain refused to function, becoming a void. Her certainty over the monitor positions had gone unchallenged, never wavering, until that moment. If Vincent had not been a monitor, if he didn't remember Tanya being appointed either, where did that leave her? Adrift, and that was something she couldn't allow to happen.

"Still there?"

Vincent sounded uneasy and she suppressed a wild urge to laugh. He had every right to be. He didn't know he was talking to a potential crazy person.

"Yes, sorry. I was thinking." She squelched the panicky voice in her head that didn't want her to say the next line, but she said it anyway. "Fancy having lunch?"

The pause grew just a little too long, and she was on the verge of echoing his question back to him when he spoke.

"Yeah, why not?"

"Do you remember the Chinese place up the road from the school?"

"That's still there?"

"Yes. Meet you there at two?"

"Done deal. Looking forward to it."

She gave him her mobile number, said her goodbyes and hung up. Then she gave up control, allowing the shakes that had threatened throughout the conversation to wrack her body, giving the tears free access to her eyes.

Ten minutes later, feeling drained but cleansed and with renewed purpose, she hauled herself to her feet and headed for the shower. The school was only a twenty minute bus ride away, and she had plenty of time. Standing under the cascade of hot water, she pondered on the fact that she'd never moved more than half an hour away from the school. Was it a part of her subconscious telling her that she needed to deal with the memories? At that point in time, she figured anything seemed possible.

While the bus travelled familiar streets and passed landmarks that took her back to her schooldays, she found it hard to imagine ever living anywhere else. The familiar was comforting and safe, and yet her current intentions would tear that safety to shreds. That was, unless Vincent could give her a speck of hope and recall one memory that they shared without any doubts. Was she really that desperate to stay in place? Could it be fear of stepping outside of her comfort zone that had stopped her picking the scab off of those memories for so long?

Her steps slowed as she alighted from the bus and walked toward the restaurant she remembered passing by as a child, thinking how exotic it looked with its brilliantly colored paper lanterns in the window. She'd envied the people inside, sitting in calm pools of candlelit elegance. She stopped, pretending to study the menu whilst attempting to peer through the dingy window to the seating beyond. In her rush, she had forgotten to arrange where to meet Vincent. He could already be inside. The dim lighting gave no clues.

"Still a shorty, I see."

She jumped, spun around and found herself nose to chest with Vincent. Looking up into that achingly familiar grin and soft brown eyes, she was transported to her childhood and the bittersweet pain of a first crush.

"You haven't changed," she managed before he engulfed her in a hug that left her ribs aching.

"You have." He studied her hair and winked, "No more pigtails huh?"

"I got a little tired of the boys swinging on them." She giggled and eyed the door, "Shall we?"

Vincent looked at the restaurant, glanced up the street and then tucked her arm over his.

"How about we walk up to the park, feed the ducks and talk instead?"

Surprised and uncertain, she hesitated, and he

seemed to understand.

"Whatever it is that forced your hand this morning and impelled you to ask me to meet up, I'm thinking shoving food around a plate and making small talk isn't the way to go."

"Perhaps not, but are you sure? I did promise you lunch."

"We'll grab some chips at Ramsay's, just like the old days."

Ramsay's had been a favorite haunt of adults and kids alike. It was a traditional pie and eel shop, but it had branched out into fish and chips. While they walked, Ramsay's loomed into view, still painted in navy blue and white with a ram's head on the shop sign that rocked back and forth above the door. Vincent insisted the chips, in a delightfully nostalgic newspaper cone, were his treat. Little was said as they left the shop and headed for Ryedin Park.

They paused in unison before the slender wrought iron gates.

"It hasn't changed."

She realized she was whispering, a reverential tone to suit what had once been their temple of worship. Here they had fallen out of trees, been chased off of the silken bowling green by the keepers, made houses under the trailing willows, told tales of the giant pike in the lake and shared kisses on the tire swings. The last thought brought a faint blush to her cheeks and made her exquisitely aware of the masculine presence at her side. Hoping to bury such thoughts quickly, she tugged on his arm and pointed to the kiosk.

"I wonder if they still sell bread and nuts."

"Shall we find out?"

Vincent grinned, and she could see the child she had adored beneath the faint stubble and the experience lines about his eyes.

To their mutual delight, they bought both bread and nuts and headed into the park. They passed the bandstand, and she thought she heard the faint sounds of memory, of concerts on Sunday afternoons with ice cream dripping down her fist. The bowling green was still a silken emerald sea, and she burst into bright laughter as Vincent threatened to hurdle the fence and trespass. They ran off, still giggling as a keeper emerged from the miniature hut next to the green and watched them retreat with a world-weary frown.

Around the corner, the path forked. On the left lay the lake, but to the right the path curved again and led to the rose gardens. She met his eyes, looking up the second he looked down. Their synchronicity spooked her a little.

"Rose garden?" he asked, and she nodded. "Thought so. I remember it being very little travelled. Let's hope it's the same."

"It will be; I can feel it."

Her premonition proved correct as they entered under the arch that was draped in blousy pink blooms. They ducked to avoid the cloud of bees that flew up at their appearance. Eight side-routes branched off from the straight central path. Each led to a square garden dedicated to a particular variety of rose. In the center of the main path, a fountain tinkled. Water poured from a siren's jug to agitate the water below, which was speckled with tiny orange darts. A heron stood on the lip of the fountain and eyed the darting goldfish speculatively.

They brushed through roses, interspersed with a riot of summer annuals, and settled on a rustic wooden bench near the center of the gardens. Silence enveloped them, occasionally broken by the trill of a songbird, but they might have been alone in the world for all they could hear of civilization.

"So, are you ready to get it off of your chest, Janey?"

"No one's called me that since junior school," she managed with a faint smile.

"And you are avoiding my question. I'm guessing it has something to do with those odd questions you asked me, yes?"

She nodded, suddenly engrossed in picking at her chipped nail polish, startling as his warm hand settled over hers and held her fingers still.

"Just tell me, Janey. Whatever it is, it can't be as bad as you think, right?"

"I'll let you be the judge." She stared out across the rose bushes, focused on the past, and started to relate the tale.

By the time she reached the incident in the playground, she was running out of steam. What remained was, for her, the worst of it, but she wasn't ready to talk it out until she had some reaction from Vincent. She noticed that she was still holding his hand and he squeezed it gently, but his frown was warning enough. He looked away, seeming to focus unseeing on the same spot that she had stared at for the previous half an hour, and then sighed.

"I don't think I can tell you what you want to hear, Janey. I don't remember any of this. There is something I remember that you haven't mentioned though."

She fought to relax her grip on his hand, aware that what he had to offer might be no better but willing to reach for any truth but that which battered at the base of her brain.

"Tell me, please."

"I want you to answer a question first, ok?"

"If I can." She frowned, uneasy.

"What if nothing I tell you can prove what you believe to be true? What will you do?"

"Go back to my therapist and get him to commit me, I guess."

She tried for a smile and ended up releasing a solitary sob. Vincent tucked his arm around her, pulled her head to his shoulder and hugged her briefly.

"I don't think I need to tell you any of the scenarios. I reckon you've been through them all and probably convinced yourself of the worst." She nodded against his shoulder and he chuckled. "A writer is the best person to know how to be a drama queen, huh?"

She coughed out a reluctant giggle, and he hugged her again.

"Janey, I don't think you're going to like what I tell you, but it might explain a lot. Back then, none of us knew about child abuse. I guess the adults knew, but it was a different world. Everyone minded their own business, and no one interfered, not even teachers. We couldn't have known what was happening to you, but kids are cruel. You were withdrawn, the bookworm who went home for lunch and never played out after school. You were an easy target and we, probably me as much as the rest, found it simple to wind you up. Do you remember the occult fad?"

"No." Her voice rose at the end, turning her answer into a confused question.

Genuinely puzzled, she sat up a little but decided not to forego the comfort of his arm about her—and he didn't seem inclined to let her go.

"I guess it was around the time you are talking about. You remember Janet and Sheila?"

"Gods, yes," she uttered with feeling, "The 'popular girls' who held sway over the playground. If you weren't their friend, you were no one."

"Yep, and despite your quiet disdain, I think, deep inside, you would have done anything to be a part of that group and that is why you got sucked in with the whole occult rubbish."

"I still don't remember it."

He continued as his eyes lost focus, and she guessed he had drifted back over the decades to the playground, to the girls gathered around the picnic benches and a solitary figure wandering through the school gates and eyeing the giggling girls suspiciously.

"They called you over. Perhaps some kid sense was working in me, because I almost called out to you, tried to distract you but--" He shrugged an apology and cast his eyes downward. "I was a popular kid too and with my mates. I couldn't take the risk of losing face."

"It was nobody's fault," she told him quietly. "It was what it was, and it's too late to fret over it."

"It doesn't make me feel so great. Anyway, you went over to the girls and they had some stupid game going. One of them had seen a hypnotist on the telly, and they were trying to hypnotize each other. I was close enough that I could hear it all. They were already doing it with one of the other girls when they got you to sit on the bench with them, and I could almost hear what you were thinking, could see your eyes taking in what was going on. Do you remember any of this?"

"No."

"But I know this happened."

"How?"

"Because I spoke to Sheila a couple of weeks ago and she remembered it, too. You won't be surprised to hear that she still thinks it was hilarious."

"No, I'm not. What happened?"

"Janet pretended to hypnotize you, and you did what seemed the logical thing. You copied what the other girl was saying, something about a ghost in the school. The girl--"

"Don't!"

She pushed up and stalked across the garden, ferociously blinking back tears. It wasn't difficult to imagine the vicious laughter, the snide comments. Her ten-year-old self was stumbling away from the group in tears as the woman felt Vincent take her hands in his.

"You remember?" he asked gently, and she shook her head, a single tear flying from her cheek.

"But it explains a lot, right?" he urged, and she felt him stiffen in surprise as she laughed, a sharp bark that ripped her world open.

"Not so. Maybe I did make it all up, but I don't think so."

"Janey, you must have." She could hear a touch of frustration. "I was never a library monitor and neither was Tanya. The school doors were locked at break time, and you had to ask a dinner nanny to be let in. I didn't see a ghost in the hall."

He hesitated, then finished, "Unless I made it up to tease you."

She tore away and plopped back down on the bench.

"Maybe you did, I don't know, but I never finished my story."

For the first time, she looked up and held his eyes, saw the uncertainty in him and shrugged.

"It's up to you. Stay or go."

He settled beside her, but there was no comforting arm, no soothing hand this time.

"I'll stay. I feel a bit responsible for--" He paused, seeming to search for the right words. "—for the way things have been for you."

"I suspect it wasn't you that started my madness." She saw him wince at the word. "Even if you added to it. I'll tell you the rest.

"There was a repeating dream that began around the same time. I used to dream about a little girl on the balcony at the top of the school. It was always at night, she was in her nightgown and it was dark but for a gas lamp near the head of the stairs. She'd walk forward, and then a door would open and she'd scurry back along the balcony rail, away from the woman who stepped out. A woman who looked just like the one you described as the ghost in the hall."

"I never…"

"Let me finish. Wherever the image of her came from, she was the ghost. Black dress, hair scraped back into a bun so tight it pulled the corners of her eyes up. I will never forget those eyes, black, cold and angry. I never knew what she had against that little girl, but she would advance along the balcony and grab hold of her before throwing her out over the balcony rail. I would be terrified by this point.

"Remember the old wives tale about dying in reality if you died in your sleep? In the dream, I'd be in two places at once, inside the girl, falling and screaming, and hovering above her, watching her fall.

"Stupid as it sounds; I was always terrified that I'd wake up dead. I'd watch her fall whilst being inside her, and I'd feel her hit the floor three levels down and wake up sweating and crying. At first, these dreams came two and three times a week, but once I moved away from the school and started to face other problems, it lessened. I was still having that dream until I was around eighteen. No matter how often I had it, it woke me, in a cold sweat, crying, sometimes screaming.

"Then I attended a séance with a friend and my mother. The woman set up a Ouija board, and I went along with it for a quiet laugh, completely convinced that she was shoving that glass around and coming up with random messages from her monk guide. I was close to suggesting that we all go and watch a movie when everything changed. I was suddenly freezing cold, like being wrapped in a blanket of ice in a deep freeze.

"I think I saw genuine fear in my mother's face when that glass started to fly around the table. It felt like my finger was glued to it, my shoulder was creaking under the strain and my friend was terrified. The glass kept spelling out 'Jane' and then 'Sorry', over and over, faster and faster. I don't know how or why, but I was certain it was the ghost woman. That dream had terrorized me for years. I was angry as hell, and I remember screaming out that I would never forgive her and that she belonged in hell.

"A second later, the glass flew off of the table, smashed against the fireplace, and I was thrown backwards across the room. I cracked my head on the windowsill. I must have blacked out, because the next thing I remember was being shoved into my room and told to go to bed. I probably had a concussion, but all my mother cared about was that my friend had called her mum to come and get her and what the neighbors would say.

"I have two witnesses, Vincent. Two people who remember that night and something coming through that attacked me after I refused to accept its apology. Tell me I'm making it up."

He sat in silence for a long time, and she watched emotions play across his face, a quiet melancholy settling on her heart as she realized that she would never see him again. Her tale didn't fit his safe little world. Finally, he met her gaze, but he was already shrinking away from the unknown and unbelievable.

"How do I know you aren't making this up, Janey?"

"You don't. Would you like something else to consider? How do I know which is my reality?"

He stood, hands shoved deep into his pockets, shoulders rounded, head down and eyeing his shoe as he scuffed through the gravel.

"I can't help you, Janey. I'm sorry."

She rose, hugged him briefly and smiled as she began to walk their back trail, hearing him follow her lead.

"I know, Vincent, but I am glad you came."

They were silent until they reached the gates. She could feel the itch in him, the quiet voice telling him to get away from the crazy lady, but he held out his hand and she shook it, managing to keep her voice bright and breezy.

"I'll be in touch, and you have my number," she said, knowing she would never get a call or contact him.

"Okay, well, I guess I'd better get going. The wife'll wonder where I am."

And there it is, she thought as he turned and walked away. He'd maybe thought that she'd be willing to be his bit on the side, had not told his wife about her in the hopes of keeping the two lives separate. Instead, she had dumped a double life of her own onto his shoulders, and they had ultimately proved too narrow to carry the weight of not knowing, of never being able to know what had really happened.

A memory flashed brilliantly before her eyes, and she suddenly wondered if her nana had been wiser than she'd ever suspected. She could see Nana standing at her side, watching her try on a jacket and struggling with the slender fit.

She heard her comment, "You've got broad shoulders Janey, my girl, and I reckon you're gonna need them."

Was it a true memory, or had it surfaced from Janey World, where ghosts walked, doppelgangers stole magazines and memory became clay to mold?

She found she didn't know, and it was likely that she never would. Her therapist could dig and delve all he liked, but he would never be able to tell her the truth; because, in the end, there was no way to prove what someone said. Someone who wasn't there could never know for certain where the truth lay. She realized then that she had a new problem. How could she ever verify anything she considered to be a part of her past? Could she cope with learning that no one remembered things she held as unshakeable truths? Perhaps more importantly, could she cope with knowing that she lived in two worlds and that, for her, they were both completely real?

Walking towards the bus stop, her fingers sought through her wind tangled hair and ran over the faint raised scar on the back of her skull. Had it come from the séance incident or from the time her mother had put her head through a window? She didn't know, didn't know if either incident was real. How could she live, survive, in what others considered to be reality, when she would never know what was truth and what was lies? As the bus pulled up, she realized she would spend the rest of her life finding out.

THE REPLICATOR

By Nancy Smith Gibson

"Hurry! Come on," Danny called to his companion while they ran across the field.

"I'm coming. Hold your horses."

The two boys came to a stop behind the rundown house, threw themselves on the ground and peeked around the corner.

"She's home. Now what are we going to do?"

It was the most trouble Danny had ever been in, and getting out of it was going to be just about impossible.

I'm just going to have to be resourceful, he thought.

Resourceful: That was what his mother had taught him to be.

They'd had to be resourceful to survive the previous five years, especially the most recent few months.

Danny had been seven years old when his dad had taken off. The day he had left, his dad had sat on the front step and said to Danny, "You're going to have to be the man in the family until we are all back together again. I have to go to Nashville and meet up with a man about a recording contract. When I get some money I'll send for you and your mom, and we'll be together again. But until then, you be the man and help your mother all you can. Okay?"

With that, he had taken his guitar and duffel bag and left.

At first, he had called home, collect, once a week, but then he had missed weeks and finally he didn't call at all. Danny had received a birthday card from his dad with five dollars in it the first year, but that had never happened again.

Danny was good at being the man in the family; his mother told him so. He made his bed and picked up his toys and helped carry in the groceries. He and his mother had done fine until the plant where his mother worked had closed. She had a real good job there, assistant to the sales manager, but everyone who worked there had lost their jobs. She had told Danny it was something called a "recession". There weren't enough orders for the car parts the plant made, so the company that owned it had closed it down.

At first she had thought they could make it until she found another job. The problem was, lots of people in town were looking for a job and there weren't enough to go around. She had unemployment, but the two of them had to cut way back. They had cut off the cable TV and stopped going out to eat and to the movies.

She was going to use her retirement money until she found another job, but then she found out some crook had taken all the money the people who worked at the plant thought they had saved. They had lost it all. That was when Danny could tell she was worried. When the unemployment money ran out, she told Danny they were going to have to be resourceful.

There were no jobs in their town, she told him, so they were going to have to go to where the jobs were. She used Danny's college fund to pay the last couple of payments on their car.

"I'll start you a new college fund when I get a job," she said. She sold all their furniture, they packed up their clothes and some blankets and pillows and a few other things and started out to find a town with a job.

They went from town to town, looking for work, and Danny could tell she was really worried. They bought stuff to eat they didn't have to cook and had picnics along the way. It was like a game at first, like camping out, sort of, but they slept in the car. They used the rest room at rest stops and parks and service stations and used the washcloths and towels they had brought with them to wash up. Sometimes they found state parks with showers and then they could really get clean.

In some towns she found a day or two of work, but nothing permanent. Sometimes she would get typing jobs or computer jobs that lasted a week or two, until the project was finished. She sometimes made enough that they could eat in a café occasionally, and she put away money to have enough for gas when the jobs ran out.

While she worked, Danny played in the city park, if there was one, or read books in the library. Sometimes there was a dollar matinee at a movie theater, and he would go to that. However, sooner or later, the job ran out. When she couldn't find another one, they moved on.

That's how they ended up in Centerview. It looked like a nice little town, clean and neat with lots of stores. When they stopped at a red light, Danny spotted the sign.

WAITRESS WANTED

"Look, Mom. A job!"

His mother glanced over at the Coffee Cup Café. When the light changed, she went around the block to look at it again. She pulled into the parking lot, where there were several cars parked.

"We'll go in and get something to eat. Now, don't say anything about the job, Danny. I want to see what kind of place it is. There are some places I wouldn't want to work, so you just be quiet. Okay?"

They went in and sat in a booth at the front. "Don't you want a hamburger and fries, Danny?" his mother asked him when the waitress arrived. "And a glass of milk?"

Danny nodded.

"And I'll just have a glass of milk for myself. I ate something just a while ago," she told the waitress.

Danny knew she hadn't eaten, but he didn't know how to get her to order something. He wondered if they didn't have enough money to pay for more food.

While they sat there, Danny and his mother looked around. It looked like a nice café. The booths were all red vinyl, and they didn't look like they had any cracks or holes, and Danny thought it looked clean. He knew how important it was to his mom that stuff was clean. The other people eating there looked nice too, not like they were bums or bikers or anything like that.

When the waitress brought his food his mother said, "This looks like it might be a good place to work."

"It sure is," the waitress said. "The owner, Sue Bailey,

is a good boss if you are a hard worker and not a slacker. Are you looking for work?"

His mother took a deep breath and said, "Yes, I am."

"Well, we're looking for a morning waitress. Billie Jo just up and left, and we're real shorthanded. Have you ever waited tables?"

"Yes, I put myself through college waiting tables," his mother said.

While Danny ate his hamburger and fries, his mom went in the back to meet Ms. Bailey. When she came back to the booth, she was smiling and she had a tee shirt in her hands. It was like the one the waitress was wearing: yellow with a big picture of a cup and the words *Coffee Cup Café* on the front.

"This seems like a good place to work, Danny. I start first thing in the morning."

Danny was finished eating, so they paid up and left. His mother left two dollars for a tip, although she usually only left one.

"I don't want them to think I am cheap," she explained to him. "I'll have money starting tomorrow--tip money-- and I'll get paid every Friday."

When they left, she drove around town and spotted the two places that were important to Danny: the library and the park. They were close to each other, which was convenient, since that was usually where he spent his time while his mother worked.

"I have to be at work at six o'clock in the morning, so we're going to have to be up early and ready to go."

Of course, getting ready when they lived in a car just meant pulling on his jeans and shoes, then she would drive to a place with a rest room so they could brush their teeth and wash their faces. It was easier for Danny than it was for his mom. He didn't have makeup and pantyhose and stuff like that to get right. His hair was easy to comb and get looking good, not like a girl's hair.

"It'll be easier for me to get ready for work, since I can just wear jeans and that shirt," she told him. "Now let's go find a place to park for the night."

A place to park was always a problem. The cops sometimes ran them off when they tried to stay at a park or a business. The trick was to find a place where no one would notice them staying in the car. They saw several police cars, so she drove farther out from town, hoping there weren't a lot of sheriff's cars in the county.

Finally, his mother went down a narrower road that looked like it wasn't used often. It looked like an abandoned driveway. After about half a mile, they came to a tall fence with barbed wire around the top. There was a gate, but the chain and lock that had held it closed was rusty and had fallen away, leaving the gate standing open.

His mother stopped and looked for a while, and then said, "Let's see if this will do, shall we?"

She drove through and down a road that looked like it had been years since anyone had driven on it. The pavement was cracked and there were weeds and grass growing up through it.

They had driven just a short distance when they saw a row of houses. It didn't look like anyone was living in them. The grass and weeds had grown up around them, and the paint was peeling. There were no cars or people around. There was no sign of life anywhere. His mother pulled the car around behind the houses.

"I think this might do. If anyone comes around, there is plenty of room to drive away."

"Can we look around? See what's in the houses?"

"It's getting dark. We'll do it tomorrow after I get off work. I only work until the lunch rush is over, or maybe until the middle of the afternoon."

The next day, they were at the café by six o'clock. Danny slept some more on the back seat of the car, then woke and ate a cereal bar and drank a box of juice for breakfast. He put a couple of packages of cheese and crackers in his pocket for lunch, put his little metal cars in the other pocket and set out for the park.

He played there for most of the morning, testing out all the playground equipment and then building roads and towns with sticks and stones to accommodate his cars. When he was tired of that, he ate his crackers and then went to the library down the block. There he first went to the restroom to wash up. He didn't want to get the books dirty when he read them.

When the big clock on the wall read two o'clock, he put away the book he was reading and walked back to the café and sat in the car to wait for his mother. It wasn't long before she came out, and she was smiling.

"I think this is going to be a good place, Danny. Everyone is friendly, and I made good tips today. I'm glad you saw that sign yesterday."

On the way back to their place to park, she went through a drive-in and got Danny a chocolate milkshake.

"That's for being such a good, resourceful boy," she said.

While she drove, she told him what she had found out about the abandoned houses. "There used to be a big government facility out there," she said. "It was very hush-hush. No one knew what went on. Those houses were for the workers. They didn't hire anyone from town; they brought them in from other places, and they lived out there and didn't associate with the people from town. No one has lived out there for over four years, since they closed the place down. When the last president needed more money for the war in the Middle East, they cut the funds for whatever it was they were working on and this place closed up."

"So can we look around in the houses?"

"Sure. That shouldn't hurt. But they are just old empty houses."

As it turned out, the houses weren't altogether empty. The first house had a kitchen table, but no chairs. It had a stove and a refrigerator in the kitchen and a couch in the living room. There were two bedrooms, and one of them had a mattress on the floor and a chest of drawers with one of the drawers broken. They went into the other houses. There were a few pieces of furniture in some of them, and two doors down they found another mattress.

"Let's take it back to the first house, Mom, and we'll both have a mattress to sleep on," Danny said. They worked together to get it back to the house where they had started. Then they grabbed two kitchen chairs from the last house in the row and put them at the kitchen table at their chosen house.

"Now we have a real house." Danny was surprised to see his mother sit down at the table and cry.

"What's wrong? Aren't you happy we found this place?" he asked.

"Oh, Danny. What a place to live in. Yes, I'm happy

we found it, but we used to have such a nice house. I'm so sorry you don't have a better home."

She took out a tissue and started to wipe her eyes. "I'm sorry I can't provide better for you."

"Don't cry, Mom. Please don't cry. I'm doing fine, really I am. We'll have a real nice house again someday. I know we will."

He put his arms around her and rested his head on her shoulder.

"I know we are okay." She hugged him. "We have each other, and we have more than some folks do. And I just know this new job is going to work out for the best. We'll be back on top in no time."

She stood and started looking around. She walked over to the sink and turned the handle. Water shot out the faucet, dirty looking brown that turned clear after a few seconds.

"Will you look at that! The water is still on. I can clean the kitchen and the bathroom and mop the floors. And we can flush and take baths." She looked around the room again. "Look there in the corner--a broom. I'll sweep, and tomorrow after work, I'll buy some cleaning supplies."

Danny walked to the refrigerator and opened the door. "Look, Mom! The power is on. We can use the refrigerator."

His mother came and looked in it.

"It just needs a good cleaning. I wonder about the lights."

She went to the switch beside the door and flipped it. The overhead light came on.

"This is great, but I am not sure we need to have lights on after dark. Someone is liable to see the light and come see about it. It is nice to know we have them, though."

The next morning, Danny talked his mother into letting him stay home. That was the way he had started thinking about their new place: home. It looked like it might rain that day, so his mother finally said yes, even though she was reluctant.

"This is a safe place, Mom," he said. "I'll sweep and look around in the other houses to see if I can find anything we can use. I'll be okay."

She went to work and left him there. He explored all the buildings and found more furniture: three small tables for the living room, a bed frame he thought would be good for his mother's mattress, a small lamp, and some dishes. He took it all back to their house in between rain showers.

When his mother came home, she brought cleaning supplies. They cleaned everywhere, scrubbing out the bathtub and toilet and the refrigerator. Danny wiped down all the kitchen cabinets. Then Danny took a shower and his mother took a bath and washed her hair.

"It sure feels nice to feel really clean again," she said.

From then on, Danny was allowed to stay home every day. He explored all around where they lived and often played with his cars under the big oak tree behind his house. His mother bought a small radio, and on rainy days, he stayed inside and played while he listened to music.

After a couple of weeks, he became bored and decided to explore farther from home. When he walked about half a mile to the east, he happened upon another tall fence like the one they had driven through to get in. He could see a big building on the other side.

"This must be the government facility Mom told me about, the one that closed down," he said, although no one was around. Danny turned left and followed the fence until he was in front of the building, where a road ran up to a gate in the fence.

GOVERNMENT PROPERTY

NO ADMITTANCE
AUTHORIZED PERSONNEL ONLY

The signs on the property warned. The gate was locked up with chains and padlocks.

Danny turned back to the right and followed the fence back to where he had started and kept going that way. Soon he turned another corner and then he was behind the big building. After walking a few yards, he found another gate, and on that one, there was no chain or lock.

Danny didn't think it was really trespassing to go inside the gate, like it would have been if the place were still being used. He figured he wasn't going to bother anything, just look around.

First he circled the building. In the front, there was a set of double doors. He tested them, but they were locked. There was a keypad with numbers beside the door, but he didn't bother it. It might set off an alarm or something, since he didn't know the code to get in. The place where his mother used to work had one like that, and he knew someone had to know the right numbers to get in.

He continued around the outside. The only windows were about ten feet off the ground, so he couldn't see in anywhere. There were several doors along the outside and some of them had keypads and some didn't. When he finally moved around to the back side of the building, he came to a door that not only wasn't locked, it stood open a couple of feet. He hesitated for a minute, and then went in.

He went all through the building and looked at the rooms. There were windows in the ceiling all over the building, so there was light to see everywhere. There were offices in the front part. Most of the furniture was gone, but he could tell they were offices. There was a desk with a broken leg in one, chairs in a couple, and a computer monitor sat on the floor in another. One smaller room had shelves on three sides and there was paper still on them, and pencils and pens. Danny picked up some paper, two pencils and a pen from the floor. He didn't think anyone would mind since they left them there when they moved out. He liked to draw but hadn't had any paper in a long time.

Danny noticed there were signs beside the doors of some of the rooms. The sign beside the door that had the paper and pencils said: **SUPPLY ROOM**. There were rooms that said **LAB 1**, **LAB 2** and **ELECTRONICS**.

Finally, he was back to the room where he had entered the building and noticed it had a sign that said **REPLICATOR**. There were several large metal objects in the room. They looked like cabinets, with doors of various sizes, and there were dials and lights, buttons and switches. It was all very interesting to Danny. Some of them had labels, like "carbon input" and "pressure gauge".

Looking at his watch, Danny saw it was time to go home before his mother got there. He had a feeling she wouldn't like him playing in that place. When she asked him later about the paper and pencils, he told her he found them in one of the other houses.

From then on, Danny played in the factory. That is how Danny thought of it, as a factory, even though there was no sign it ever made anything. Some days he sat in an office and drew pictures. Other times he ran up and down the long halls. Usually, he played in the room with the odd cabinets with the doors and dials and switches.

One day he was playing cars there, pretending the cabinet was a car factory. He put his little red car in one of the cubby holes, shut the door, and punched a couple of buttons, then flipped a switch. The machine's lights came on, and it made noise.

Danny jumped back, startled and wondering what to do, when a rattling sound caused him to look at the chute at the end of the machine. To his amazement, his little red car rolled out the end.

"Wow," he said to the empty room. "It shot my car through it and out the end. Cool!" He picked up the car to put it back in and do it again, but when he opened the door, there was his car, right where he put it.

It made me another car! he thought. He looked at both cars closely. There on the new car was the scratch that was on his original. Then he took his blue car and put it in the compartment. He had to think a while before he remembered which buttons he had pushed, but after a couple of tries he got it right, and out came another blue car.

By the time he had to go home, he had expanded his collection of cars to eight cars, three trucks, two motorcycles, and three police cars. He thought he was in trouble that night, though, when his mother saw how many he had.

"Danny," she said, "Where did you get so many cars? I thought you only had four or five."

"I found them in the houses. I guess the kids that lived there went off and left them behind."

His mother looked doubtful, but didn't say anything else about it.

One day Danny decided to take his lunch with him to the factory, so he took the half-full jar of peanut butter and a sleeve of crackers, along with a knife for spreading. He amused himself by drawing pictures and making more cars until he was hungry. While he ate, an idea came to him. He put one cracker, spread with peanut butter, into the factory machine, pushed the buttons and out came another one.

This can save Mom money on groceries, he thought.

He made two more jars with peanut butter and several sleeves of crackers to carry home that afternoon.

The next day he started making more groceries, but he had to be very careful not to have too many cans in the cabinet or his mother would notice. He tried making fresh fruit too. He took a banana and made a second one, then ate the first one.

When his mother asked him why he didn't eat the banana that day, he said, "I forgot about it," and ate it the next day.

Danny felt good helping with the expenses by making more food. His mom wouldn't have to spend as much for groceries and could save up more money. She had talked about saving money so they could rent a place in town. It would be time for school to start before long, and Danny had already missed most of one year because they had been on the road.

"It's important to get you back in school," she said. "You are a smart boy, but I know you're behind in your studies. If you study really hard when you go back to school, maybe you won't be put back a grade."

Danny hoped so. He was willing to work hard if it meant not having to repeat a grade with all those kids who were younger than he was.

The big day, the day *it* happened, Danny was playing in the factory room one morning when he heard voices coming from the front of the building. He crept to the door into the hall and listened. It sounded like two men talking. He heard one say, "Here it is, in this office."

And the other one said, "It sure was careless going off and forgetting to check to see if you had all the records."

Then the first voice said, "Let me show you around while you're here. This was some important place when we were working, let me tell you. A lot of hush-hush experiments going on. Let me show you the replicator room."

Danny thought later he should have left by the back door, but it was pouring down rain, so instead of going home, he ran to one of the big metal cabinets in the factory room, got inside and closed the door. Soon he heard the voices inside the factory room, but inside the cabinet he couldn't tell what they were saying. The voices faded away, but Danny stayed where he was.

It's better to be safe than sorry, Mom always says, he thought. *And I don't want to have to explain what I am doing here.*

He worried he and his mother would have to move, and he thought it was a pretty good place to live.

After about ten minutes, as near as he could tell, Danny decided it might be safe to get out. He was cramped up and tired of sitting in one place. Just as he reached to push the door open, there was a really loud clap of thunder. It sounded like it was right there on top of him, and suddenly he was glad he hadn't gone out the back door and started home. He might have been struck by lightning.

The air around him quivered, and the cabinet shook. When it was still again, Danny opened the door and stepped out into the room. That's when he saw the other boy. The boy who looked just like Danny sat on the floor where the chute came out of the side.

"Hey!" said the boy. "How did I get from the cabinet to here?"

Then he looked around and saw Danny.

"Holy Cow!" he said.

The two boys circled each other, saying nothing. Finally, Danny reached out and touched the second Danny on the arm.

"You feel real," he said.

"Of course, I'm real, doofus. I'm Daniel Ryan Colburn, and I'm as real as can be."

"How can you be Daniel Ryan Colburn when *I'm* Daniel Ryan Colburn?"

The other boy had no answer for that.

Finally he added, "Boy, is Mom going to be surprised. And mad. There's two of us. What are we going to do?"

They sat down on the floor to think about the situation.

"I'm the one who got out of the cabinet, so I'm Danny number one," said one of the boys. "You are Danny number two."

They remained quiet for a few minutes. "How about if you be Danny and I be Ryan? I've always liked my middle name," said Danny number two.

"Me too! I've always liked my middle name too."

When they thought about that, they laughed so hard they rolled around on the floor.

When they stopped and sat up again, Ryan said, "When I was little, I thought I would like to have a twin brother, like two boys in my class."

When Danny said, "Me too," it started the laughter all over again.

They went over all the memories they had from the first time they could remember anything. At noon, they put the sandwich and bottle of juice Danny had brought into the smaller factory machine that made the toy cars and made a second lunch for Ryan. By the time they headed home, they were all talked out.

"This is really cool, having someone just like me to talk to," said Danny, and Ryan agreed.

"But," Ryan said, "We don't want to ever, ever make another one of us. It would be too confusing."

Danny agreed. They also agreed on something else: They needed to wait to tell their mother. It would be too big a shock to just walk in and announce there were two of them. She might have a heart attack or something. It would take some planning before they told her. After all, it would take more food and more clothes and more everything. They would have to figure it out by the time she got enough money saved up for rent and a deposit on a house or apartment in town. She would have to know by then she had two sons, not one like she thought.

Before she arrived home from work, they took

Danny's sleeping bag and enough food for supper over to another house. They decided to take turns sleeping in another house at night until they could tell their mother what happened. Ryan volunteered to be the first one to stay alone. He said he wasn't afraid, but Danny knew he was, just a little bit, because Danny was a little bit afraid thinking about staying alone the next night.

The two boys spent the next week running races, tossing the ball back and forth between them, and playing with all the toy cars they had accumulated. One rainy afternoon, they spent it listening to the radio, drawing pictures and planning what to do. When they had it all figured out, they went to work on their plan. Danny and Ryan hated to do some of the things they felt were necessary, but they just couldn't see any other way to handle the situation. They had to make sure their mom didn't worry.

They spent some of their time making a second set of clothes for Ryan. One day when they were running a race, Danny fell and ripped his second best pair of jeans. That's when they decided to make an extra of everything that was still good, so if something got torn they'd still have a good pair.

"We don't need more than one extra, I don't guess," said Ryan.

"Yeah. Mom said yesterday I was growing like a weed and she was going to have to buy me a new pair of jeans and some new shoes. We don't need to make more of things that we're outgrowing."

They continued their plans so they would be ready when the time came to present Mom with her new son.

Finally, one morning before work she said to Ryan,

whom she thought was Danny, "I think I have found a place to rent in town. I'm going to go by after work and give them the deposit and first month's rent. Then, when I get home, we can start packing to move. It shouldn't take very long. We don't have much. That way I can get you enrolled before school starts."

That's when the boys knew they had to be ready. They practiced their speeches and prepared everything for that afternoon. However, when they made the trip back across the field from the factory that last day, their mother was already there, early.

"We're just going to have to be resourceful," Danny said. "I'll go in and start, just like we planned, and you get it ready and stay in the kitchen until the right time. Okay?"

"Yeah. Okay." Ryan took off for one of the decrepit houses that the boys had designated headquarters, carefully keeping out of the range of sight of their home, just in case their mother was looking out the back door.

Taking a deep breath, Danny stood up and entered the house that had been home for several months.

"Hi, Mom," he said.

"Hi, yourself. I took off a little early so we could get moved. I looked for you and called, but I didn't see you."

"Oh, I was off in the field. But I came home," he added unnecessarily. He twisted the tail of his shirt and stared at his shoes. Despite their practice, he couldn't think of any good way to start the conversation.

"Well, I can see that," she smiled. "Why don't you go start getting your things together. Here, take a couple of garbage bags to put your things in. I swear, everything expanded when we took it out of the car. It seems like we have twice as much as we did before."

She emptied the kitchen cabinet while she talked. "I guess a lot of it is food that we didn't have in the car."

She looked puzzled when she took two jars of peanut butter from the back of the shelf. "Now how did we end up with so much peanut butter? I've already packed one jar and here are two more."

"Mom? I really need to talk to you about something. Can you come sit down in the living room for a minute?"

"Can't it wait until we get packed, Danny?" She turned and saw how serious he looked. "Are you okay? Are you hurt? Did you break something? What's wrong?"

"No, Mom. It's not like that, but it's really, really important that I talk to you right now."

"Okay, Danny. Let's go in the living room and talk."

When they sat, she on the old worn out sofa and Danny on the threadbare chair, she asked, "What's the matter, honey? Whatever it is, I'm sure it will be all right."

"Mom, when we first started staying here, remember the stories you heard about this being some kind of secret government place, real hush-hush?"

"Yes."

He could see by the way her eyebrows drew together that she was even more puzzled than before.

"Well, after I played around here for a few days, I got bored so I walked over to that big building inside the tall fence. There was a gate in the back that was open, so I went in and walked around the building for a while until I noticed a door standing open, so I went in."

"Danny! That was trespassing!"

"Mom, living here is trespassing, but we aren't hurting anything and nobody cares."

"But there might be dangerous chemicals in that building. Something to make you sick."

She grabbed Danny by the shoulders.

"Are you sick? Is that what it is? How do you feel?"

"No, Mom," he leaned away from her. "Please, just let me tell you."

She sat back. "Okay. Tell me."

"For a while I just played over there. There's a little bit of broken down office furniture, and they left plenty of paper and pens and stuff, so I drew pictures. Mom, I'm sorry I lied to you about finding that stuff in one of the houses."

"That's okay, Danny. I'm sure no one would mind your using the office supplies they left behind. Don't worry about it," she said, as she started to stand.

"Please, Mom. Let me finish. That's not all of my story!"

She settled back on the lumpy couch.

"After a while, I started playing in this great big room that has these metal things. They're sort of like a cross between cabinets and machines. There are different sizes and all of them have a hundred million dials and switches and buttons and stuff on the front and all kinds and sizes of doors and drawers. I would put my cars in and pretend it was a car factory. One day I did that and punched a couple of things and there was this noise and another car just like mine came out the chute at the end. So I made a bunch of cars and trucks.

"Mom, I'm sorry, but I lied to you about that, too. That's where I got the extra toys. I made them with that machine.

His mother sat there with her mouth open.

* * *

245

Danny continued. "That's when I got to thinking about saving money on the grocery bill, so I made cans of vegetables and fruit and other stuff. I would just put something in the door, punch the right buttons and click the right switches and another can or whatever would come out the chute. That's why there was extra peanut butter in the cabinet.

"Remember the time we had green beans for supper one night, then you found another can? And you thought you had bought an extra and forgot about it?"

She nodded her head.

"Well, I had made that extra one."

"Danny! It might be poison! It might make us sick!"

She leaned forward and grabbed his wrists, eyes wide in alarm.

"We've been eating it, Mom, for weeks, and it hasn't made us sick yet. I'm coming to the important part. Let me tell the rest of it, please!"

She let go of him and sat back quietly again.

"One day, I was playing over there and some men came."

"Danny! Did they hurt you? You can tell me. Are you in trouble with the government?"

Danny looked pained. "Please, Mom."

"Okay. Okay. I'll listen."

"It was storming outside, so I went and hid in one of the machine cabinets until the men went away. Before I could get out, there was this big clap of thunder and the machine shook and rattled and made weird noises--."

"And I slid out of the chute," said a voice from the kitchen door. Danny's mother looked from boy to boy in shock.

"So now there are two of us," said Danny to the silent woman. "I'm Danny,"

"And I'm Ryan," said the second boy as he advanced from the kitchen.

"See I'm the first one, the one who got into the cabinet, so I get the first name."

"And I'm the one who came next, so I get the second name."

When their mother burst into tears, they hurriedly surrounded her with hugs and assurances.

"It'll be okay, Mom."

"We both love you, Mom."

They expressed their deepest fear, the one thing most frightening to them.

"Please, Mom, keep both of us."

"Please don't get rid of one of us. We'll be good; we promise."

"Yeah, we really, really like each other. We're twins, but better than twins because we have every single memory just the same, and we can talk about everything."

"Please, Mom, please keep us both."

She put her arms around them.

"Of course I'll keep you both. How could I do anything else? You are both my sons and I love you."

She closed her eyes for a moment, and then opened them again.

"It may be harder to provide for three instead of two, but we'll manage, somehow."

She kissed one on the forehead, then the other.

"Twice the clothes, twice the food, twice the college funds — but twice the love. Yes, we'll make it."

Danny jumped up and headed toward the kitchen.

"Mom, you don't have to worry about that part of it," said Ryan. He rushed to join his brother. Together they pulled a big duffel bag into the living room and placed it in front of their mother.

"We've got the college fund taken care of," Danny said.

Ryan opened the duffel and let the bills spill out onto the floor.

NANCY SMITH GIBSON

Nancy Smith Gibson lives in the country near Hot Springs, Arkansas. On the trip to town she listens to NPR radio. One afternoon a scientist on the "Science Friday" program said someday everyone would have a cabinet-like device connected to their computer and when they want to order something online, the information will be sent to their home device. Upon paying, the order will be produced immediately in their home from the carbon-stocked apparatus.

Hmm, she thought, what trouble could a kid get into with such a piece of equipment?

Thus "The Replicator" was born.

PAST REALITIES

By Laurie Darroch-Meekis

Cobwebs in the attic room,
draped across the eves and corners of old wood,
as time passes slowly in the dark.
No voices heard in countless ages,
to break the silence with life.
Cramped spaces between bits of lives,
        piled high in disarray,
threatening to tumble down in dust on the slatted floor.
Stored here to be retrieved by future generations,
where ancestors and old accounts are kept,
in weathered trunks and boxes,
shut tightly with brass locks, ancient keys to life,
metal in a dark patina aged with the years of neglect.
Every box holds memories, enshrouded in stale air,
a treasure trove of history packed away to be discovered,
or not meant to be found
wrapped in satin ribbons,
and yellowed newspapers brittle with time,
tucked safely between sheets of tissues,
        and signed documents,
long faded photographs in boxes tied in twine,
secrets lovingly stored away until another time,
unremembered pieces of lives that built the present,
Past realities, encased in silence,
at the top of the stairs…waiting patiently.

SHANNON LAUSCH

Shannon Lausch has a lifelong love of books that has most recently culminated with her writing her own stories. After graduating from North Central College in Naperville, Ill., in 2008, she wrote for several websites and did editing work for a video game company. Joining the Accentuate Writers Forum, she soon discovered the joys of making stuff up.

Considering fantasy allows this more than any other genre, it is what she most likes to write. This is her first work of fiction. Besides wandering around in this new-found world of fiction, she enjoys exploring the "real" world's past through archives. As time machines have not yet been invented, she feels archives are currently the best mode of travel. Hollinger boxes will have to suffice until physicists get around to manipulating time and space. She is currently pursuing a master's degree in library and information science at the University of Illinois Urbana-Champaign.

THE INTERVENTION THAT WASN'T

By Shannon Lausch

"Cut!" Aiko cried.

Ken could feel his blood pressure rising. His interview subject, the junior senator of Virginia, smiled sheepishly.

"What is it this time?" Ken snapped.

"Boom mic shadow," Aiko said.

"Ah, well. At least it's a gorgeous day to be outside, am I right?" said Senator Clement, squinting at the sun.

It was perfect weather: dry and warm with a gentle, cool breeze. A shot of Ken and Senator Clement chatting and strolling along the senator's expansive lawn seemed ideal to close what had been a pleasant interview.

"Sorry," the boom operator said.

Ken snorted. The operator's very existence bothered Ken. He didn't trust men who were a head shorter than him or who wore what was probably secondhand clothing or chewed gum on the job. However, most vexing of all was the man's intentionally modified pointy ears.

Ken shook his head.

"Five, four, three..." Aiko signaled to Ken to restart.

"So, Senator Clement, what will you do to change the culture of corruption in Washington now that you've been elected?" Ken asked.

"Why, Kenny, as a Washington outsider, I aim to shake things up. Put an end to earmarks and wasteful spending. It's ridiculous the hold lobbyists have on politicians. We need to remember that we serve the American people."

Ken mentally rolled his eyes at the canned response. The senator was a rising star in Ken's party of choice, so he let the answer go without an argument.

"But your opponents would have otherwise, wouldn't they?" Ken replied. "Are you promising to take them on?"

"I promise," Senator Clement. "I—"

"Cut!"

Ken clenched his fists. It was times like those Ken wished he were older, so a vein would pop out in his forehead or neck for dramatic emphasis. He had to settle for a glare and several deepbreaths that tacitly said, "Look how hard I'm trying to calm myself down, but you've made me so angry that I don't know if I can."

"Boom mic got into the shot," Aiko explained. "Almost clobbered you on the head, actually."

"Ah, geez. You've got a newbie on board, huh? That's an industry term, right? Newbie?" Senator Clement said. He laughed.

Ken brushed off the senator's question and marched over to Aiko, almost trampling a bed of well-groomed Pink Moss.

"Why don't you just fire the little bastard?" he hissed.

"Why? Why don't I fire him?" Aiko hissed back. "Because of *you*! No one wants to work with you. These are all," she lowered her voice further still, "bottom-of-the-barrel techies. And if you try to intimidate this new guy into leaving, I swear I will end you."

Ken bit his lower lip. "I'm warning you," he said, choosing to ignore every word she said. "This is the last shot I'm going to do. And then I'm through! It's either me or him," and he jabbed a finger toward his newest nemesis.

Ken jogged back to his place before Aiko could give another scathing reply, so she followed him. Rather than confronting Ken, she went to the boom operator and instructed him on how to put the mic over his shoulders the proper way.

That was her problem, Ken deduced. Forty-two, and she was still working at that pint-sized station, because she didn't have the heart to mow down incompetents and look out for herself.

Aiko finished her impromptu lesson and signaled to Ken the cameras were once again rolling.

"So, Senator Clement," Ken restarted. "What will you do to change the culture of corruption..."

Then, Ken realized that Senator Clement was no longer beside him, and Aiko was no longer in front of him. Or the cameras surrounding him. Or the emerald green lawn below him. Or anything at all.

He was in a pitch black void.

∞∞∞

Aiko dropped her clipboard and rushed to the unconscious Ken. Senator Clement was already stooped over Ken, checking for a pulse.

"Hey, Kenny! Wake up! C'mon. Wake up!" he shouted.

"Does he have a pulse?" Aiko asked.

"I can't find one."

"Move it!"

Aiko shoved Senator Clement out of the way. She gripped Ken's wrist and prayed she would feel a beat. Relief flooded her when she felt a little throb underneath her thumb. His breathing also seemed regular.

"Call an ambulance," Aiko yelled to one of the camera operators. "His vitals are fine as far as I can tell. But he just won't come to."

"Huh," Senator Clement said. "Never realized the dangers of boom mics."

"It doesn't make any sense," Aiko said. "Boom mics aren't even heavy. It must have been something else. Maybe he passed out for other reasons."

"Wait a minute. Where's that newbie?" Senator Clement asked.

Aiko looked around for the boom operator, but he was gone.

"Damn," she said. "Lost another one."

⋘⋙

Ken blinked a few times. He was sprawled on the ground. He pushed himself up off the hard dirt and scanned his surroundings. Tall grass stretched around him for a great distance, maybe miles. Everything was blurry.

He didn't know how he'd gotten there or what he'd been doing before he arrived. He wondered if he'd been dreaming, but it didn't feel like a dream.

Two indistinct figures slowly approached him, breaking his thoughts.

"So Nark actually came through?" one of them asked the other.

"It would appear so, though I imagined a much grander personage than this mere fellow."

Ken squinted. Two young women stood before him, one wearing a deep green dress. Blond curly hair flowed down to her waist, and her bemused brown eyes stared through him. The other had short-cropped brown hair and an oval face. She was dressed plainly in a tan cotton blouse and dark brown wool trousers. Curiously, both wore formfitting steel breast plates.

Ken smiled. If it were a dream, it was turning out quite nicely.

"So, ladies," he said, winking at the woman in green. "Do you like loofahs?"

"Loofah? What is a loofah, Elen?" asked the brown-haired woman.

"I think he's being vulgar, Brigit," Elen said, grim-faced.

Ken wondered why the women weren't all over him yet. If it was a dream, it was his dream, after all. He figured everything in a dream should obey his thoughts. He thought he might need to be a bit more straightforward.

"Ladies, come on, off with your clothes," he said.

"*What*? You cretin!" Brigit exclaimed.

"Pervert!"Elen said, and she slapped his face.

His cheek stung as though hot pins had pricked it. Ken was confused. That slap had hurt. Dreams weren't supposed to hurt. His blurry vision and senses sharpened, and a dreadful realization slowly built in his mind.

"Where's Nark and Lugh?" Elen said. She put her hand against her forehead to block the shining sun and looked off into the distance.

"Who would know when or whether Lugh may return? But I would expect Nark to rejoin us any moment now," Brigit replied.

"Nark better get here. I can't believe he dumped this creep on us and took off," Elen said.

"I had to go change," a hurt voice announced.

Ken jumped. Out of nowhere appeared someone familiar. The face was the same, but the clothes were different, at least, somewhat; they still reeked of second-handedness. He was wearing a rusty breastplate, torn wool trousers and a long-sleeved linen shirt smudged with dark marks.

"Dammit, Nark! Stop popping up on us," Elen said. She gave him a playful shove.

"You!" Ken managed to sputter.

The man grinned.

While Ken would normally be more concerned with a man materializing out of thin air, his state of mind could only concentrate on the mundane under the outlandish circumstances.

"You're that idiot who can't even hold a boom mic the right way!" Ken spat, his memory fully restored.

"Oh, come on. It was my first day on the job. You could've given me some encouragement, Mr. Bryce," the man said, giving a deep frown.

"I want to know —"

Elen interrupted. "Nark, are you sure this is who we need? He's not that impressive."

"I dunno. I just got who Brigit told me to get," Nark replied. He yawned and rubbed the back of his head.

As Elen and Nark argued over whether Ken was suitable for whatever it was they wanted him for, Ken massaged his eyes and paced around the field, muttering. Everything was real, he realized. He had spent his first moments there too dazed to concentrate. However, there was no denying that what he was going through wasn't a dream. While it was easy to mistake a dream as reality, there was no mistaking reality for a dream.

Ken noticed something else he hadn't before: All three of the people in the field had swords strapped to their waists. He could see the plain steel hilts sticking out of their sheaths.

He wondered how he'd ended up there. He mentally retraced his steps: he woke up early that morning for his special interview, he ate breakfast at the studio, he went to Senator Clement's estate, he was wrapping up the interview with the senator outside, and that's where his memory stopped.

What he didn't know was how long had he been with the loonies. Piles of small bags and knapsacks were strewn across the ground, barely visible through the tall grass. It looked as though they'd been camping there. He had no idea how they'd managed to kidnap him.

"What the hell did you do?" Ken shouted. "Knock me out? Drug me? Where am I?"

Nark turned away from his argument with Elen. Elen wrinkled her nose and sighed.

"Same place as you were ten minutes ago. Albeit," Nark said, with a little cough, "on a different plane."

"Plane? You mean like dimension?" asked Ken. "Do you really expect me to believe that?"

"I thought you'd get it the first time I did it," said Nark, and he grabbed a handful of Matua prairie grass.

"See? Look."

The grass vanished in the palm of his hand.

"So, you're a magician. I bet the grass is up your sleeve," Ken sneered. He dug in his pockets for his cell phone, but it was gone. "So, you stole my cell phone, huh? Well, it doesn't matter. There has to be someone around here. I'll walk."

"You really shouldn't leave," Nark said.

"Really? What are you going to do? Attack me with a sword?"

"It's dangerous out there," Nark explained. "Of course, if you want to leave, we can't stop you. But there are monsters out there."

"I'll take my chances," Ken said. "If I come across any monsters, I'll tell them you said hi."

"Right," said Elen. "You do that then."

Ken marched away from the trio, stumbling in the thigh-high grass and tangled brush.

"But this is foolish," Ken heard Brigit exclaim. "We must stop him. Why not bind him with ropes?"

Ken strained his ears to listen to the rest of their conversation, but he heard nothing. When he glanced back, the trio was huddled together, whispering.

Ken continued his slow escape. Swarms of tiny insects buzzed around his head. Swatting them proved to be only a temporary fix, since they would cluster back together the moment his arms stopped swinging. To help ignore them, he amused himself with thoughts of how his kidnapping was unfolding. He wondered if anybody knew yet and whether or not he'd make national news for it. Ken scoffed at his own question. *Of course* he would make national news. CNN and Fox News were both competing to hire him. They would surely run a story about the disappearance of an up-and-coming political commentator.

Ken smiled. His kidnapping would surely skyrocket his popularity. Maybe he'd even be considered heroic. He could envision the headlines: *Commentator Single-handedly Escapes Deranged Attackers.* Fox News or CNN would probably scramble to give him an even better offer after the whole thing was over. Ken mused about how he could trigger a bidding war between the two networks.

After an hour of walking, the scenery remained unchanged. Doubts seeped into Ken's mind, while he asked himself questions: *What if I have to sleep out here tonight? What if I'm days away from any kind of civilization? What if I can't find any water?*

Ken resolved to find a road somewhere. That was his best chance of finding someone who could help.

He was somewhat surprised that he didn't feel the least bit tired or hot, which was unusual considering he was wearing a dark suit. Not even continually swiping at the troublesome bugs was taxing. Maybe he didn't give his stamina enough credit.

A rustle in the grass interrupted his musings, but he figured it was probably a snake or a small rodent. He shuddered at the thought but took another step forward. That's when he tripped over something—something big.He landed on a smooth, hard surface.

"What the hell?"

Picking himself back up, he examined the object. He ran a hand over its surface. A few ridges marred its otherwise glassy exterior. A dull brown, it resembled a turtle shell. Ken estimated it was about a foot and a half tall and four feet long. He kicked it. No response.

Ken decided to move on. No sense wasting time on a rock. He continued his aimless journey.

"*Garrrooouuu.*"

Ken threw a nervous glance back. He'd never heard anything like that before.

"*Garrrooouuu.*"

Shit, thought Ken. *Shit, shit, shit.* There was no mistaking that a living—*angry*—thing was making that sound. He ran, but he soon met another massive rock, almost falling over that one too.

"*Garrrooouuu.*"

Ken's heart dropped when he realized the growl was emanating from the rock in front of him.

He spun around. The same rock he examined only moments ago was right behind him. The two moved to pin him between them. Ken tried to run to his left, then to the right, but two more were scuttling toward him in both directions. Squinting through the undergrowth of dead grass, Ken could see horrifically thick crablike legs coming from underneath what he decided must be shells.

He was surrounded. He jumped onto the back of the nearest rock crab, leapt off and tried to run.

Before he could move even a foot away, a claw shot out and snatched his leg. A sudden pull caused him to fall hard against the ground. The pincer squeezed his leg. Ken tried kicking the claws, but the creature's grip only tightened.

"Shit," Ken mumbled. *This is it.*

Ken suddenly found himself twirling around on the ground. When he reoriented himself, he saw his attacker had been turned upside down. In fact, all four of the creatures were on their backs, their eight legs flailing in the air. Still stuck in the pincer's grip, Ken tried to pull away but failed.

"Need some help?" a voice called.

"What do you think?" Ken shouted. He struggled to sit up before the three could see him in such a vulnerable position.

A smiling Nark and Brigit appeared before him.

"What are these things anyway?" Ken said, continuing to struggle as though he were perfectly capable of helping himself.

"Garous," Nark said. "Can you guess how they get their names?" he added in a cheerful voice.

"Very creative," Ken grumbled. "So, what, are they trying to eat me?

"No, silly," Brigit giggled. "They eat nutberries. They're delightfully friendly creatures. They were doubt-less curious about what you are." She rubbed the over-turned monster's abdomen. It cooed and released Ken's leg.

Ken scrambled to stand up. He brushed his jacket's sleeves with his hands, but stopped when he realized not a touch of dirt stained his suit.

"Garous are a nuisance," Elen said. "And really dumb."

Brigit narrowed her eyebrows and frowned slightly.

"Would you like our company now, Mr. Bryce?" Nark asked with a smug smile.

"Hell, no. I want you to send me back to my plane with your voodoo magic. Right now," Ken said.

"Oh, so now you believe me," Nark said, arms folded.

Ken scowled. "Just do it, okay?"

"No. Not unless you do us a favor," Nark replied.

"Forget it then. I'll find someone else to send me back," Ken said, and turned away.

"No, you won't," Elen said. "Nark here is one of only two plane crossers on this entire continent. The other one, well, he's not as nice."

"I'll take my chances," Ken said and continued his hike.

"Suit yourself," Elen said, "but if garous give you trouble, you're really not going to like the man-eating raiders."

Ken stopped and whirled around. "The *what*?"

"Giant birds. Who like to attack humans," Elen answered. "Especially ones that travel alone. Thanks to me, our group can blend into the background, and we don't attract any nasty monsters. That's how we followed you without your noticing."

Ken muttered and kicked dead grass into the air. "Fine. I'll do you a favor. What is it?"

Brigit gave a wild cheer and clapped her hands.

"Perfect," Nark said. "All you have to do is come with us, unlock what we need, and I'll send you back. I promise."

"How long is this going to take?" Ken asked. "I'm a busy man." He lifted up his sleeve to look pointedly at his Rolex watch, only to discover that, too, was missing.

"We need to stop at an inn about a mile away to see if Lugh is waiting for us there. If he has the key, this whole adventure could be over in hours," Nark said.

"Well, why didn't you tell me all of this earlier?" Ken asked.

"You were headed in the direction we wanted to go anyway," Nark said, shrugging. "It was easier not to argue with you."

The group trudged off, leaving the struggling garous behind.

"They'll get back on their feet eventually," reassured Elen to a concerned Brigit. The sky became a deeper blue as the afternoon wore on. Chipper chirps and sweet songs from unseen birds unnerved Ken so much that he walked much closer to his new companions than he would have liked.

After some time of silence, Ken pointed at Elen and said, "So, you can turn us invisible."

"I suppose if you ignored all the nuances of my power, yes, you could say that," she replied.

"And you," Ken continued, pointing at Nark, "are an elf who can teleport and travel to different dimensions."

"What? I'm not an elf! And I can't exactly teleport. I *cross* planes," said Nark. Ken was pleased to see Nark looked as though he sucked on something sour. Ken enjoyed it when he discovered a person's greatest insecurity.

"Why can't you *cross* into my world and grab a gun? Or some other kind of weapon? You wouldn't have to hide from monsters anymore, and you'd be the most powerful guy here," Ken said, and he snapped his fingers. "See? I haven't been here two hours yet, and I could figure out how to exploit your power better than you can."

"Things don't last long here when they're from another realm. They'll stay three minutes at best," Nark said stiffly.

"So, wait a minute, why didn't I go back?" Ken asked, eyes wide.

"I found a way around that for people," Nark said.

"Well, don't tell me everything at once," Ken muttered. A few more silent minutes passed.

"And what's your power, um, Brigit, is it?" Ken asked.

"I'm the greatest poet in all the land," she said proudly.

"What the hell kind of sucky power is that?" Ken said.

"I'll have you know that *I'm* the one that solved the riddle and knew that *you* would qualify as our gateway key," she said, fists clenched.

"I helped," muttered Nark.

"What do you mean, 'key'?" Ken asked.

"We may as well tell you," Elen said. "We're hunting for a treasure. A very valuable treasure. We need keys. We have the Bane Key. Our partner Lugh went to get the Chaste Key. But the key that unlocks the treasure itself is a sentient, otherworldly person. Brigit?"

"The riddle was inscribed on the base of the Tower of Nysokani, where we found the Bane Key. I translated it from its original language in Cipet," Brigit explained.

She closed her eyes as though in a trance.

Otherworldly disseminators of doom,
Self-proclaimed seers forever forecasting gloom,
Climbing in power ever higher,
Straying watchers by their desires
Shall unlock what lies beneath
Their utmost wish within reach.

"In other words, we needed to find a rising, successful pundit from your world," Nark said.

"I still don't understand what—exactly—pundits do, Nark," Brigit complained.

"First, it's political commentator, not pundit,'" Ken said. "Secondly, we analyze the news and give our take on

it. That helps people watching us make their own deci-
sions. We watch out for our viewers."

Nark snorted.

"How nice for you," Elen said. "It must be fantastic to
be paid to just run your mouth."

"Oh, please. My opinions are *very* valuable. I make
and break politicians. But why? Why take me?" Ken
asked. As much as it pained him to admit it, there were
many others who were rising stars in the world of broadcast journalism.

"Your studio was hiring," Nark said with a shrug.
"Plus, you were closest to the Telurei Cave, which is where
the treasure is."

Ken let silence wash over the group again. They were
soon steadily climbing over one of the few hills and —
cottages, blessed cottages — appeared over the horizon.
Ken breathed a sigh of relief. He always thought that cob-
blestone cottages with thatched roofs in the twenty-first
century were for deluded romantics. But at that moment,
he welcomed them as a sign of civilization.

One lonely, dusty road separated the rows of homes.
Ken heard sheep bleating somewhere in the distance and
saw a lone person tending to a garden in front of one of
the cottages. Ken was relieved to see nothing unusual in-
habiting the plot, only broad green leaves poking out
through the ground.

"C'mon," Nark said. "The inn's this way."

The only distinguishing feature separating the inn
from the rest of the cottages was a wooden sign hanging
above the entrance. It depicted a coat of arms with a poor-
ly drawn black horse standing on its hind legs. The words
"Halworthe Inn" painted in spiky handwriting stood

above the illustration.

The bare wooden floorboards creaked when the group stepped through the threshold. The smell of beer and poorly-cooked meat greeted Ken's nose. It was packed inside. There weren't enough tables or stools for even half of the patrons. But the part of Ken that had relaxed when he felt some sense of normalcy when he entered the village vanished when he examined the clientele.

Ken groaned. What he saw inside the inn helped him to appreciate Nark as a full-fledged human. Humans far outnumbered the other *things* at the inn, but one nonhuman patron, in Ken's opinion, was too many—let alone dozens.

A group of squat, muscular beings with squashed noses were the second largest group populating the inn. They looked as though someone took a tall, brawny person, tried to squish them into a four foot tall frame and painted them a grayish-purple.

Ken's limited knowledge of fantasy creatures placed them under the general heading of trolls. The other humanoid creatures were translucent. Most were tall and thin, as though they had been stretched out. One winked at him. Ken turned away and shuddered.

Most of the crowd was congregated into small groups. The room buzzed with conversation, and an occasional burst of laughter rose above the din.

Ken then noticed someone who walked among his group as though he were a member.

"Who the hell are you?" Ken blurted out.

"Seshat, the scribe," the man answered without looking up. He was pale and lean man and dressed in plain black robes. He moved his right hand in a series of swishing motions. Ken tried to peer over the man's shoulder, but Seshat turned to block his view.

"He's the artist who's been assigned to us," Nark explained. "He's normally invisible, but there are anti-magic shields in this inn. Seshat serializes our group's progress and publishes it on a weekly basis."

"Wait. What?" Ken asked. The group jostled through the crowd with Brigit leading the way toward somewhere in the back of the room.

"We're not the only ones looking to unlock the treasure. It's a competition," Elen explained. "Whoever finds and unlocks the treasure wins fifty thousand gold coins. Every week, scribes send in their latest renditions, and they're mass-produced somewhere. They sell them all over the continent. Or at least we've heard. They run at least a month behind."

"If we don't win, we at least gain some fame," Brigit added. She stood on the tip of her toes, Ken assumed to obtain a better view of the crowd.

"But wait, do you get the treasure *and* the gold coins?" Ken asked, narrowly avoiding a barmaid who rushed by with two goblets of red wine.

"No, just the gold. The treasure is probably some rare artifact, but it doesn't matter anyway. Whoever's running the competition is making more than enough money by selling the chronicles," Nark said.

"How many people are competing?" Ken asked.

"Who knows? I've heard inns all across the Eastern seaboard have been serving as gathering points for hundreds of groups," Elen said. "There's even other teams at this inn right now. I know that's the Esprit Team over there," she pointed to the translucent beings, "a team of departed spirits. They're a bit unsociable. And that's the Brutes over there." She pointed to a group of trolls.

"Bunch of copycats," Nark muttered. "Ripped off our name of Celt Squad."

Brigit shrieked. "Look! Lugh is here!"

She streaked past humans and brutes to someone who looked like a combination of the two. But, Ken reasoned to himself, it was mostly the man's cumbersome armor that gave the impression of bulk, and of course the large pack sitting atop his back. With some disapproval, Ken also noticed black hair tumbling down to the man's shoulders.

A few trolls stared when Brigit hugged Lugh, who was leaning against the far-right corner.

Ken found a nearby wooden stool and grabbed it before anyone else could claim it. He sat, his chin in his hands, while Nark, Brigit, and Elen gathered around Lugh.

"Got it," Lugh whispered. Ken could see him try to surreptitiously show the three a cobalt-colored key. In the center of the key's head, a white opal glistened. Ken stared at the key while the others listened to Lugh's tale.

The flickering candlelight played with the opal's iridescence. Flashes of luminous yellows, oranges, greens and blues invaded Ken's mind. Ken felt the lids of his eyes drooping. He tried to refocus on the group's reunion with Lugh, but his eyes would not cooperate. His lids closed, and sleep seized him.

⋙⋘

Aiko looked at her watch. A quarter past five.

She didn't want to be there, but when she heard Ken's

closest family lived twelve hours away, she felt someone had to look over him until they arrived. Alas, she had drawn the shortest straw back at the studio.

The off-white linoleum floor and bare walls didn't help her discomfort. Neither did Ken's presence only a couple feet away, attached to all kinds of tubes and machines. She focused on the nurses who bustled around outside the door.

"Well," the doctor said, whishing into the room, "we've analyzed the MRI results. There are no abnormalities as far as we can tell."

"Any theories?" she asked.

"No, none so far. Besides the fact he's in a coma, he's perfectly healthy," the doctor replied.

Aiko grunted. "So it's a medical mystery, then?"

The doctor sighed and scribbled on her clipboard. "We'll run some more tests. I'm sure we'll find the cause soon."

Aiko sank back as much as she could into her armless, cushionless chair. She glanced at Ken and sat up straighter.

"Hey! Did you see that? His eyelids just twitched!"

＊＊＊

"Hey! Hey, Ken! Yoo-hoo! Ken! We're leaving!"

Ken woke to see Elen frantically waving her hand in front of his face. Elen's voice and the tinkling sound of glass breaking somewhere had roused Ken from his stupor.

Lugh and Brigit stared at him with concern. Nark was ashen-faced.

"I'm in the hospital?" Ken asked, blinking.

"Forget it," Nark said. "This will all be over with

soon."

The concerned look on Nark's face relaxed as he managed to gently guide Ken off the stool.

"Aha. I see what's happening now," Ken said, catching his balance.

"What?" Nark said, his voice a little higher than usual.

"I know what this is about," Ken said.

"Yeah," Elen said, tapping her foot. "We just told you about the competition--"

It was an intervention, Ken decided, a spiritual intervention. Growing up, Ken always loved the movies *It's A Wonderful Life*, *A Christmas Carol* and *The Wizard of Oz*. Something similar was happening to him. He knew it. The universe was trying to guide him through a lifelike dream. It wanted to show him something, but he didn't know why. He was generous—sort of. People needed a kick in the ass sometimes, and Ken thought it was his role in life to be the ass kicker. Or maybe the universe was simply encouraging him to stay the same. He didn't know, but he was curious.

"We've got to get going," Nark urged, his face still pale. "C'mon, the cave's an hour walk from here."

The group left the inn. The sun was setting, but instead of creating golden, heavenly laces across the sky as Ken expected after a revelation as holy as his, the sunset was rather dull. The sky was merely turning a darker, deeper blue with a flare of red where the sun met the horizon.

"Did you blend us, Elen?" Brigit asked.

"Of course," she replied.

Ken looked back. Members of the Brute Squad poked their craggy heads out the door. One held a club with spikes.

"Thought they could steal our keys from us, huh?" Lugh said with a smirk.

The group continued eastward. The grass gradually became stubbier and sparser until rocks eventually took over completely. While the happily reunited group chattered away, Ken was once again lost in his thoughts. He wondered if anyone in the quartet was his spiritual mentor and what part he had yet to play in the dream world. But if the journey was all in his head, he wasn't sure it really mattered.

The group stopped when they reached something that looked like a solid mound of rough rock. It was as big as one of the cottages back at the village. Elen ran a hand across the front of it.

"Sealed," she said. "But it's definitely hollow right through this area." She rapped the rock with her fist.

"Lugh, I think you know what you need to do," Nark said.

"Gotcha."Lugh took a pickaxe out of his enormous pack and hacked away at the rocky exterior. In no time, the front façade crumbled to reveal an entrance.

Ken couldn't see anything ahead. Brigit lit a candle. It must have been imbued with some kind of magic, Ken guessed, since it lit up its surroundings with an intensity that belied its small size. A seemingly endless steep slope lay before them.

"Here we go," Elen said.

Down, down, down they trekked. Nark stumbled a few times, but the overall path was smooth with a few pebbles here and there. Ken was surprised how dry the cave seemed. He expected to hear echoes of water trickles or see moisture gathering on the rust-colored rocks. He couldn't hear any signs of life — only the labored breaths of the Celts as they journeyed deeper into the earth's depths.

After what seemed like hours of walking, they reached what appeared to be a dead end. Lugh, who was drenched with sweat, lifted his pickaxe again.

"No, no, Lugh," Elen said, and Ken noticed her hair looked limp and frizzled. "I think there's a switch here." She pushed a protruding stone next to her. The wall in front of them rumbled and rose shakily into the rock ceiling above. Red dust fell, and Brigit coughed.

Ken gasped. The cavern ahead of them was brilliantly lit. Blinded at first, his eyes slowly adjusted to the burst of light. Ken saw a narrow stone path leading to a dais the size of a small stadium. A shimmering cerulean semisphere cut the platform in half from floor to ceiling. It buzzed with a slight hint of malice. More alarming, however, was the pool of molten lava gently lapping the bridge and dais fifty feet below.

On the center of the dais, a man stood alone, his back to the group. Dressed in a gray suit, the man did not seem of the world Ken had spent the day in. Except for his mop of chocolate brown hair, he looked like he could almost be Ken himself.

After carefully crossing the bridge, Ken hurried ahead of the group, mouth agape. The man turned, and Ken stopped mid-stride.

"Ah, welcome," the man said. In Ken's opinion, the best word to describe him would be folksy. He exuded a benign energy. Whether it was his friendly smile or the way his eyes crinkled with happiness, the man had charisma.

"Senator Clement?" Nark said, as stunned as Ken.

"Glyndwr," Brigit whispered, her limps trembling and her eyes growing wide.

"Glyndwr? That's Glyndwr?" Nark said. "Damn it. I thought he'd be, you know, a little more demonic based on what you've said about him. I could've told you that I saw him."

"Nark, when has Brigit ever not resorted to hyperbole?" Elen asked.

Clement, or rather, Glyndwr, cleared his throat.

"The rumors of my—" He paused for emphasis. "...*wickedness* are greatly exaggerated. Now give me the keys, and the reward is yours."

The forcefield behind him created a bright glow along the edges of his frame.

"What's the treasure?" Nark said.

"Oh, it's something that *you* no doubt would very much like to have. Unlike you, I keep tabs on other walkers," he replied. "But we have a deal. You get the gold, and I get the treasure. Keys, please. Including Kenny. Now."

He outstretched the palm of his hand.

"I'm not letting you have anything that you would want," Elen said, hands on her hips. Lugh, Nark, and Brigit nodded in agreement. Ken looked from them to Clement and back again in confusion.

"Ah, non-cooperators?" Glyndwr asked. "Strange time to try to be noble."

Elen squinted her eyes, concentrating.

Seshat suddenly reappeared among the group. Ken looked at him and saw his eyes widened.

"I'm afraid I'll allow only my powers to work down here. Sorry I had to disturb you, Seshat, but Elen there was trying to blend. We can't have that," Glyndwr said, giving them a classic toothy grin.

Elen, Lugh, Nark, and Brigit drew their swords.

"Ah, how adorable," Glyndwr said. "Fine. If you wish to fight, I suppose I'll have to disarm you."

Glyndwr muttered for several seconds, and his feet lifted off the ground. He rose about a foot. Ken was trying to determine whether he should be impressed when he heard cries behind him. He whipped around to see.

The shadows cast by the Celt Squad rose from the ground. Paper thin at first, they gradually filled out and became inky blobs that replicated their owners' physique. As they formed, the group desperately tried to hack at them with swords, but the weapons became lodged in them as though the shadows were made of tar. Seshat stood still, quill limp in his hand.

"Hey, Clement! Cut that out!" Ken shouted. He looked over his shoulder at the evil man.

To Ken's surprise, Glyndwr lazily drifted down to the ground.

"Oh. I didn't think that would work," Ken said, then turned back to his friends. Each shadow had successfully restrained its counterpart and covered its owner's mouth with an inchoate hand.

"Dammit, Clement, I said to leave them alone," Ken said.

Glyndwr smiled. "Forget them, Ken. Come to me."

"Let them go, Clement," Ken said. "I'm not helping you."

"Why? They were only using you. I can send you back

myself."

"Wait a minute. *You're* the other plane crosser?" Ken asked. "If you're a plane crosser, why didn't you just take me yourself? Or someone else? Why the contest?"

"Ah, yes," Glyndwr said. "Frankly, I didn't know it was possible to yank someone's spirit out and cross it over. I expected the contestants to locate a plane portal, find a target, drug them with Satargido and bring them back here. Why not make money *and* get others to do the work for me? I got the idea from your world. *The Amazing Race* is a fantastic bit of programming, by the by."

"Wait a minute. My spirit was yanked?" Ken frowned and patted himself up and down. "Look how solid I am."

Glyndwr seized on Ken's question. "You're a particu-lar-ly concentrated spirit. That man," he pointed at Nark, "stole your spirit for a game. He could've killed you. All because his group was trying to take a shortcut. Satargido is a legendary plant that delays otherworldly organisms from quickly departing back to their realm. It's much saf-er."

It wasn't a spiritual intervention, Ken realized. He was simply a pawn, a tool, in some dumb game. Bitter and feeling foolish, he was at a loss for words for the first time in his life. Ken could vaguely hear the muffled cries of the Celt Squad behind him.

"Come to me, Kenny," Glyndwr said, breaking the si-lence. "We'll unlock the telestone together."

"Telestone?" Ken asked. "Why should I care about this telestone?"

Glyndwr sighed. "The telestone is an ancient piece of magic that would allow me to permanently take objects with me on my jaunts. Do you understand what this means?"

Ken blanched and backed away. "Oh, no. You're crazy if you think I'm going to let you take all kinds of wackos into my world."

"I assure you, your world is safe. Do you know how much time it would take to clean it up? It would be far too much work."

Ken's forehead wrinkled first in confusion and then in frustration when he realized Clement had insulted his world.

"As senator and member of the Armed Services Committee, I do have access to some very nice weapons this world has never seen."

Ken realized the Clement had thought along the same lines he had thought about weapons when he'd first awoken in the new world. He felt a little ashamed to be sharing those types of thoughts with the strange man.

"What do you say? I'll let you have your world if you let me take mine. I could give you magicks here that will help you on your way to the top. You could even obtain the presidency, if you wish."

There it was: the classic good versus evil choice. But Ken realized that it wasn't a test; it wasn't a divine intervention after all. If Ken chose the good, he figured there was no way Glyndwr would let him walk away. If he chose the evil, he wasn't so certain he'd get to walk away then either. When it came right down to it, Ken figured he was screwed no matter what he chose.

"Make your decision, Ken," Glyndwr said. "I'm tired of explaining things to you."

Ken stepped toward the force field, but he said nothing.

"Good choice," Glyndwr said. "Now, place your hands on the center of the shield, and I'll take the other keys from those filthy degenerates."

When Glyndwr turned around, Ken ran, racing along the width of the dais.

"Wait! Where do you think you're going?" Glyndwr shrieked. Ken could see a long shadow lifting from the floor behind him, but it would be too late.

Ken dove off the platform. In the short seconds it took to fall, he fervently hoped, and even quickly prayed, that if he died in that world in spirit, he would survive in body in his world. He closed his eyes just before the red hot lava lapped up and made contact with his flesh.

❦

There was a bang on Ken's dressing room door. He pulled it open and saw Aiko standing there.

"What is it?" Ken asked.

"Breaking news," she announced breathlessly. "Senator Clement's been missing for six days. No one knows what's happened to him. His staff has been covering it up." She pushed past Ken into the room. He followed her and sat in front of his make-up mirror.

"Hmm." He picked up a comb and ran it through his black hair, examining his reflection in the mirror.

"That's all you can say, just 'hmm'? This is major! You interviewed the guy last week. Granted, it was an incomplete interview, but it was apparently the last time he was seen. The cable networks are going nuts."

When Ken didn't respond right away, Aiko said, "Speaking of which, have you decided yet?"

"Yep."

"Okay," she said, drawing out the last syllable. "Who

are you going with?"

"Neither," Ken said, putting down his comb.

"What? But that was your dream," Aiko replied.

"Well, you know, they only wanted me to act like a nutcase. I want to be taken more seriously," Ken said, straightening his tie.

"Since when?"Aiko asked. "Look. Maybe you should go back to the hospital and have them reexamine your head. They never did figure out what was wrong with you."

"I'm fine," Ken insisted.

Aiko looked at him suspiciously. "Are you sure?"

"Excuse me?" a young intern interrupted, poking his head into the room. He held up a dark blue jacket. "This is Mr. Bryce's drycleaning."

Ken gazed at the jacket. A small wrinkle disfigured its otherwise pristine appearance. He turned to an intern and asked, "Did you hang this up in your car, or did you just throw it in your trunk?"

"Erm…" the intern mumbled, shifting uncomfortably and not making eye contact.

"Get the hell out of my sight! And take it back to the cleaners!" Ken snapped.

The intern scampered away.

Aiko sighed. "Do you think you can start working on your people skills next?"

"We'll see," Ken said. After all, he knew change wasn't as easy as television made it out to be.

UNSTABLE GROUND

By Gillian Taber

Rain gurgled in the gutters and downpipes and streamed into the unknown depths beneath her feet. Rachel looked at her shoes and felt the anger she had been struggling to hold at bay rumble up and explode. She stood at the curb and screamed her frustration to the heedless storm that continued to flash and thunder overhead.

People stared at her, morning commuters who couldn't know or care about her ruined shoes, soaked stockings or the fact that she was about to lose the biggest story she had ever been given the chance to cover. All down to the man in the red car who had decided that day was a good time to screech around the corner, cut around the stationary bus and blithely careen through the standing water to save a couple of seconds in his selfish world.

She stood in a growing circle of emptiness, people shuffling away from the crazy lady in the dripping business suit who brandished her umbrella like a sword and bellowed abuse at the receding red blur that had probably ruined her career.

She hurled the umbrella after the car, glared at everyone around her, then rummaged in her pocket for her mobile. She flipped it open and promptly dropped it in a puddle on the ground. She picked it up, heard it give out a pathetic distorted bleep and screamed again when it expired in her hand, drops of water running over its blank screen in mourning. Frustrated, she dropped the phone from fingers numbed with cold and ground it under her heel. She was deeply satisfied with the grinding metallic crunch.

When she straightened up and peered through the sodden curtains of her hair, she saw the bus approach. For a moment, a fleeting, optimistic second, she considered getting on and continuing to the interview. When the doors slid open, they revealed a look on the driver's face that she assumed would be followed by a sentence containing 'not' and 'my bus' with the possible inclusion of 'filthy street walker'. She turned stiffly on her heel and headed into the downpour. She would have to walk to the interview.

She trudged steadily along, distantly aware of the sucking squelch each time her feet hit the ground. Presently, laughter threatened to overtake the anger and frustration. She felt it deep in the pit of her stomach, a burbling, tickling sensation like incipient hunger. The thought of that made the sensation evolve. The skin over her cheeks twitched, tightened, lifted, and the tickle wriggled up through her chest. All the while, rain soaked hair caught in her collar and dripped icy cold water down her neck. She shuddered; although, whether it was from the rain or the creeping giggles, she wasn't sure.

She was hungry. After all, her editor had nicknamed her Ravenous Rachel. Rachel was always the first with her hand in the air, the pick-me girl of the journalism staff, willing to take any story--including the "Hatches, Matches and Dispatches" so despised by reporters at the beginning of their careers. It had paid off, though.

The previous night, she had received **The Email.** Even in her head it was capitalized, bold, underlined. It was the big one, the one that was going to take her to the heady heights of the front page. Her editor had given her the chance to interview a local activist, one of those long-haired greenies who chained themselves to trees on ground about to be plowed under for a shopping mall. It was an opportunity to raise some hard-hitting questions.

She'd imagined asking the questions that most re-porters were too afraid to ask, fearful of rocking the boat, making waves, losing their jobs—the ones about fat cat government that oppressed the little people, taking away their few remaining open spaces and clean air whilst swanning around in limos and private jets. She would ask those questions of the politicians as well as the activists. All she had to do was be at Blue Lake Park by ten-thirty in the morning. Later was not an option, because the bull-dozers were due to move in. After that, all arguments would be as redundant as the mangled remains of trees and grass.

Over, she thought grimly of her career. She kicked soggily at a pebble, missed, tripped and sprawled to her knees, straight into a puddle.

Of course, she thought as the laughter, no longer in her chest but erupting from her throat, howled into the open. She laughed until her stomach hurt, her smart pin-stripe suit turning even darker blue by slow degrees as it soaked up the puddle. Her baby pink blouse turned a deeper almost reddish color with the mingled rain and tears dripping from her chin onto the thin fabric.

A pair of shoes loomed into her view, stopped at her side. They hesitated. The thought of hesitant shoes sent her into further peals of breathless laughter, her throat raw and tasting coppery, her ribs a solid band of pain, her vision almost completely obstructed by tears and rainwater and thus preventing her from seeing the hand that hooked under her elbow and lifted her to her feet.

"I think you need to calm down, miss."

The laughter abruptly disappeared, and she unceremoniously jerked her arm out of his grip and scrubbed at her bleary eyes with her sodden sleeves. She looked up and made out a face to go with the voice. Beyond that, it didn't matter. She turned away, one aching knee causing her to limp. She could feel eyes watching her back while she hitched toward the corner, and she glared back over her shoulder.

"What?" she spat.

He shook his head, turned and walked away without a word. That was worse than any answer he could have given. She felt he thought she wasn't even worth his time, his words. Tears started in her eyes, and she rubbed them away, hoping she didn't leave muddy streaks on her skin.

An hour later, the rain had progressed to torrential, and her clothes were so saturated they were no longer absorbent. She walked into Blue Lake Park, her gait restricted by her drenched skirt that clung, limpet-like, to her legs. To her left, she could see the signs warning of imminent work, bulldozers resting under tarpaulins and the faint sound of men chattering in the Nissan hut behind them. She thought it strange that the very same rain that had ruined her life had given the park a reprieve from its fate.

Hysterical laughter coughed its way over her lips once again, short, maniacal barks that cut through the pounding, incessant sound of rain bouncing off of the gravel path. From the corner of her eye, she saw a large tree, broad and sheltering, and considered taking its offer of a haven. Tiny snippets of pain came from her feet as gravel scattered by the raindrops clipped her skin. Lightning streaked across the navy sky and left her with brilliant white striations across her vision. For a few seconds, thunder drowned every other sound, and in the split second of silence that followed, she heard something that sent her running over the path, desperate to be anywhere but the park.

It hung in the air, a heavy, expectant weight, an absence of sound that invited her to wait for the explosion to follow. Her heel parted company with her right shoe as she fled. She kicked off both shoes and pounded onto the grass, immediately sinking into the mire. Whilst she struggled to haul her feet out of the cloying mud and roots, she felt the impact behind her and heard the impossibly high whine as the lightning struck the tree, followed by a second of silence. It wasn't long enough. She hadn't run far enough, bogged down and immobilized as she was.

There was a single crack, and she drew a relieved breath a mere second before the shockwave hit her. The pressure built at her back, pushing at her like hands in warm gloves, slowly, inexorably shoving her forward, off balance. A second sound exploded: immense, deafening, turning the air about her into a maelstrom of flying debris as fire screamed up from the heart of the stricken tree. She looked up just in time to see a branch sail past her, missing by inches as the force of the madness behind her finally tore her from her feet and sent her face down onto the grass and mud. She could hear things careering over her, dragging the air, distorting it into unnatural patterns. Something struck her calf, piercing and sharp. It was quickly followed by another dagger of pain in her shoulder.

She fought to drag herself to her hands and knees, aware of the urgent need to get away from the crackle of flames and the flying detritus of the shattered tree. Her hands sank deeper into the mud, and she screamed her frustration, her voice lost to the insanity around her. Something hard and unforgiving slammed into the back of her head, and the darkness was complete.

It was the noise that finally brought her back to a species of foggy consciousness. It crept into her brain, gurgling, sucking, insistent. She panicked briefly, unable to breathe until she realized her nose was clogged with grass, her mouth filled with mud. She spit and sneezed while she fought her way back to her knees and gasped as she sat back on her heels and agony seared through her leg. She eased forward, steeled herself, then tipped sideways onto her hip. A five inch piece of wood stood proudly out of her calf. How much was embedded, she refused to contemplate. Her automatic reaction was to pull it free, but something in the back of her mind muttered about severed arteries and she hesitated.

Better to hobble to the nearest help, she decided.

Her decision brought the Nissan hut to mind. She flicked her dripping hair out of her face and felt it catch on something. She gingerly reached over her shoulder to feel something brittle, contorted and metallic buried in her left shoulder. Her mind tried to ask why a tree would have metal in it, but pain slowly flooded from both wounds, pulsing to the beat of her heart, and she couldn't think of anything.

The Nissan hut.

She looked across from her, barely noticing the flaming torch that had once been a tree, and felt her strength drain. She took in the lump of molten twisted metal that had been the workmen's retreat only minutes before. It was unrecognizable, a landscape from a surrealist nightmare. She couldn't comprehend the scene, couldn't imagine one lightning strike eradicating the hut, turning it from a joke-filled haven from the storm to a molten tomb.

Two questions occurred to her simultaneously:

Why weren't there rescuers — ambulances, fire fighters, anyone at all? Aside from the ubiquitous hammering of the rain about her, there was nothing. No flashing lights, no wailing sirens. Even the flames roaring out of the throat of the sundered tree lacked any voice, as if the world had been muted.

The other question was more than her brain could deal with. *How had both the tree and the hut been hit by a single bolt of lightning, when they were on different sides of the path?*

"An error. It happens," a voice near her said.

"Huh?" She startled at the unexpected statement, not having seen anyone since before the lightning strike.

Through the bouncing, twisting, tormenting rain, she vaguely made out a familiar shape. She looked at his shoes, the fact that they appeared dry, failing to completely get a hold on her swirling consciousness.

The hesitant shoes.

No laughter this time, just incipient panic and the thought that maybe she had tipped into insanity after the stress of her morning.

"No, you are sane. Time to go."

On the verge of asking where, she became aware that a sound battered at her ears. It reminded her of the garden after a storm, that slightly unsettling sucking noise as the earth vacuumed up the excess water. It tickled her mind, irritated her eardrums and scattered her thoughts as it grew in volume, gradually drowning out all thought. She clapped her hands to her ears and then shrieked when she felt a pull on her body.

She looked down and realized her legs had begun to disappear into the quagmire beneath her. A bolt of pain shot up from her calf while the sucking stopped being mere noise. She struggled wildly, but the pull continued unabated. She slammed her hands against the ground, trying to brace herself, a second before her traumatized brain warned her against such foolishness. Instantly, her hands began to sink through the grass and mud, tiny stones scraping against her skin as her wrists disappeared before her disbelieving eyes.

"It's easier if you don't struggle. I can't get you down any other way."

She'd forgotten about the man with the hesitant shoes, but now she turned a terror-ravaged face to his. Her question faltered on her lips and was gone while she watched, with all the fascination of a rabbit ensnared by a weaving snake, the whites of his eyes slowly fill with blue threads. It was perhaps a blessing, she thought, that she became trapped there while she sank to her chest. It stopped her mind from hysterically bleating about suffocating when the ground eventually closed over her head.

She vaguely noted that he seemed to be sinking with her, a slight smile on his blue lips.

Blue lips? That couldn't be right. Something about breathing difficulties tried to dredge itself up in her mind, but the ground closed over her chin at that moment, and death became her sole focus. Mud tried to ooze through her clamped lips. She made the mistake of trying to take a final breath, and his eyes, which had turned completely blue, were the last thing she saw. The mud engulfed her head.

In later years, that sinking, sucking, horrific journey through the earth would haunt her nightmares and her daydreams. She could see nothing, but she could feel — and she fervently wished she could not. At first, her body seemed to slide through slippery mud, buffeted by occasional stones and the cold, clammy slithering of worms blindly going about their business. They made her think of coffins and decaying corpses.

Worm food.

She was jerked out of that thought into another as the world about her changed and became steadily drier. The mud became shifting earth, grainy and elusive, as she tried to dig her fingers in for purchase.

The sucking became more urgent and forceful, and she felt stretched thin, elongated as she was pulled through the dry earth into the fine shale beneath. She wanted to scream in pain when she bounced over rocks that grew larger the deeper they went — some of them hot to the touch, which caused her to wonder just how deep she was. Her mouth refused to open when jagged edges nicked her flesh, and she belatedly realized that she had some kind of clear mask over her face, protecting her from the ravages of the journey.

When had that appeared? Did he do it, perhaps whilst I was unconscious?

Her brain had more important things to consider and shoved the thought aside.

She wondered why she couldn't have been totally encased in the same material when the pain started in the base of her spine and bolted up to her neck, finally exploding in her head. It took a couple of seconds to realize her downward fall had ceased and that she was sitting on a blackened, hot floor.

A hand took her elbow and lifted her to her feet, and she gazed around at the cavern. Engrossed, she barely noticed the mask being removed, now a flaccid sheet that resembled cling wrap. Everything glistened, the black walls appearing to sweat in the constant heat. Vibrant red veins caught her eye, running vertically at regular intervals and disappearing into the layers above.

"Where the hell am I?"

"My home," Hesitant Shoes answered, unhanding her when she showed no signs of collapsing without his support.

"I'm dreaming all this, right? I'm unconscious and my mind is wandering."

"As you wish."

To her disbelief, he turned and walked away.

The pain in her calf was all too real, and she tried to stagger after him.

"You're just going to leave me here?"

"Apparently not."

He watched her limp toward him, irritation in the tic under his right eye. His eyes gleamed with what looked like unshed tears overlaying the azure blue. He turned and continued his march away from her.

"A little help?" she snapped. She wished for something to throw after his retreating back.

"Someone will deal with you in the infirmary."

The thought of any kind of medical facility in the depths of the earth further convinced her that she was in some kind of crazy coma dream, but following him seemed to be her only option. She could feel the drag of the wood in her leg and the twist of the metal in her shoulder and gave herself over to self-pity. They traversed a narrow stone bridge across what appeared to be a lake of steaming water and entered a warren of tunnels, each lit with blue-white light given off by glowing stones in the walls.

He stopped by a roughhewn opening and waited for her to wearily lurch up to him. He jerked his head to the opening.

"They'll patch you up in there. I'll be back for you in a couple of hours."

He turned on his heel and disappeared around a bend. Stunned and uneasy, she peered through the gap into a scene of unexpected tranquility. A handful of figures walked back and forth, all dressed in pale blue robes, some carrying trays that gave off glints from metal implements, others carrying papers or linens. When she stepped through the door, one of the figures detached itself from the others and approached, smiling.

"Ah, the overworlder. Come, you must rest and heal."

The woman's arm about Rachel's waist gently encouraged her to move deeper into the strange room and eventually to a stone box, identical to a dozen others scattered around the room. It was roughly cut from a single piece of black granite, and her guide tipped back the lid to reveal what looked like a sarcophagus. Rachel backed up instantly and winced when her legs bumped and pain flared in her calf.

"Please, it will take no more than two hours, and you will sleep through it, I promise." The blue clad woman smiled reassuringly.

"Through what?"

"The healing, of course." Rachel's would-be nurse frowned, and then her face cleared with realization. "Of course, your kind does not have this process. It is simplest if I show you."

She beckoned Rachel to the adjacent box and slid back a hidden window in the side, offering Rachel the chance to look inside while her nurse explained.

"This poor soul was caught in the backfire of a lightning strike on a pylon. He will need several days of healing, I'm afraid."

Beyond the clear crystal window, a body floated in a bath of viscous fluid, his eyes closed, his breathing slow and rhythmic. Even while she watched, Rachel saw the liquid flow together over a badly burned patch of skin on his arm. It seemed to sink into the wound, tiny flecks of dead skin drifting away, sucked out of the liquid by some process she could not imagine and tight new skin replacing the damage.

"How does it work?" she asked when she straightened.

Her nurse shrugged. "It is not for us to ask. It is enough that it does what we cannot. Come. Lamar will expect you to be ready when he returns."

Rachel allowed herself to be led back to the box and helped into it, but then she paused and frowned.

"Who is he? Why did he bring me here?"

"It is not my place to know. Sit, please. You may lie down when the water is high enough to float your injured limb."

"You said I would be asleep!"

Panic threatened to overtake Rachel when the nurse moved to close the lid. The woman smiled, her words enigmatic but soothing.

"You will. Do not doubt it."

The lid closed, and water seeped in through the stone sides and the base. Rachel tensed in the darkness, more terrified of the enclosed space than at any time during the storm that had been the cause for her ending up there. Even while she felt her nerves tauten, the fingers of claustrophobia skittering over her spine, a phosphorescent light began to fill the box, a light that seemed to emanate from the water that had reached her waist. The return of vision helped a little and she eased down, pretending it was a bath to calm her mind. Gradually, she became surrounded by gently lapping waves, their ebb and flow establishing a rhythm that rocked her, lulled her, eventually sending her to oblivious sleep.

A change in the light woke her, and the still-smiling face of her nurse appeared over the rim of the box when the lid lifted away. The water rapidly receded, the stone seeming to suck it up like a sponge, and Rachel accepted a hand out of the healing box.

"How do you feel?" the nurse asked.

Rachel noted an absence of pain when she ran her hands over her body. She gingerly felt down her calf, finding nothing but smooth skin. An exploration of her shoulder yielded the same result. Just as strange, no trace of moisture remained in her clothes or on her skin.

"How?" she managed, and the nurse shrugged, indicating the box.

On the bottom lay the wood that had been buried in Rachel's calf, as well as the contorted metal shard that had torn through her shoulder.

"The water heals," was all the answer the woman gave.

She had no opportunity to inquire further, because quick footsteps sounded behind her. She turned and saw Lamar leaning against the doorway, arms folded across his chest, that impatient tic jumping under his eye. The nurse gave her a light push towards him, but Rachel found herself strangely reluctant to find the answers to the questions swirling in her head. She had the feeling she wouldn't like what she heard. Left with no options, she closed the distance and hurried after him when he turned and headed down the tunnel. The way twisted and turned until she was hopelessly lost, and she knew she could never find her way back on her own.

He halted before a heavy wooden door, studied her critically for a moment, and then nodded and pushed the door open.

"Inside."

She stepped over the threshold and felt her knees buckle under the onslaught of screams that hit her. They rebounded from the high vaulted ceiling, echoed from the walls and rippled the surface of the lake in the center of the cavern. The lake appeared to be fed by a waterfall that cascaded from a distant point near the ceiling. The lake water foamed wildly beneath the onslaught, but nothing could drown the howling, pathetic screams.

Lamar's regard was less harsh than before, his words softer as he took her hand and led her to a deep alcove in the cavern wall. The sound of the screams was muted there, and Rachel drew a shuddering breath, trying to gather her thoughts.

"Painful, isn't it?" he asked, and she nodded.

She finally managed to get her words out. "Where is it coming from?"

"Up there." He pointed at the ceiling. "From your world."

"What is it?"

"The dying screams of every living thing that is killed by man's greed... incompetence, heedless destruction of the world that sustains a pitiful existence. Every reckless action results in those screams."

"I don't understand."

"Of course you don't. You are a mortal, and mortal understanding extends as far as the edge of your daily existence — as far as the next junk meal, the next gadget, the next choice that will deplete the planet further."

His bitterness was acid dripping from lips that she saw were indeed blue. It provoked the inevitable question.

"What are you?"

"I am Vodyanoi."

She gave him a blank look, and he sighed.

"A water spirit. Does your kind no longer tell the old

legends?"

"Not really. We don't believe in sprits."

"Yet, we are forced to believe in you because of what you do to our environment."

"But we're real!"

"And I am not?"

He grabbed her arm, his grip hard enough to bruise, but she was fixated on the texture of his fingers. They were soft and spongy, and when he let her go, they left faint moisture and the clean smell of fast running water.

"I'm dreaming this."

"What will it take?" His anger was vivid, his actions abrupt as he shoved her out of the alcove. The screams poured over her, and the sound battered her to her knees. The hands she clamped over her ears were no barrier to the constant shrieks and cries that soaked into her deepest being.

"Those are my people that you hear. Every one of those voices, millions of them, those dying cries. They drown in water so polluted they cannot breathe. They are poisoned by toxins poured out of your factories and die in agony on riverbanks and seashores. They spend their lives trying to repair the damage done by the humans who deny their very existence. They die of acid burns and septic wounds from the rubbish man leaves behind. But do you have any idea what breaks my heart?"

She could barely hear him above the continuous death cries. She was shaking her head, but whether in negation or confusion, she wasn't sure.

"Thousands of them are dying, simply fading from existence, wasting away because they see no future. They have lost all hope of stemming the tide of poisons that spread ever deeper into the water that sustains us. That sustains you!"

He bellowed the last while he dragged her from her knees and propelled her across the cavern to the shore of the lake. He grabbed the nape of her neck and forced her to look into the waters that boiled for a second and then became crystal clear. She tried to back away, unwilling to see the horrors that floated just below the surface, but he held her still. Contorted, blackened bodies washed back and forth with the ripples created by the screams, limbs missing or ravaged by burns and necrosis.

It was the eyes that finally gave her the strength to pull away, to turn her back on the empty, water-filled orbs that stared hopelessly, vacantly, distorted by the water's movement, black and empty eyes that had once shone as brightly as Lamar's.

Her tears fell, but selfish anger was what poured out of her when she faced Lamar.

"It's not my fault! Why drag me here? Why make me see this? I didn't do it!"

"You never dropped a single piece of paper and walked away as it blew into a stream, into the ocean? You never used a bus, uncaring of where the company dumped its old oil? You never let a tap run when you cleaned those pearly white teeth? You lived a perfect life, spotless, guiltless?"

His calm tone threw her, and she shot a glance at him, at the emptiness behind his eyes, the sag of his shoulders. He looked to her like a soldier who'd seen one too many battles. The thought sparked something in the back of her mind.

"The guy in the healing box. The nurse said he'd been

near a pylon. What was he doing near electricity?"

"His job."

"Sabotage."

It hit her as hard as the lightning had hit the Nissan hut, with the same crystal clarity. Lamar looked uncertain for the first time, his eyes shifting to the water.

"Why?"

She took a step closer while she spoke, laid a hand on the fluid skin of his arm, watching blue blood flow through veins that glowed beneath porcelain delicate skin.

"I had to do something."

He shook her off and began to pace.

"Your kind is taking our world from us. Nothing we did was enough. I had to stop you. Don't you see?"

"Perhaps, but putting the lives of your people in greater danger? Sending them out on what amounts to suicide missions? Has it not occurred to you that it isn't working? I haven't heard one report of downed lines, power outages, or even bodies washing up beside waterways or shores."

He stopped abruptly and spun on feet that she noted were bare, a trace of webbing between his toes.

"You. That's why you are here. I could have left you, but an empath--" He stopped when she frowned and rolled impatient eyes before he hurried on. "My people have a degree of empathy—telepathy—and you were broadcasting on every available frequency. From the moment I walked by you just after the car drenched you—"

"Where were you going?"

His fists balled in anger at her interruption, but she

held her ground and he shrugged.

"It doesn't matter now."

"It does to me and should to you if you want something from me."

"The power plant."

She distantly recalled seeing a rucksack slung nonchalantly across his back while his hesitant shoes had carried him away after helping her to her feet..

"You were going to blow it up!"

"I changed my mind."

"And saved your stupid life too. You would never have made it. Don't you know about security, men with guns and short fuses?"

"Something else you can gloat over. You saved the life of a lesser creature. Make you feel important, does it? Superior?"

"Stop it." She held a hand up, palm out. "Your anger, this bitterness, it isn't helping you, and it certainly isn't endearing me to your cause. Why did you stop?"

"Because I could hear you leaking your anger at losing the story, your chance at the lead. I realized you were a reporter and that I could use you."

She snorted and laughed once, sharp and sour.

"Reporter, yeah... right."

"You work for a paper and write stories for that paper. It is all I require."

"What for? I write fluffy little pieces about the local knitting circle and book day at the school. I cover kittens stuck up trees and the occasional excitement of a new release at the cinema. I'm no one. Why me?"

"Because you know how to use human words and I need someone who can speak to humanity."

"In this backwater burg? Who do you want to reach? The hippy misfit who lives on the edge of town in his foil-shielded caravan, listening for aliens? He's about the only one in Stepfordville who will take any notice, believe me."

"Every ocean begins with a single drop."

"And you want me to be that drop? Lamar, I'll be lucky if I make a puddle, let alone an ocean."

"Come."

His tone was less abrupt than before. He waited for her to join him and slowed to her pace while he led her from the howling lake room through tunnels that led steadily downward. A shift had taken place in their dynamic. She realized she accepted him for what he was, or what he said he was. Perhaps it had been the lake with its burden of lost souls or the dying screams, but a switch had flicked. She knew she wasn't walking a dreamscape but something real, something tangible that would affect her life directly.

"Sooner than you think."

Lamar's telepathy was unsettling, but the simple room before her chased such emotion away, leaving her drained and speechless. Two great stone bowls hung from a thick chain of silver links that passed through a monolith in the center of the room. One bowl contained roaring flames, but she could see nothing in the other, which hung considerably higher.

"Go closer," Lamar urged, and she crossed the floor to the steps below the higher bowl. Dread dogged her steps, knowing what she would see. More what she would not see. She stood on tiptoe, straining to see into the bowl. It proved to be almost empty, a sluggish pool of water, no more than a foot deep, forlornly reflecting her face. She looked across to the flames that soared into the air from the opposite bowl and then to Lamar.

"What does it mean?"

"The Vodyanoi have been the keepers of the balance since our creation. It is our task to ensure the waters are pure, in balance with the consuming flame. You see for yourself that we are losing."

"We did this? Humans?"

He nodded, and she stepped away from the sad tale told by the scales.

"How much longer?" Those three whispered words held the weight of a world and every life on it.

"No more than a decade."

"They'll think I'm insane if I try to publish any of this. They'll fire me, and nothing will change."

"Not if you fund your own paper."

"I don't have that kind of money, Lamar."

"Come."

She followed him once again and watched him haul open a stone door. She was almost blinded by the contents of the room. Shielding her eyes under her hand, she stared about and then looked at Lamar.

"I've never seen that much gold in my life!"

"My people collect it before it can taint the water when it falls from wrecked ships and drowned men. We have no use for it, but it may be enough to help you."

It was clear to her he had no concept of how many lives she would have to live to spend even a quarter of what sat in the storeroom.

"I can start my own paper, a website--heck, even my own TV channel. If you are serious about this, Lamar—"

"Why would I joke? My people will die out as readily

as yours, likely before, if the balance isn't corrected."

"Do you have any idea how cranks, eccentrics for a more polite term, are seen in my world? I'll be a laughing stock. They won't believe me, Lamar."

"They will if you show them."

From a small table beside him that had been hidden in his shadow, he lifted a box and offered it to her. She smiled slowly when she lifted the seashell encrusted lid and surveyed the brand new video camera within.

"They'll still think I made it up."

"For every drop of rain that winks out on a concrete slab, another falls into the puddle--"

She finished for him. "And becomes an ocean."

ASTRAL VOYEUR

By Robert L. Arend

Body at rest, eyes lightly closed,
A white screen springs from a cone;
A face from the past was whom he chose
Whenever his soul felt alone.

Warmth coursed from feet to thighs,
Swirled at abdomen before moving to chest;
Loosening vibration before the soul did rise
From the body, no longer its guest.

Near the ceiling came the roll
When seen the deathlike container:
That heavy, dense thing that had harbored the soul
That must return to sooner, if not too much later.

Then, at the speed of thought, stood in a foyer,
Just beyond, she, first love, surfing the Net;
Unaware of the invisible voyeur
Who blinked into her living room near where she sat.

Thirty-five-years older, no longer as pretty,
Yet still possessed the twin soul that made both one;
And on a short stack of mail was address and city,
But a search for phone number found none

On the sofa, he sat beside her.
Chilled, she buttoned her sweater.
Side-by-side, as once they were
Upon a time, when love was new and better.

Then into the room walked a tall balding man,
Who rudely sat on and through the soul;
He dared to kiss the bedazzled woman.
A kiss she returned, long and full.

The heartbroken soul followed them up the stairs;
Inside a bedroom she closed the door,
Leaving the soul out in the hall, alone with his tears,
Until dragged back to his body once more.

ABOUT THE EDITOR: MICHELLE DEVON

Known online as Michy, Michelle Devon is a writer, editor, poet and professional dreamer. She is also the owner of Accentuate Writers, the managing editor of the now fourteen-year-old company Accentuate Author Services, and the founder of Twin Trinity Media, LLC, the publishing company that produces the Elements Series and Expressions Series of short-story anthologies for the Accentuate Writers Forum.

Her own writing has seen three books published through three small presses, inclusion in two short-story anthologies, as well as having essays included in *Cup of Comfort* and *Chicken Soup for the Soul*. In addition to numerous online writing awards and contest wins, Michy won a People's Media Award and one of her essays was a finalist in the *Redbook* magazine's *Your Love Story* contest. Her first novel was a semi-finalist in the 2010 Faulkner-Wisdom Creative Writing-Novel Contest. Her second novel, as yet unpublished, made the short-list in the 2011 ABNA contest. Another essay was a finalist in the *Thin Threads* contest and yet another was a finalist and published in the *Editor Unleashed* "Why I Write" contest.

Michy lives with the philosophy: "You are what you help others become." To that end, she created and based Accentuate, TTM and the contests that produce this very book on the premise that helping others become successful ensures both their success and hers. Her goal and mission with TTM, LLC and Accentuate is to help launch writing careers, while helping unpublished and underpublished authors get the support, encouragement, coaching and accomplishments they deserve to keep them motivated to move forward with their chosen writing career.

Join us at: http://AccentuateWriters.com